I0653243

Copyright © **2018 by Melissa Bender**

Typewriter Pub, an imprint of Blvnp Incorporated
A Nevada Corporation
1887 Whitney Mesa DR #2002
Henderson, NV 89014
www.typewriterpub.com/info@typewriterpub.com

ISBN: 978-1-64434-006-6

DISCLAIMER

FORGIVING YOU

MELISSA BENDER

Bailey. Mason. Everly.
Your mind will always believe what you tell it.
Remember, you are so loved.

PROLOGUE

"Jesus . . ."

"Oh god . . ."

". . . fuck me."

Unfortunately, we weren't in the throes of lovemaking.

We were both wide awake, annoyed, and cursing at the fact it wasn't even 6 AM and the guy in the apartment beside ours was using what sounded like a sledgehammer and bashing it loudly into a wall.

"Maybe he's having wild, crazy sex, and it's the headboard banging?" I suggested, trying to calm my husband who was growing more annoyed each second.

Chris looked over—unimpressed—with his brows scrunched together, eyes giving me the 'you're kidding' look. "Maybe he's doing renovations like last weekend without proper approval, and I should draft up a suit to toss at the prick."

Always the lawyer, even when at home. "Oh? Based on what grounds?"

"For waking me the fuck up."

I had to laugh as I rolled half asleep to face him. He really could be such a grump for a morning person. "How will you cope when we have a newborn at home? Crying all hours of the night . . . keeping you awake? God forbid you'd miss some beauty sleep." I toyed with the idea of our future family.

He raised a brow at me. "Babies?"

1

We hadn't talked much about babies since we got married two months ago, but we wanted them.

Chris, however, looked surprised as he raised a dark brow mid-yawn, glancing over at me. "Are you trying to tell me that you're pregnant?"

I rolled my eyes. I think if I were pregnant, he would have known about it by now. "Umm, not that I know of."

"Do you want to be?"

A smile grew on my face as I shrugged, acting all shy and coy. The thought did excite me. "I mean, I love babies and would love to have one or four with you."

His fingertips were warm as they stroked against my cheek. Leaning in closer, I could feel his warm breath hit against my skin as he spoke; his tone was soft, yet confident. "I think we should have one."

"What? Now?" I laughed, immediately wrapping my legs around his waist as he moved in closer, finally settling between my legs, and resting on top of me.

Naked and so warm, Chris engulfed me in a hard embrace. "No." I could feel his smile grow against the crook of my neck as his growing erection pressed against my smooth, waxed mound, nudging around until he sunk inside with a slow thrust. "We'll *make* a baby now."

Pulling back with a slight surprise, I wasn't sure if Chris was serious. My brows dipped slightly in confusion as I cupped his face. "Chris, do you really want to make a baby? Right now? What about our plan? Spending a year in newlywed bliss before moving to the suburbs for mum-and-dad life . . ." We had decided about that on our honeymoon.

"Char." He smiled, gazing into my eyes in a way that made me quiver from the inside. "Fuck the plan. I want a family."

CHAPTER ONE

"Let me help you with those?"

My hands were full as I slowly turned around, dipping both feathered brows in confusion and mostly to squint past the downpour of rain as I looked up at the man standing in front of me. "I'm sorry?"

"Let me help carry your bags to your car. I couldn't forgive myself if you fell and broke your neck in this weather." He grinned.

Unfortunately, I had chosen the worst time to walk to the store and grab a few groceries for dinner. Glancing around, I felt embarrassed for some reason. "Umm, I actually don't have a car. It's okay; I don't live too far ahead anyway."

His face crumpled, and he stared at me as if I had just grown another head.

That's how I ended up sitting in his car, soaking wet, and giving directions to my block, which was twenty minutes away in the traffic. Not looking bothered as he jumped out in his light grey joggers and a navy jumper, he opened the back door and took out my three bags while I fumbled around in my leather bag, searching in a hurry for the keys to the apartment I lived in. Just as I pulled them free, a loud clap of thunder startled me, and I dropped them down in a puddle, cursing at myself on the inside.

"Wasn't it meant to rain next week?" I pointed out.

"It was forecasted for this evening; looks as if it came early." He shouted over another rumble of thunder. "Let's make a run for it before the rain gets worse."

The rain didn't let up, and by the time we both made it to the apartment, we were soaking wet. I looked over at the man standing in my kitchen with droplets of water coming from his jet-black hair down his face as he sat my bags on the counter. He looked like he had taken a shower fully dressed. I took a breath, realising I didn't know who this man was, and suddenly, stranger danger was singing into my brain.

"I'm Charlotte," I said. "Just figured you should know my name."

"Chris." He managed a smile and brushed a hand through his hair. "I should head off anyway."

I looked towards the window; flashes of lightning lit up the sky as the rain grew louder. "No, you can't drive in this. It's dangerous."

He smirked. "I'm a big boy. I think I can manage."

"Please. Stay for dinner," I insisted. "I will get you a change of clothes—my way of saying thank you for the drive home."

I walked to the spare bedroom where my brother sometimes stayed to source the closet for a change of dry clothing.

He was in the bathroom, changing, when I heard him call out, noting the amusement in his voice. "Should I be worried about these clothes? I mean, your boyfriend won't come home and murder me for being in them, will he?"

I had to laugh, popping my head around the door and immediately blushing as I caught sight of the toned torso and strong muscled arms as he had his arms raised above his head, pulling down the red t-shirt. Christ. What I would do to run my hands all over . . . and then I realised he was looking straight at me.

My cheeks flamed red as my gaze dropped to the floor. "Umm, my brother. No boyfriend, so you're safe from that." I smiled, walking back to the kitchen.

*   *   *

Taking a swig of his beer, Chris began to tell me more about himself while I started preparing dinner—an easy pasta that I regularly made. He was a lawyer—well, a partner—in a law firm. It was the same law firm that had

4

contacted me about doing their new business cards they were having next week, and I had been asked to take each employee photo. So, we were going to be seeing each other again soon.

The small talk was easy, and dinner was the same. Nothing too awkward until the power went off, and I couldn't see a thing. I

"Do you own a torch? Candles?" Chris asked, pulling open a cupboard to search around. "Anything?"

"Umm . . ." I had no clue. "I have a fireplace though." I had to laugh; I really sucked in a crisis.

The living room lit up as we both sat opposite each other; the blazing fire keeping both of us warm. Looking around, I couldn't help but laugh. "This looks kind of purposely romanced." It was something out of the movies.

"True." He agreed, his voice deep but still soft. "But it's not romantic until I do this."

I hadn't caught on to what he meant until the last second when he was leaning in closer, cupping my cheek as he lowered his mouth to mine, kissing me ever so tenderly. It was almost perfect.

"Are you sure you're not dating someone?" he asked, pulling away all too quickly.

With a roll of my eyes, I had to laugh. "No. Now get back over here and kiss me more." I bit my lip, eagerly leaning in closer for another kiss, but this time, with more passion.

It was by far, the most memorable way to pass the storm.

*   *   *

Today was meant to be the happiest day of our lives. The day we had been waiting nine long, tiring months for; the one day I needed him the most, more than anyone in my life.

I really needed him today.

Aside from the day we married, this was our next best day ever. Or, so I would have assumed.

I waited hopefully, anxiously.

For five days, I waited for a phone call or a visit. I waited for something to let me know everything was okay.

Instead, I was met with nothing.

He was meant to be the one next to me—my own husband who was meant to be holding my hand and helping me through this as I delivered our precious, absolutely breathtaking baby girl into the world. The baby we made with love and happiness, knowing that we were starting a family together.

However, he was nowhere in sight. He wasn't there to cut our daughter's umbilical cord or hold her. We didn't get the birth photos of the moment we became a family of three. I had to do it all alone with the help of a wonderful midwife, as she offered words of encouragement when I wanted to give up. I cried because Chris was the one who was supposed to be by my side, doing it all like we had planned and talked so often about.

The last time I had heard from him was when he had kissed me goodbye at the breakfast table, and then he had leaned down and placed a kiss over my burgeoning stomach, telling our unborn child just how much she was loved before he left for work.

The pain had become stronger when I called him almost immediately on the phone when my water broke. He sounded so excited and promised that he was on his way home to take me to the hospital. I could hear the elation in his voice as he told me that he couldn't wait to greet our baby earlier than expected.

But when an hour passed, and nothing came except stronger contractions, I had to drive myself that half hour. I tried to ignore the pain as I cried, screaming for my dear life as I waddled up the steps to the emergency room. I called him several times, but I kept being sent to voicemail.

I considered the possibility that Chris had been in a meeting or court, but that didn't seem likely; he had promised to be there for me.

I even tried to leave a message with his secretary, who then rudely told me that Chris had taken a meeting with a client and couldn't reschedule. I thought, perhaps, he would instead meet me at the hospital. My hopes faded to disappointment when I realised he wasn't coming.

I didn't call again after that.

I didn't tell him that I had given birth. I didn't tell him how much his daughter weighed, or even that she had trouble breathing after the emergency C-section, which was due to the umbilical cord wrapped around her neck.

Anger bubbled inside me as I couldn't believe how someone could do this to the person they loved the most. However, as angry as I was, I was in love all over again, with a small human being who needed me the most in her life.

I would show my daughter just how loved she was in this world.

My parents were both furious when I mentioned Chris not being around for the birth. Mum wanted to strangle him, unable to comprehend how a man could just leave his wife on the day that was in labour. I would love to know the answer to that. My parents had been abroad, travelling in their caravan, and weren't supposed to come home until next month. They changed their plans and came back home to be with me. I was grateful because I really needed them right now.

*   *   *

Chris and I had always been happy, having a typical whirlwind romance—dating five short months before becoming engaged, then marrying six months later. Three months after we said I do, I became pregnant. We may not have been together for long, but I had been blissfully happy and so in love. He was older— thirty-one—when we began to date. I assumed he would be serious, mature, and mindful of what he wanted in life. That was how he came across when we spoke about settling down. I, a young twenty-four-year-old, was foolishly unaware of just how much this man could break me. I didn't know a thing about love, but Chris showed me what it could be, and for that, I adored him even more.

His family loved me, and I loved them the same. We got along so well, and they were thrilled about having their first grandchild. We never found out the sex of the baby. I didn't want to know, and neither did Chris; he wanted to be surprised. It turned out I was the one being surprised.

I had wondered if Chris had been seeing someone else or having an affair with that leggy brunette from his office who always eyed him up and down and scowled at me whenever I visited him at work. The glares got worse as I became pregnant and my stomach started growing rapidly. I even asked him once if anything was going on between the two of them. I was having a bad day, I felt ugly, and he came home later than usual. He insisted there wasn't, then took me out for the weekend to make up for working so much. I still felt that maybe he was. The leggy brunette was his age and was always calling him, even on his days off.

I had tried to rack my brains as to where I went wrong.

How did I not see the signs when everything was perfect in my eyes?

We still made love quite often; he was always up for that, and I would make sure he was happy in the bedroom. We had even slept together the morning before he left for work. He had woken up in a rather playful mood, so I don't know how he had changed from being so happy to not wanting to be with his family in a matter of hours. It just didn't make sense to me.

I was even more furious when I drove myself home from the hospital. The doctor told me I wasn't allowed to drive, but I had no one to pick me up and take me home. Well, I could have called Adam—my brother—but like my parents, he was away for work purposes, and the humiliation of having to relive why I was alone and asking for help was unbearable.

My heart broke as I held the capsule. My darling girl was soundly sleeping as I rode the lift to our home in constant pain as I struggled to even walk with the numbness and the stinging in my lower stomach; it was all stitched up. But, hey, I was on some awesome painkillers.

There was no denying that I was hoping Chris was here with one hell of an explanation, but instead, all of his things were gone, and a letter addressed to me was placed on the table.

> *Charlotte,*
>
> *I'd appreciate it if you signed these. I will pick them up on Friday afternoon. Don't make this harder than it must be. Everything I believed was wrong. I don't know what made you do it, but I can't even stand to be near you at this moment. Leave the papers at the front desk.*
>
> *Christopher*

I looked at the paper behind the note and let out a scoff. Chris must be joking; he wants to get a divorce. I scanned over everything and what he was offering me. He wanted to settle quickly: two million dollars a year, the penthouse, and the car.

I never once thought he would try and buy me off this way. Yes, I was well aware just how wealthy he was. After becoming engaged, I assumed I would have been asked to sign something, but he never brought it up.

I scribbled a very fancy *go fuck yourself* message in a black marker over each of the divorce papers and placed it back on the bench. He can have everything: the house, the cars, and the money. The one thing he wasn't getting was our daughter, and I would get my own damn lawyer to make sure that happened. Hell, I would get my brother to represent me against him.

I had my own savings from when I was working. Chris and I never spent anything from that account, and fortunately, it was only in my name. Chris couldn't touch a cent in it, and even though there weren't millions of dollars in there, it was enough to keep me settled until I found a job. I could take a year to spend with my daughter, Lucy, then go back to work part-time doing what I loved.

I only packed my clothing and essentials for Lucy. I didn't need anything else. I called up the concierge, Leighton, from the front desk, and he helped bring the things down to my car, loading it up in my Jeep as I set off for the long drive I was about to embark on.

Chris would have never expected me to go to a place like this. We loved the city, living a fast-paced life of dining out and luxury. We had a penthouse in the city, and although it was amazing, it wasn't where he and I wanted to raise our children. We would spend weekends, visiting open homes in the suburbs, but could never find a home to our liking or one we agreed on.

A place to relax in peace, which wasn't going to happen anytime soon with a newborn, but one can wish.

My amazing friend, Vanessa—or Ness as I usually called her —lived along the beach in a caravan park for travelling tourists. She loved it so much that she bought one for a permanent residence. I didn't blame her though. I was only staying here after she mentioned her neighbouring one was vacant. Three bedrooms, probably too big for me, but she was out finding me a crib and changing table. I hadn't told her the exact reason as to why I was coming down, but that's one of the many reasons I loved her. She never pressed for details unless I was ready to talk, and at this moment, I wasn't quite ready. It was a face-to-face conversation and preferably a large glass of wine, though I probably wouldn't be able to have the latter anytime soon.

I pulled over twice, breastfeeding before getting back on the road and driving yet again. The radio didn't distract me as I kept replaying everything in my mind. What went wrong? How? Why? Who? It was doing my head in. Tears ran down my cheeks as hormones played with every emotion my body could go through.

From anger to heartache, I just didn't understand. Chris had been to every appointment and every scan, and *always* made the effort. My late-night cravings didn't bother him. He was always eager to run down to the store and fulfil my hunger for those evenings. Pizza had been my main craving, which he loved because he was never one to complain about eating that. Pizza was now the last thing I wanted.

Checking my messages after I parked the car beside Ness', I noticed that I had missed calls or messages. Nothing at all—not from Chris, nor his family. They all knew I was due, and I honestly thought that maybe they would have called. His sister, Samantha, and I were close, so it really surprised me she hadn't called to check in on me.

More tears filled my eyes as I thought about how easy it was for him to leave me. He promised me we would be together forever, and that I was all he needed in life. He was the same to me.

I guess they were just words—nothing but empty promises.

CHAPTER TWO

Tonight was the night I was going on a date with Chris. A proper date where he picked me up and took me somewhere of his choosing.

Excitement consumed me.

It was hard to believe that we had only met a mere week ago, but something had felt so right between us. Chris' age didn't bother me, and he didn't care that I was somewhat younger than he was, which was a relief.

His age attracted me, knowing he was mature and not going to screw me around.

The night we had shared a kiss, Chris stayed over. We never slept together, but he did share my bed, and he held me close to his body all night as the loud rain poured heavily against the windows.

I guess we were kind of dating, but nothing was official.

The only thing I was worried about was my brother. If Adam knew I had let a man spend the night in my bedroom—one I barely knew—he would flip. Protective was an understatement.

There was a loud, short knock on my door. I froze, then I walked over with shaky legs to open the door. I was met with a handsome-looking Chris who was in a casual V-neck shirt and dark blue jeans. Instantly, I smiled, unable to hold back as he grinned down at me. "You look beautiful."

I was only in red skinny jeans, a black baggy shirt, and black slip-on shoes—the opposite of sexy. "You look better." I grinned, biting my lower lip as my heart rate picked up when he stepped in closer to me.

"I missed you all week," he murmured, my hands wrapped around his neck and I stood up on my toes to meet him halfway for a kiss. I liked his height; it made me feel small and safe in his arms as he towered above me.

Chris drove; we were heading out to see a movie. It was very cliché, but we had similar taste in movies and there was a new comedy that I was eager to see. Two and a half hours later, we walked out of the cinema hand in hand, trying to keep a straight face from the heated make-out session we had done in the middle of the cinema. I could have easily straddled his lap, and ground us both to a happy ending, but there were other people around.

I was expecting to go home, but he led me towards the road instead of heading to his parked black BMW. "The date isn't over yet." He wrapped his arm around my waist, pulling me closer against his side.

"It's almost midnight." I stupidly pointed out, looking around at the near-empty park as we walked across the road.

"Just come for a walk; we won't be long." He bent slightly, pressing his lips to my temple.

We walked through the park and down to the lake. There was absolute silence this time of the night; nothing but a few splashes in the water from the ducks waddling away from us. It was peaceful and nice; quite a change from the loudness that normally fills my day.

"Charlotte, I have a feeling you may freak out a little, but I need to get this off my chest before anything else happens. Hell, I'm fucking worried." Chris cleared his throat, sitting down on the park bench and bringing me down on his lap.

"Do you not want to see me again?" Christ, had the date been that bad?

"Quite the opposite, actually. I'm not looking at this as something short-term. I don't have time to play games. Work keeps me busy, and it's been my life for quite some time, but since meeting you, I know I want a lot more with you than I ever thought, especially since we barely know each other." He looked up at me, worry clear in his expression.

I smiled looking back at him, my hands cupping his face as I rested my forehead to his and let out a relieved breath. "I have no objections to that, councillor."

13

*　　*　　*

I spotted Ness near her car in front of a building. She was waving and smiling brightly as she walked out of her cosy little cabin. She rushed over, opening the car door for me, and as soon as I stepped outside, she brought me into a big warm, welcoming hug.

"I can't believe you're really here!" She squealed with delight.

"I know. Me either." I couldn't, because I didn't think I would be. My hormones played up again, and I was fighting the urge to burst into tears and break down. Now wasn't the time; I had a baby I needed to be strong for.

Dangling the keys in front of me, she wiggled her brows. "Ready to check out your new place?"

I could only smile; she knew how to distract me all too well. "Heck, yes! Show me the way."

She had sold herself short describing the place; I loved it already. There was a small, but simple kitchen that was off from the open living and dining area. I followed her down the hallway, passing a bathroom and two rooms until she opened the end bedroom. The first thing I noticed was the oak wood bassinet; it had pink bedding with a small light grey bunny that was beside the king-sized bed. "It's perfect, thank you."

"Oh no, you haven't seen the best part yet." She spun on her heels as I followed with Lucy in my arms. Going to the other bedroom, she said: "For your parents or brother. And now, for the main event . . ."

"What have you done?" I laughed, pressing my lips to Lucy's soft head of black hair. "I'm nervous."

"Don't be." She winked before pushing open the last door and walked inside. "Welcome to your bedroom, Lucy."

I stood, staring in disbelief at what she had created in such a short time. Ness had created a dreamy, beautiful nursery. There were no words for how I felt right now, and I was afraid to speak, knowing I would burst into tears at any second. Finally, it felt like hours before I could say anything. "Thank you," I whispered, unable to use my normal voice. "Lucy will love it. Heck, I even love it."

I felt Ness' hand on my back as she rested a head against my shoulder and stroked her fingers gently against sleeping Lucy's cheek. "I will always be here for you whenever you need me. Both of you."

"You're amazing." I smiled. "You truly are."

"I know. Anyway, tell me how you chose Lucy's name. It suits her so well; so dainty and delicate. She's just perfect."

That she is.

Smiling, I switched arms as Lucy stirred against my chest but stayed asleep. "Chris' nan, she passed away a few months ago, and I know how close they were. I wasn't going to tell him, and I knew deep down he would have liked to name his daughter after her."

*   *   *

It was a relief to take a shower. Ness eagerly held Lucy whilst I cleaned myself up. Bleeding heavily, aching and swollen breasts—it wasn't the most attractive feeling. My pyjamas were giving me comfort as I walked outside onto the deck and found Ness with a glass of wine, whilst still cradling a sleeping Lucy.

I sat down with a hot tea in hand and sighed. My eyes still stung from the hot tears that I wasn't able to hold in any longer.

"Char, what happened? Everything seemed to be so well when we spoke last week when you did that maternity photo shoot."

15

I shrugged, feeling more tears springing to life, but also smiling at the same time. "Chris left me. I called when I went into labour, and he said he was on his way, but he never showed up. I haven't heard from him since then. I thought maybe he was in an accident, or something went wrong, but nothing at all." I wiped my eyes, shaking my head, annoyed. "Oh, wait. If you call, leaving divorce papers for me to sign on the kitchen bench hearing from him, then yeah, I heard from him this morning when I went home," I said bitterly. I was never an angry person; always seeing the good in people, but right now, it was difficult to see him in a good light.

"You're joking, right? What the actual hell! Like seriously, what would make him not show up to the birth of his firstborn, and then slap you with a divorce?" Ness shook her head angrily.

I bit my lip, looking at her. I honestly had no idea how to answer that. I really didn't.

I didn't want a divorce, and I wouldn't sign. Well, not until I knew the reason Chris left us.

We sat outside for a while longer. Ness wanted the gory details of my labour and birth; I eagerly gave them, unable to hide my amusement as she cringed and crossed her legs with horror and refused to ever have children.

Sitting out here, I breastfed again and stared down at my daughter. She looked so innocent, unaware of any heartache and hurt the world could throw at her. I would do everything I could to protect her and keep her safe. I would do my best to move on, take care of her, and make sure she had all she would ever need.

If her father didn't want her, then that was his issue. But for me, I had fallen in love with a small version of myself and would make sure she knew how loved she was every single day.

CHAPTER THREE

"Move in with me?" he asked with a daring smile.

My brow shot up, excitement coursing through me unexpectedly. I hadn't even considered that an option, especially after just four short weeks of dating; nor was I planning to answer Chris the way I did. "Yes."

"Wait, really?" Chris grinned, putting his chopsticks back down into his Thai takeout box. "You're teasing?"

I laughed, shaking my head. "Aren't you meant to be a lawyer or something? I thought you could tell when someone is bluffing."

"I can never tell with you," he muttered, leaning back in his chair.

Standing up, I made my way around the glass desk and over to him, leaning forward as I sat on his lap. "Christopher, when would you like me to move in? Or, would you like to move in with me? I have a nice apartment that's all cosy and warm."

He laughed, his palms on my thighs, slowly running up and then back down again. "Your apartment, while it is nice, it's too small. Move in with me this weekend."

I let out a groan, playing with him for a moment. "I don't know. I mean, your apartment is so clean, and I might mess everything up. You love to clean, clean, clean." I laughed, leaning in closer, our mouths almost touching. When his hand slipped beneath my dress and moved closer towards my inner thigh, a soft moan escaped, and I sucked in a breath. "Mmm."

"Mess my apartment up. I don't care. I just want you with me," he said, and I felt his fingers brush against the fabric of my panties.

17

"Chris . . ." I moaned, my eyes closing on their own accord. "You'll need to meet my brother . . . my parents . . ." I trailed off, losing all of my concentration.

His fingers stopped moving as my eyes opened. I had my hands working on loosening his belt and tugging his shirt out. "I'll meet anyone you want me to."

Slipping my hand inside his navy slacks, I leaned in, our mouths still close but not touching. "I want you."

"Not here," Chris said. His hand went to mine, stopping me from moving into his boxer shorts. "I want you. Oh, fuck do I want you, but I'd rather do it on a bed for our first time."

We parted briefly, and I slumped back against his desk. We hadn't done anything, and I was starting to feel the sexual tension between us and what we were both craving for. I wanted him so badly. "When?"

Cupping my cheeks, he leaned in once again, pressing his warm soft lips to mine. My whole body reacted to his touch—a simple touch that drove me wild. "When I can spend hours exploring your body, making you come, and then doing it all again the next morning."

I half moaned, gripping his tie tighter. "Oh, I love you." The words slipped effortlessly.

Expecting him to pull away, freak out, or say he had work to do, he snaked an arm around my waist and pulled me in close. Our eye contact never once broke as he cupped my cheek and whispered, "I love you. I want to make love to you."

Our mouths finally met again, and we kissed. Slow and sensual, his tongue took sweet dominance. Holding me tightly, as I held on for dear life too.

*　　　*　　　*

In the seven days that I had been here in my new place, I hadn't heard from Chris. Nothing at all. Did I want to hear from him? *Oh, so desperately.*

18

The only plus about this whole situation was that I was settling into a routine with Lucy, and we were going fine. Yes, nighttimes were hard especially with my stomach pain, but it was slowly getting better each day. Lucy woke every four hours, and when I was too tired, I would do a cheeky feed in bed where she would fall back asleep quite quickly. I should have napped during the day when she slept, but I was unable to take my eyes off her, a terrible but wonderful way to waste time.

My thoughts of Chris were still there. I wasn't going to deny that he wasn't always on my mind. He was. There were times when I wanted to call him. I needed him, my husband, my lover—the man I loved with my whole heart. How could I just walk away from that? It was hard to think that we would never have what we once used to. Did he really not love me? Was this him just trying to say he had a change of heart?

Every day, I worried more and more.

Lucy had her father's jet-black hair and dark blue eyes. She was so much like him, even with her long lashes. She would be a heartbreaker, that's for sure.

We had settled in here better than I had expected. Yes, there were times when I just cried randomly, and I was grateful that Ness was here, helping whenever she could. I loved to sit out on the balcony, staring off into the sunset, or waking up early to catch the sunrise. Each morning gave me a newfound hope that Lucy and I would be alright and that one day I would look back on the pain, and it wouldn't hurt as much. That day was far from close, but I still held onto hope.

My rings were fixed on my finger, unable to slide off the white gold promise I had made the day we married. Maybe he had already disposed of his, thrown it over a bridge, or tossed it out the window at his firm.

How was he coping?

I think every woman's first thought in this situation would be assuming their loved one was finding comfort in another woman, fucking someone else to get over the woman in their head. He once told me that he didn't believe in one-night stands, but nothing made me feel sicker than to think he was deep inside some random woman from a bar.

Walking back into the bedroom after the quickest shower I ever took, I bent over Lucy's bassinet and smiled to myself. The number of photographs I had taken of her each day was crazy. She was just perfect, truly incredible as she slept peacefully. So content, without a care in the world, and not knowing the heartbreak that would come later in life.

Still in my pyjamas, because I didn't feel the need to throw on something pretty and do my makeup, I laid back down on the bed, reaching for my Mac laptop. I had managed to avoid Adam, and that was only because he was still away. I replied to his texts, but that was about it.

Plugging in my camera, I waited as the photograph files downloaded, until an email popped up in the right corner of the screen. The sender's name had my heart racing.

Message after message appeared, my heart pounding furiously in my chest as they were all from Chris. I had turned off all alerts on my phone so that I wouldn't be bothered or tempted. But for my laptop, I hadn't, as today was the first time I got all the notifications since everything had gone down.

Eight.

Eight unread emails.

Two from my brother, Adam. Just updating me about his travel and whereabouts.

My heart raced as I read the familiar name of the sender of the rest of the emails. *Christopher Rivers.*

"Delete them," I whispered to myself, biting my lower lip as I clicked on the first one.

-Go fuck yourself? Nice, Charlotte.

I rolled my eyes and clicked the next.

20

-As you have refused to sign, I have sent the contract again. Please sign. I'll give you more money. Just sign the damn paper.

-Leighton called and told me that you hadn't been home since last Wednesday. Where are you staying so I can send them there? Who are you with? You're with him, aren't you?

-Where are you?

-Charlotte, where are you? No one has heard from you. Why aren't you answering your phone?

I almost laughed. Chris had to be delusional if he thought I was going to speak to him.

The last one, I read over and over, wanting to believe he meant it, but I knew better.

-Please, just tell me where you are. Char, I need to know that you're both okay and that nothing has happened. I tried to call the hospital, but they wouldn't tell me anything. Please, just tell me you're okay.

"Too late for that now," I muttered, rolling my eyes. He never even asked about his child.

Tears pooled in my eyes, hot with anger as I typed back. Emotional emailing was never a good idea.

Christopher,

I am fine. Email me the divorce papers, and I will send them back to you signed. I don't want your money; keep it all. I don't need, nor do I want anything else from you. All I ask is full custody. I will fight you through hell if you dare object to this. Thanks for asking about your daughter who, by the way, almost died during childbirth. You might be a great lawyer, but you won't be winning Father of the Year.

Enjoy your whore who's been sucking your dick.

Much love,

Charlotte

I pressed send and turned the computer off.

Out of sight, out of mind.

I left the bedroom before my pacing woke Lucy up. *With him? Who the hell was he referring to? Did he mean Adam?* He was the only other guy I could assume it would be about.

My soft cries turned into a loud sob, as my legs gave way and I fell to the floor in agony. I couldn't stop; every single breath felt like my heart was breaking even more. I couldn't breathe. I couldn't think. My head was going to explode. "Fuck you!" I screamed, to no one. I leaned my head against the wall, eyes shut tightly as I punched the floor, cursing him.

A pair of strong arms startled me when I felt them wrapping around my body and drawing me into his chest. The familiar calming scent filled my nose, and even though I felt safe, I felt relieved to have him here as I cried, clinging tightly back.

"Don't cry, sweetheart." Adam's soft, deep voice cooed against my cheek.

"He doesn't love me anymore, and I don't know why . . ." It was the question on my mind, which I was begging for an answer. "Why?" I just didn't have the answers I needed.

"I don't know," he replied quietly. "But, I'm here now, for as long as you need."

I had no idea how long we sat here on the floor in my brother's arms. It would have lasted longer, but Lucy woke, and her cries broke us apart. I had to be strong for her and show her that I would love her forever and give her everything no matter what. She didn't need her father; she had me.

"So, I have a niece?" Adam smiled, watching by the door as I changed Lucy's diaper and dressed her in another light pink onesie.

I lifted her up, giving her back a soft rub. "You sure do, and Lucy would like to meet her uncle."

Lucy's little eyes opened, and a yawn escaped as Adam held her in his strong arms. He sat back in the chair, smiling. "She's beautiful and so small, just like a doll."

"She is. I know babies are small, but I feel like I'm going to break her at times," I admitted.

"You won't, but I understand the feeling." He laughed. "Hence, the reason why I'm sitting down."

"I don't think I've ever seen you so scared," I teased, catching sight of my reflection in the mirror as I made my way over with a coffee. Christ, I was more than a hot mess. "Anyway, tell me how you've been."

"Mum called." He ignored me and looked at me like the lawyer he was. "She's worried about you."

"I am doing okay," I assured, realising I was lying to a lawyer and not even believing my own lies. "I'm doing the best that I can. It's hard; my husband left me the day I gave birth, and I struggle with it. I don't know why he did it, and it kills me because I love him so much."

Adam looked at me; I prayed he didn't delve for more information. Remaining quiet, he sighed. "I went to see him." My eyes snapped to his, and I urged him to talk more. "It took every ounce of me not to break his fucking face, but I had to know what kind of man just walks out on his family like that."

My hands shook, chest tight as I licked my lower lip and hesitantly asked. "What did Chris say? Did he tell you why he left?"

Adam looked down at Lucy, and then back to me. "It's not good."

"Tell me," I urged, needing to know. He remained silent. "Tell me, Adam," I pushed again, harsher this time.

"Chris doesn't think she is his child." As soon as he said the words, I wanted to throw up.

"What?!" I half shouted. This was insane. "Of course, she is his."

He nodded, not mincing his emotion. "I know. Fuck, just one look at Lucy, and you can see that she's his daughter. The hair and the eyes . . . she's a dead ringer for her father."

23

I couldn't, for the life of me, think why he would assume I would be pregnant with someone else's child. That made no sense, and it infuriated me beyond words that he could ever believe such a disgusting lie.

He was the one who wanted to fuck for hours, trying to make a baby.

"Did you tell him where I am?"

"No. I told Chris you deserved better, called him a few choice words, and walked off before I knocked him out." He shook his head angrily. "What type of man just leaves his family like that? A fucking weak man that's who."

"Clearly a man who thinks his wife is cheating on him," I said quietly. I was stunned. My mind went blank; I was literally out of words. I didn't know how to respond. "He didn't even ask me if it was true or not. I haven't had the chance to defend myself. I've just been assumed guilty." I always and only had eyes for one man, and one man only—my husband whom I gave everything to. "Do you know he filed for divorce?" I asked sitting my cup of tea on the coffee table

I heard the heavy breathing flaring out of Adam's nostrils. "No," he answered, as he kept his eyes on Lucy.

"He thinks that giving me two million a year and our apartment will keep me happy. He never bothered to ask about his daughter; he doesn't even know we had a girl." I blew out a breath, trying to control myself.

I heard my phone vibrate, and the devil himself had sent me a text. Chris had replied to my message.

-Tell me where you are so I can send you the papers or drop them off.

I rolled my eyes typing a quick reply to him.

-I was happy to sign and be out of your life for good, but that was until I found out you thought I cheated on you and accused our child of not being yours. I have left the city; you'd need to catch a plane to drop them off.

That was a lie, but I hoped he would get the picture as to how mad I really was.

I looked back over at Adam who was almost falling asleep in the chair. Lucy was tucked in on his chest as he laid down, holding his hands over her back. One of his eyes peered open, looking at me. "You know I'm staying with you until I think you're going to be okay on your own, right?"

I smiled, leaning back in the chair I was on. "Good. I wasn't going to let you leave yet anyway."

Adam had made it quite clear that he wasn't going anytime soon. The main hint was him hanging his shirts in the spare bedroom as he unpacked his suitcase. He was making the room his. Always the perfectionist, rearranging and decluttering. He was always like this when we used to share an apartment before I moved out, and in with Chris.

It was probably why I was a clean freak as well.

My brother was on the deck, lying back in the sun without his shirt on. His light brown hair was freshly wet from taking a dip in the water, and now he was sprawled out with Lucy on his chest. Every chance he had gotten, he was holding her in his arms. I loved it.

"Have you heard from his parents?" he brought up.

I was in the middle of taking a photo of the two of them, assuming he had dozed off to sleep. I assumed wrong. "Nope. They probably hate me too," I said with a heavy sigh, rolling my eyes as I sat the camera down on the ledge briefly, so I could fix the white cotton sock that had slipped from Lucy's tiny foot.

Adam's hand caught my wrist, and his voice went stern. "None of this is your fault. You do know that, right?" I nodded, already over this conversation. I just didn't want to sit here bashing my husband, because as much as I loathed him right now, I still loved him. It'd only been a week after all. The wounds were still raw.

25

"Anyway"—Adam cleared his throat—"Don't babies cry all the time? I haven't heard her cry much."

I grinned. "She's a good baby. But you haven't been here for a night yet, and she usually wakes a few times for milk."

"True. Ask me in the morning if I still think the same then." He winked and moved upright as Lucy stirred.

I looked up when Ness walked out, joining me and taking the seat Adam had only moved out of a few minutes ago when he went to take a call. I filled her in on my day and the events of what had happened with Chris; talking it over, getting her opinion on everything, and making me feel like I wasn't going crazy. My head was spinning, and she looked like I had spat in her coffee when I mentioned the emails about Chris wanting to know if we were okay.

"Like he gives a shit. If he did, then he would be here himself with you." She scoffed. "He's full of shit."

"Adam is here." I gave a genuine smile, feeling happy that I had my brother with me.

"I know. He called me last night and asked me to keep it a surprise for you. It was hard to keep my mouth shut, but I managed." She winked. That explained the phone call she took outside last night. "I just wish Adam would have punched Chris for us all."

I would love to punch him right now. "Yeah, tell me about it. I bet that cow told him I was cheating, and he believed her. She always pisses me off. I can't stand the sight of her."

"The cow?" Adam asked, popping his head outside looking slightly confused.

"That bitch who takes his calls." I rolled my light blue eyes. "Looks like a supermodel but drools every time Chris walks past her desk." Heck, I even drool at the sight of him. He was beyond sexy, and even more so whenever he wore a suit.

That seemed to have refreshed his memory because my brother's smile grew from ear to ear. "Ah, Katie. Yes, she is a bit of a . . . uh, she's very friendly. Anyway, that was Mum asking how

26

you are and wanting to know if you're on the verge of a breakdown." He bent down and scooped Lucy back up into his arms. "Can I feed her?" Adam asked as my daughter let a little cry out.

Ness laughed loudly, slightly snorting. "Why? Do you want to give breastfeeding a go?"

Adam shot her a glare but smiled. "No, I want to give her a bottle. I could help during the nights if you wanted. I don't mind getting up if you feel like sleeping."

I stared at my brother and saw the happiness spreading on his face. To think my own brother was excited about getting up in the middle of the night to help feed my daughter was beyond me. "I guess I need to go buy a pump then."

His brows rose, and he looked confused. "Pump?"

"You'd be familiar with a pump, wouldn't you? But I guess only to make something else bigger." Ness teased.

I should have known he would come back at her. "Trust me. It's too big to fit inside a pump." He walked away, muttering something else under his breath.

"You know, you're horrible to him." I laughed, sitting up and standing with a stretch. "I need to shower."

"I know, but he loves it. Plus, what does he expect after all those years of picking on us?" She grinned. "Let's go into town and buy a breast pump. You may as well take his offer on the night feeds."

*   *   *

Showered and dressed in a pair of navy shorts and a white tee, I was ready to go. With makeup on, I felt slightly more human than earlier. My blonde hair was tied in a twisted-up bun, and I had a pair of black Ray-Ban glasses on. I was enjoying an almond milk chai latte, while Adam pushed Lucy in her pram. It was the first time I'd left the cabin since coming down here.

"You know, anyone would think she's your daughter with the way you're acting, Adam." Ness raised a brow at him.

"You're just jealous because she loves me and lets me hold her without screaming," he retorted, unbothered.

"Whatever," she grumbled. I had to laugh at them both with their back-and-forth banter and constant bickering.

The weather was warm, and the streets were busy as we walked along the pathway. Adam handed the pram back over to me, and it didn't feel normal as I pushed it. I needed to get out more often and take Lucy for walks. I peered into where she was laying; her tiny body dressed in a pastel pink all-in-one short jumpsuit with a little blue bird on the front. She had more clothes than me, and it was easy to get swept up in the excitement of buying more.

I spotted my brother and Ness walking back out of the shops with three large bags and big smiles on their faces. When they reached me, they handed the bags over to me so I could place them in the bottom of the pram.

"Where to next?" I asked.

"Pump and bottles," Adam said, grinning.

"Words I never want to hear again from you." I laughed, shaking my head.

CHAPTER FOUR

"*Are you nervous?*" *I whispered against Chris's ear, nipping his lobe with my teeth to try and lighten him up.*

"*Yes.*" *He smirked back, sliding his hand lower from my waist until he cupped my ass. "Don't tell anyone that or I will deny it strongly."*

I couldn't help but giggle, pulling away to sit on the stool beside him, my hand resting against his thigh. "Oh, the big bad lawyer is scared of something after all." I bit my lip, as he laughed slightly, lifting his tumbler filled with his usual scotch, and then downing the last of it, motioning to the bartender for another.

"*Only around you, my dear.*" *He smiled, taking hold of my hand, placing a gentle kiss. "Your brother, how old is he? What does he do?"*

I scanned the bar, checking by the door and smiled as I spotted Adam walking in. "Your age; he's here. Relax, and play it nice."

We had decided getting drinks for when they met would be a little easier. Plus, my brother loved this bar, so I was hoping he was in a great mood already. The subject of family hadn't really been brought up; we were too busy in our little bubble. But since we had decided to move in together, we needed to the do whole meet-the-family thing. And starting with my brother was the first move.

Unfortunately, one thing I didn't plan was for them to already know each other, and judging by the look on Adam's face, he wasn't happy about this at all. His brows scrunched, eyes darting from Chris to me.

"*You're dating my sister?*" *Adam's jaw clenched as he stared down at Chris.*

"Adam." Chris was taken aback for a moment but cleared his throat and stood up. "I should have put two and two together. I had no idea. I would have said something if I did."

Running a hand through his hair, Adam scoffed. "Fucking hell, Charlotte. Out of all the men to pick from, you just had to choose the guy I work for?"

My mouth fell open, and then closed again, unable to find the right words to say. It should have dawned on me weeks ago when I met Chris, all his talk about being a lawyer, and the firm . . . but it didn't. I clearly wasn't thinking about that. It was only when Chris had placed his hand on my lower back, giving a reassuring rub that I was able to snap back to reality.

There was so much to say, yet, the only words that came out were "I love him."

"You don't know him; how can you love him?" Adam raised a brow. My brother didn't believe in love. Well, not anymore. He was a cynic when it came to love.

"We've been together a month. Since that storm, he was the one who drove me home and things just kind of happened," I answered, picking up my drink for a well-needed mouthful.

Bad choice of words as Adam's glare hardened. "So you fucked my sister? What? You give her a lift, so you expect her to put out in return?"

"No. I didn't fuck her at all. I gave her a lift because she would have been stuck on the streets in that storm. She offered dinner as thanks; nothing happened," Chris replied, his tone showing he was now getting pissed off. I had to hand it to the guy for standing up to him. He also made a wise decision to leave out the part about us kissing and sharing a bed together.

"Do you love her? Or, are you just stringing her along to pass your time?" Adam asked, eyeing both Chris and me.

"Of course, I love her. If I didn't, I wouldn't be asking her to move in."

"Fine. Live together in sin, but I swear if you hurt her, make her cry, or even look at another woman, I will put you six feet under. Boss or not, I don't fucking care," Adam said, then his scowl turned to a grin. "And you're

clearly shouting drinks and dinner tonight." He winked, leaning over to place a kiss on my forehead.

*   *   *

Adam and I both froze when there was a loud firm knock on the door.

It wasn't even 6 AM. Who the hell would be visiting at this time? Adam and I had been up with Lucy for a good part of the night. She pretty much screamed the place down from 10 PM and only stopped whenever there was a breast in her mouth.

I didn't know what the matter was; she wouldn't stop crying. I thought maybe it was a tummy ache or acid reflux. We googled and searched, did every self-help option that we found, and nothing seemed to work except a breast in her gob. Then each time I tried to lay her back in the bassinet, or if I moved, she woke with a loud cry and it was back to the start again. Not even a bath was calming her. We had taken her for a walk in the pram, circling the walking track multiple times. She did stop crying. However, there was no sleeping; only her beady bright eyes staring back at us.

It was only half an hour ago that she had chucked all over Adam, and then dozed off on the bed.

Adam's face was so funny when she did it. He then took a shower, and I was starting to fall asleep when the knock woke me.

"Do you think Ness is coming to complain about the noise?" I whispered, carefully getting off the bed to answer the door before the persistent knocking woke Lucy.

I'd possibly smother anyone if they woke my baby up right now.

Adam cracked a grin as I tiptoed to the door, him quietly walking behind me. As I opened the door, I was beyond shocked.

There stood our parents, dressed and ready for the day. Their car was parked beside mine and the boot still popped open.

Mum had her black leather handbag on her shoulder, whilst Dad carried two plastic bags in each hand, filled with groceries. We must have looked like death as their faces suddenly broke out into wide smiles.

"Welcome to parenthood, kids." Dad grinned, slapping Adam on the back as he walked past us.

"Thanks," Adam and I muttered at the same time.

"For goodness sake, Adam, put a damn shirt on." Mum laughed, pulling on his dark spread of chest hair. I had to hold in my laughter as I looked at him looking tired, wet hair sticking up all over his head.

"They're covered in spew," he defended, pushing her hand away. "And don't talk so loud; Lucy has just fallen asleep."

"Who knew your brother would be quite the mother hen?" Mum laughed softly, giving me a nudge.

I smirked, biting my full bottom lip, then let out a tired yawn. "He's the best big brother ever."

"I'm your only big brother," he pointed out, yawning as well.

We went and sat outside to talk; I was too worried that Lucy was going to wake up and scream all day again. I couldn't help but notice how happy my parents seemed. They had a wonderful life of always travelling every six months. Just packing up the caravan and taking off to a new town or just randomly driving anywhere they desired. I would love to do that: the life of the retired. Both of them had worked hard and saved, and now they're enjoying their lives to the fullest.

"When can we see the little princess?" Dad raised a brow; Mum and Dad both wanted to sneak into the room and have a peek at her.

I half rolled my eyes; I still hadn't slept a wink, and I feared Lucy would be screaming the place down again if the slightest noise was made.

"When she wakes up." I just smiled, sipping on my second hot tea.

I had my legs up on the railing to catch the sun that was now shining brightly, trying to get a tan. When I looked beside me, I saw Adam glaring directly at our parents. I hadn't thought anything of the silence, until now.

"What's going on?" I asked, not understanding why they were looking like they're ready to kill each other. Not even two minutes had passed, and the whole atmosphere had change drastically. It was thick with tension.

"Nothing is the matter, Charlotte. Just ignore them." Adam tried offering me a reassuring smile.

I wasn't buying it. "What? Is everything okay?"

"I won't sit here and pretend nothing is wrong. What the hell happened between you and Chris? He won't speak to any of us." Dad's gruff voice growled, making me jump slightly. "Talk to us. Tell us what happened."

I pulled on the oversized jumper that was once my husband's; I had taken it the day I packed up and left. This wasn't something I wanted to talk about right now. I was tired, and just sick of talking about Chris and him leaving me. "We're getting divorced, end of story." Saying those words hurt each time somewhat more.

"She's joking; they aren't divorcing." Adam shot me a warning glare.

I knew he was just trying to calm Dad down. But I was confused to why he would say that to them when it was the truth; Adam knew Chris wanted a divorce.

"You need to go back and fix your marriage, Charlotte." Dad shook his head, turning his full attention to me as he leaned forward.

I was automatically in defense mode. "Me? I didn't do anything wrong!" I put my feet on the ground, getting ready to stand up.

"You took off with his child; no wonder the man is asking for a divorce!" he bawled, shaking his head. "Jesus, Charlotte."

Tears were prickling in my eyes; *how could he just accuse me of taking off like that?* I hadn't done anything wrong. My heart rate was increasing as I sighed shaking my head. "No. He left me before I had given birth. I came home, and he had divorce papers already drawn up. I didn't do anything wrong," I defended, feeling like they assumed me guilty already.

"You just took off and gave up on your marriage. Just like how your brother did with that girl of his." Dad shook his head, waving his hand through the air with annoyance.

I couldn't believe he was siding with Chris on this, and to throw my brother's old relationship into the conversation was a harsh blow to Adam.

Adam's situation was completely different from mine.

"Both my kids got married then divorced a year later." Mum sighed, looking ready to cry. "Did we raise you wrong? Did we not teach you about love and marriage?"

Her reaction surprised me because I had expected her to be a heck of a lot more sympathetic with me. She was my mother, and she knew how hard it could be with a newborn, lack of sleep, and no help. It was as if my parents were rubbing salt into fresh wounds.

When I felt the small cry from inside, I bit the inside of my cheeks and stood up, pointing at them both. "Don't you dare come here and tell me I'm the one at fault. Chris doesn't even think Lucy is his daughter. As for Adam, he was eighteen, and his girlfriend cheated on him with his best friend. So thanks for coming here, making me feel worse than I already do, *and* for waking Lucy up."

Fresh tears pooled in my eyes as I went back to the bedroom and locked the door. I picked Lucy up, holding her close against my chest and rocking gently. My head was pounding, and my eyes were tired. I decided to take a shower to clear my thoughts and calm my body down. I stripped myself and Lucy naked and made our way into the shower.

Lucy's cries slowly subsided as the water cascaded down her bare back, soothing her. Her little hand fisted a firm grip on my wet hair and gently tugged it. It wasn't until I was ready to finish up that I noticed her fast asleep, eyes firmly shut and mouth slightly parted, soft breathing coming out. Maybe this was what she needed? Just close skin-to-skin contact.

All my anger vanished instantly. Lucy was the most precious thing in the world to have fallen asleep while we were in the shower. I made my way out, still naked and dripping wet. I picked up my camera and took a quick photo. Yes, I was nude, but hell, I was a mother, and this was too much of a precious moment to miss out on.

Laying Lucy's little body down slowly on the fluffy white towel that I had placed over the bed, I gently wrapped her up to keep her warm. Quickly, I dried myself off and changed into a pair of blue cotton boxer shorts, and a singlet top then went back to Lucy, still passed out as I unwrapped the towel and grabbed a nappy and a singlet to put on her.

I sat on the bed just staring at her as she was still fast asleep in her bassinet. I had managed to move her without her waking. I should have lain down to sleep, but as I said, she was a time waster.

My bedroom door opened slowly, and I thought it might be Adam, but when I looked up, I caught sight of my mum walking in. She said nothing at first. Her eyes gazed over to me quickly as she closed the bedroom door and made the walk over.

She stopped and peered in the bassinet, and a smile spread on her face. "Oh my," she whispered, her voice sounding as though she might cry any second.

I knew she was referring to Lucy being a spitting image of Chris.

She sat down beside me, holding my hand softly. "She's beautiful, absolutely breathtaking," she whispered again.

I nodded keeping my eyes on Lucy. "How could he leave me?" I whispered back. "Us," I corrected.

"I have no idea. Adam told us that you spoke with him last week. What did he have to say?" she asked softly.

"Nothing. He's too angry with me." I shrugged it off as if it didn't hurt. But that had been the worst part: Chris believed whoever had been filling his head with lies.

"We'll just see what happens then. Your father and I will be in town for a couple of days, so we can take little Lucy for walks and to the park."

She reached out, running a fingertip over Lucy's cheek. "Your father didn't mean to say what he said; he's just angry and upset about the situation. Adam had a word with him while you were taking a shower. I put a load of washing on, so your brother can have some clean shirts."

"Thanks. It was pretty funny when she threw up on him." I smiled, slightly trying to keep the noise down.

I lay down on the bed hugging my pillow, wishing it could have been my husband who was always there to hold me tightly against his chest. I missed his touch. His smell. Just the fact he would always find a reason to touch me.

Mum stayed on the bed staring at Lucy, not wanting to look away from her.

I started to feel my eyelids get heavier and slowly felt myself drift off into a deep sleep.

*　　*　　*

Someone was holding me tightly, a warm and strong body pressed against my back as I stirred, waking up. "Chris?" I mumbled as I felt an arm wrapped around my waist, holding me slightly tighter.

"No." A deep sleepy voice spoke in my back. I moved quickly, and my eyes started watering. How could I have been so stupid to think that Chris was here with me? I don't even know why I would think or dream about him. Adam pulled me back to him, rubbing my arms. "It's okay. You were crying in your sleep when I came to check on you."

"It's fine, Adam. I went to sleep thinking about him." I yawned, rubbing my eyes. "Why would I think he was here with me when he's not?"

"It's not fine, Charlotte. He should be here. He should have fucking come and begged you to take him back, that's why I haven't killed him yet. My own mate ditched my sister, and I have to watch how it affects you. I watch how it kills you every morning you wake up." He sat up, running a hand through his hair.

"Should I call him?" I asked, wondering why the hell I would even suggest that for.

He gave me a look to say *are you fucking crazy,* but then his eyes softened. "If he wanted to talk, he'd have called you."

I hated that he was right.

I shrugged, not knowing what to do. I felt stuck between a rock; part of me wanted to call him and let him know where I was to let him see what he did, but the other part never wanted to speak to him again.

"Why is it that I always give in and feel like I am the bad one?" I hated that I felt this way.

"It's because you're such a good person. You have a pure heart; this isn't your fault." I went to peer over at Lucy, but Adam grinned. "Mum and Dad took Lucy for a walk not long ago. She woke up just before I came in. Don't worry; I gave them an hour limit. Otherwise, I will call the police to report a kidnapping." He winked.

I rolled my eyes at him. There was no doubt about him; he was definitely a mother hen.

Temptation caught the better of me; my stomach swarming with butterflies as I rang the number. I didn't bother to block the call. He would see my caller ID and either answer or send me to voicemail. I guess I needed to talk to him; we had things to discuss if he was adamant about leaving me.

It rang three times before a breathless woman answered, *"Hang on. Let me put my top back on."* There was more shuffling in the background, and then she spoke clearer. *"Hello?"*

It was on speaker, so Adam could hear as well. I thought I had the wrong number until Chris' deep voice spoke too. "Hello?"

My heart dropped; Chris was with another woman, and she was getting dressed. How could he do that? How the fucking hell could he do this to me? Rage hit me. "We aren't even divorced yet, and you're already fucking your secretary. Are you trying to fucking kill me even more than you have been?!" I shouted angrily into the speaker.

"Charlotte?" His voice came through, panicked.

I didn't hear anything else. I hung up and tossed the phone on the bed. I was fuming to a point where if I were in the same town as him, I would have marched to his office and thrown the bitch through his large floor-to-ceiling length window from the top floor of the building.

My head was lying on Adam's chest as I clutched his shirt, holding it tightly as I cried. This wasn't like any other cry; it was a realisation that Chris was moving on. He was moving on and leaving me behind.

I had lost something so good, and I didn't even know why. He promised me he would never divorce me and that he would never sleep with another woman. He even promised that if I died, he still wouldn't move on. He would never be able to get over me. But here he was.

He completely broke my heart.

I was wrong. Everything he said meant nothing to me now, and hearing the woman on the phone was just validation that Chris didn't care. I didn't know this type of heartbreak existed.

It was pure torture to know the man I pictured spending the rest of my life with had moved on.

CHAPTER FIVE

Two car trips later, I was fully unpacked.

I had moved into Chris's penthouse that overlooked the park and city. It was beyond amazing.

Adam had gotten over the fact I was dating his boss. He didn't freak out when I had turned up at work to see Chris. Well, when I visited last week, he was a little creeped out about the image of his boss slamming his little sister over the desk—his words, not mine.

Chris and I had lunch together each day due to my insane workload. Summer was wedding season. We both try to see each other when we could, in between my weekends of rushing from job to job. I had a wedding to photograph tomorrow, and I had to be there at 11 a.m., so my day with Chris was cut short, but he assured me he was taking Monday off to spoil and fuck me senseless.

I couldn't wait.

A set of arms wrapped around my waist, and his mouth placed feather kisses against the base of my neck as I stood in the living area, looking around. "You want to hope my brother doesn't see you kissing me like this; he might get jealous."

"Well, I better be quick." He laughed, spinning me around and lifting me up as he carried me towards the bedroom—our bedroom. My legs automatically wrapped around his waist, holding on tightly.

His body was moving over mine as he lowered me to the bed. "I want to make love to you."

"Oh, that's really romantic. Isn't the honeymoon over now that we live together?" I grabbed the base of his shirt, lifting it up, exposing his toned chest, and pushing it further to catch sight of the dark spread of chest hair. He sat up to finish removing it, tossing it aside on the floor.

"I'll make sure the honeymoon never ends." He smirked, bending back down, peeling my shorts off.

"And if I say no?" I questioned, tugging his belt off completely then unbuttoned his jeans and kicked them down with my feet.

"Then you may find me jerking off to you in the shower each morning." He grinned, sliding his hand up my top, pulling it up, and throwing it over to the pile of clothing on the floor.

The only clothing left on us was my bra and panties, and his boxers that were looking a little too tight around the groin area. I ran my hands over his bare back, slightly scratching with my nails. "Well then, boyfriend, I suggest you make love to me before I change my mind."

"I love you, Charlotte," he said as he pulled my panties off, and then moved to my bra.

"I love you more, Chris." I smiled, as I pulled the top of his underwear down.

"Not possible, baby. I love you more with each breath I take." The words were sexy and arousing, driving me wild as his mouth came crashing down over mine.

*   *   *

I was still staring at the phone—the phone that kept on ringing. I had already ignored it twice, and it was now ringing for a third time. I looked up at Adam who didn't say anything except to let out a loud sigh. He then reached out and pushed the phone closer towards me; I knew he wanted to me answer, or Chris wouldn't stop calling otherwise.

I felt myself giving in yet again. Damn him. *"What?"* I answered through the phone in a loud, harsh voice. My tone surprised me.

"That wasn't what it sounded like. I swear nothing is going on with me and her. There has been no one else, Charlotte." He rushed out probably thinking I was going to hang up again.

"Then why did she answer out of breath and say she was getting dressed?" I accused, feeling more tears coming on. *"Don't lie to me. I'm not stupid."*

"I don't know, but I am at work, Charlotte." He sighed. I could only imagine him running a hand through his hair, something he often did when he was annoyed.

"Didn't stop you from screwing me on your desk each week." Yes. I just had to throw that in there to piss him off even more.

"Seriously? I didn't want to know that, and I sit in that office and touch that desk each day," Adam hissed in a whisper.

I stuck my tongue out at, him enjoying how uncomfortable he looked.

"Look, Charlotte. I'm too busy to fight. Did you call for a reason or not?" Wow. He was now angry again. I could tell by the way he said my name.

"Have you had the new papers drawn up?" I asked, staring down at my chipped navy nail polish.

There was nothing but silence on the other end. I heard a loud smash followed by a low curse. I knew he had just thrown something. *"Is that all you want? Full custody?"*

"Yes," I whispered, but my heart said no. I wanted him as well. *"Don't do this, Chris,"* I whispered, pausing for a moment. *"How could you leave me like that?"* I started crying; I just couldn't hold it in.

"Please don't cry, Char." He breathed out softly. *"I was so angry. I went to leave, but then I was shown photos. Jesus. Fuck! You were the last person I wanted to see."*

42

He didn't make any sense. I wasn't understanding any of it. "You will never get that day back. I never once cheated on you, and I have no idea what photos you have seen. I didn't do anything."

"You were in a fucking bed—fucking him, Charlotte. It's your naked body, and I should know what that looks like. The date is there. The same day you fell pregnant: 12th of May." His voice was loud, booming through the phone.

I was lost for words. What the hell? It made no sense. I haven't ever been with another man. "Email the photos to Adam, you fucking asshole! I hate you, Chris. I fucking hate you," I shouted and ended the call, more tears running down my face.

Randomly, my cries turned to laughter, and I fell back on the bed, groaning with an exasperated sigh. I didn't do anything wrong, yet here I was, crying over the man who hurt me—who was accusing me of lying and cheating.

"How the hell did my life get so screwed up?"

Shaking his head, Adam just grinned. I wanted to tell him that he needed a shave but left him alone. "No idea, but I have a feeling Katie has something to do with all of this. Hopefully, he sends the photos to me then we can check them out."

Oh, I couldn't wait to see these supposed photographs. "Thanks. How about I make a start on dinner; Mum and Dad should be back soon. I'm hungry, and I know Lucy will be starving for milk."

"I just hope she sleeps all night," Adam said as he yawned.

"Same. Just sleep in here tonight. Mum and Dad will expect to get your bed, and this one is big enough for the both of us." I gave him a lazy smile. "The couch is comfortable too."

We got up, and I started on dinner. I started to cut up some potatoes, bacon, and leeks for soup. Adam was on his phone, making calls. Even though he was not at work, he still busied himself with work.

The door opened, and Mum walked in with a screaming Lucy. Ah, I had forgotten how loud she could be. Mum brought her over to me, and I went and sat down in the chair I usually fed her in. Her little mouth opened widely, searching for my milk source as I laid her down to lift my top and unclasp my bra.

I laid back as she suckled and held my breast, her little eyes wandering around as she guzzled down each drop quicker than the last.

"Someone is starving," Dad noted, as he sat opposite me leaning back on the couch with his eyes closed. I was still annoyed with him from what he said earlier today.

Adam walked over, passing me his phone. I noticed the message on the screen. It was from Chris.

-I never wanted to hurt Char, but I can't, for the life of me, forgive her for this. Every day, I want to pick up that phone and tell her I still love her, but I can't. I can't get this image out of my head, and I don't know if I ever will. I'm sorry. We both should move on and end everything.

I scrolled down and looked over at the photo. It was me in a compromising position with Joel, one of Chris's friends. I was sucking him off in other words. All you could see was my back as I was naked on my knees. The next photo was of us in a bed together. I was on top of him while pushing him down into the bed. The last picture was of us exiting a hotel in town, hand in hand, but yet, you still couldn't see my face in all the pictures.

They may all have looked exactly like me, but I knew for a fact that they weren't. They weren't me at all. I had never once been to that hotel, let alone been together with him.

"They are fakes," I whispered, not wanting Mum and Dad to hear this conversation.

"Well, I didn't think you would cheat on him. I knew it wasn't true." He took his phone back, forwarding the pictures to me so I could look at them properly on my laptop. "It's why I have never asked if what he said was true or not."

Lucy had finished drinking, and I moved her off my boob, fixing myself up as Dad walked back in with a drink for me. I'm assuming he was sucking up, trying his best to fix what had happened earlier this morning.

Adam lay down on the red rug that was over the floor with Lucy who was having some tummy time. He lay down in front of her, just staring at her, holding a rattle and moving it back and forth, teasing her. I smiled, watching them play together.

"How was the walk?" I asked, turning my attention back to Mum.

"It was good. She was a good little girl and only cried as we arrived back here," Dad spoke, up moving down to the floor where he joined Adam and Lucy.

"She is by far the prettiest girl I know." Adam grinned, taking a photo of him and Lucy together.

"She looks just like her father," Dad commented. I didn't say anything because I didn't know how to respond to that. I knew fully well Lucy looked just like Chris without people bringing it up.

"Sit up with your father and brother, and I will take a photo of you all." Mum pulled out her new phone; she now thinks she is very clever because she can use a touchscreen. We had brought her one for Christmas to replace the old heavy brick she called a phone.

Dinner was soon ready. I had no appetite. Mum gave me a stern look. "You have hardly eaten, Charlotte."

I twirled the spoon around the bowl with my fingers; I just didn't feel like eating tonight. I was tired and not hungry at all. After seeing those photos, my hunger just vanished. I felt sick if anything. "I'm just not hungry," I answered, shrugging like a teenager.

"You're losing weight quickly. There's barely anything left of you," Dad said in a hesitant tone.

What was this? Attack Charlotte day? I looked up, and all three of them were staring at me with concerned faces. "It's nothing. I'm just losing the baby weight, and breastfeeding helps; my weight is fine. Trust me, I'm eating."

45

"You're thinner than before you were pregnant," Mum said. She had a way with her words to make me second guess everything. "You need to eat some more." She sighed, turning back to her soup.

"We should take Lucy to the beach tomorrow if you want?" I had to hand it to my brother. His efforts of trying to change the subject went unnoticed.

I didn't even bother to finish dinner. I just stood and picked up Lucy who was in her rocker by the table, just sucking on her fists and quietly looking around. "I'm going to put her to bed." I walked off, ignoring anything more that would be said about me.

Nothing was ever easy, and my family definitely wasn't easy.

I needed their support, not doubts and negativity: throwing the blame around, and trying to make me feel worse than I ever have.

My body needed an early night. I just didn't want to listen to my parents talk about my weight or Chris, reminding me yet again that I was going to be co-parenting with him.

I lay Lucy in the bed beside me, just wanting to have some time with her before I feed her and place her in her bed for the night. I hoped she slept better than last night. Otherwise, Adam would probably be pulling his hair out. It only took around twenty minutes before she was passed out like a light, softly breathing, swaddled, and tucked into her bed for the evening. Or for as long as she would stay sleeping.

My eyes became heavy and almost closed when my phone began to vibrate. I knew it was Chris without having to look at the screen. Keeping my eyes closed, I answered and just listened.

I could hear him breathing softly on the other end of the line. He didn't say anything, and finally, I spoke first. *"Chris,"* I said quietly.

"I'm here," he spoke back, his words almost a whisper.

"*I don't hate you,*" I whispered, thinking I should probably start with that. "*I never meant that.*"

"*I know, Char. I don't blame you for hating me after everything.*"

It was quiet where he was, and I could only assume where he was. "*Are you at work?*"

"*Yeah, I've been staying here.*" He sighed. "*Where are you living? Do you need me to transfer some money through to you? I can do that now if you want.*"

I wanted to roll my eyes. "*No, it's okay. Adam has been helping me out. I'm with Ness. It's nice here; I have a place on the water.*"

"*You really are gone,*" he pointed out. Did he not think I had left?

"*You left me. Chris, you wanted this—the divorce and everything.*"

"*Why do I feel so empty and broken?*" he asked. "*All I see is those images, and it's tearing me apart.*"

"*The photo isn't of me. None of them are. Never have I ever cheated on you, Chris. You know me, and you know I wouldn't do something like that.*" I felt myself getting worked up again as my throat felt like it was closing over. I silently lay there, crying.

There was nothing but silence. For over five minutes, both of us were quiet. I almost spoke up until Chris's voice was on the line again, asking for something I didn't think I would ever hear. "*I know I don't deserve this, and I understand if you say no, but . . . would you send me a photo?*"

I hung up on him.

How could I answer when I was in tears? I just lay there, sobbing, clutching the phone to my ear as I cried. It was the last thing I wanted to do.

Swiping my finger over the screen, scrolling through the photos I had taken since Lucy's birth, I found one on her tummy that was taken tonight. Her big eyes, almost as if they were smiling back at me with her dark, thick lashes, I smiled. Before I could stop myself. I was already pressing send with an attached text message.

-Our daughter.

Not even 60 seconds later, a new reply from him lit up my screen.

-She's perfect.

CHAPTER SIX

Who would have thought that today, I would be experiencing both pain and pleasure?

I had experienced pleasure as I was woken up with light feather kisses being placed all over my bare back whilst his fingertips wandered between my thighs. Chris woke in a very happy mood, and I was guessing he had a good night's sleep.

Right now, we stood in a small tattoo shop. A guy called Trent was covered with ink from head to toe, staring at me curiously after he and Chris exchanged hellos. Apparently, they went to school together and were still friends.

"So, do you know what you want, sweetheart?" Trent asked, grinning at me.

I nodded, looking up at Chris. He had suggested we get each other's names over our ring fingers, and I thought it was the best idea ever until I saw the actual tattoo pen. Now, I was freaked out. I hated needles with passion.

I sat down in the chair once Chris told Trent what I wanted to have done. I was still nervous but felt a slight comfort with Chris holding my other hand, as he sat in front of me, giving me ease.

"So how long have you two been together?" Trent asked as he started dabbing the pen in the black ink.

"Six weeks," Chris answered with a grin. Some may call us fucking insane.

"Shit, and you're getting each other's names inked already? Soon, you'll be living together."

"We moved in together last weekend," I answered with a laugh, closing my eyes.

I heard Trent laugh. "Are you sure you want to get this done? No going back."

"Of course, I do. We're going to be together forever." I smiled confidently, opening my eyes and finding Chris already looking at me as the pen hit my skin.

Thirty minutes later, I was sitting there, reading over the word 'Christopher' inked around my finger in cursive. I didn't regret getting this done.

Now, it was Chris's turn. He just looked relaxed and didn't even flinch as the needle hit his skin. I kept my eyes on him, looking for any sign of pain, and nope, nothing at all, which made him look even sexier. I liked that he had my name on him.

"It looks good." Chris held his hand out next to mine, our fingers side by side, inspecting the matching work.

"I love it. It's worth the pain." I smiled, leaning into his chest as we walked back towards the car.

He placed his hand on my ass, and with a firm swat, he spanked me. "I know another kind of pain you seem to love also."

Blushing like crazy, I rolled my eyes. "You wish!"

*　　*　　*

I didn't get the early night I had hoped for. One could only wish for a good night's sleep, but instead of napping while Lucy slept, I sat up with Adam, staring at the photographs he gave me. I knew this wasn't me, but how could I prove to Chris that it wasn't me straddling his friend?

The phone call with Chris was kept a secret; I didn't bother mentioning it to Adam. I didn't think it was a good time to do so. I tied my hair into a messy bun and put my glasses on, as I tried to figure out how this was done.

Being a photographer, I was used to editing a lot and often. I had pulled the images up onto my computer and started to search every square inch. Zooming in, lightening, and darkening. It wasn't until I zoomed right in that I spotted something—a small, black Chinese symbol tattoo on her lower back. To the normal eye, it was unnoticeable, but to a photographer with a keen eye for detail, it was distinct.

I only had two tattoos: one was covered by my wedding ring, and the other was inked along the base of my neckline—three small blackbirds.

I emailed these back to Chris and heard nothing. There was a huge chance he didn't believe me, because clearly not showing up to the birth of his child was enough proof that he doubted me. But innocent until proven guilty, I was damn sure I would prove and maintain my innocence.

He wouldn't have looked for the details I checked for. To him, the photo was me. The blonde in the photographs was me. He was given a 6x4 image, and he didn't know a thing about photography. Even Adam said if he didn't know better, he would think it was me too.

Twisting the wedding ring off, I traced over the small cursive ink on my ring finger, thinking back to the day we had been so happy and excited, both young and stupid in love. I knew in time I would have to take the rings off, but the white gold halo, a pear-shaped ring that Chris had given me meant too much right now to just discard and be rid of.

It could have been easier if he had cheated; I could have tossed them into the ocean or sold them. But it was impossible. I wasn't going to be able to get over him. I wasn't even going to try because no matter what, he was the only man I could love.

My heart for the time being belonged fully to him.

Slowly, I crept out of bed, pulled my hair up in a ponytail, and made my way down the hallway. Lucy was still sleeping, and I was going to try to get in a quick coffee before she woke up.

As my feet touched the cold wooden flooring, I stopped short when I heard hushed whispers. Adam and Mum were having a heated conversation, clearly about me.

"She's going to become sick again," Mum said quietly.

"No, she won't," Adam retorted.

"Adam, she barely ate her dinner. That was all I had seen her eat since coming here. She's starving herself, on the verge of—"

Adam cut her off harshly. "Chris fucking left her the day she had a baby. What do you expect to happen?" he growled. "Don't you dare say she's going to end up like that again? Why the hell do you think I am here for?"

"Well, I won't leave until I see her gain weight. I will force her on the scales every morning if I have to." Mum's voice came back just as strong again.

I finally decided to make my presence known to them. They were both standing in the kitchen, drinking coffee. Dad was also there, sitting down at the table reading the morning paper. They all looked up at me as I walked out, a little startled that I had possibly overheard their conversation.

"So, what would you like to see me eat? Pizza? Chocolate? A loaf of bread?" I asked, unable to hide the sarcasm as I pulled a bowl from the counter and grabbed the cereal from the pantry.

"Charlotte, we're just worried about you. That's all." Dad stood up, making his way over. "You're awfully thin, much too thin for someone who's just given birth."

I let out a scoff, rolling my eyes. "Jesus, I can't win, can I? I'm sorry for being so upset about the fact that my marriage is almost over. I eat," I reminded them. "I eat every day, three meals a day with Adam. You didn't see me eating yesterday because you were walking Lucy in the pram."

"Dear, it's not over. Just give him time to calm down." I looked at my mother like she had grown a second head. This was a woman who had asked why her kids were so emotionally screwed up, and now she was telling me to be sympathetic to Chris.

Was she taking his side now? Saying what happened wasn't his fault?

"I can't deal with this." I took my cereal and went to the bedroom.

Sitting cross-legged on the bed, eating in silence, I wondered if they had a point. *Was I too thin?* I stared at my body in the mirror before I showered. I mean, I was small, but I wasn't big either. My breasts were larger and fuller. My hips had more of a curve since giving birth, but I had remained fit and exercised daily during my pregnancy. I had lost weight, and no longer looked pregnant, but I wasn't as skinny as they made me out to be. No bones were sticking out; my clothes fit just fine.

If anything, I missed my belly. I missed being pregnant.

I guess I could see why Mum was worried about me slipping back. I had a hard time in high school. Being bullied and dealing with puberty wasn't the best time of my life. I wasn't overweight at the time, but the hurtful taunts had burned into my brain that I was fat and disgusting.

I just stopped eating.

If I ate, I felt guilty and forced myself to vomit each day.

No one knew about it, and then I just stopped eating altogether. I would skip meals, make myself fast, and if I had to eat something, I would work myself harder. Running each morning before my parents woke and then again in the afternoon, and I covered my body with baggy clothing so my parents wouldn't notice the sudden change in my appearance.

Unfortunately, one morning, I had been in my room changing after a shower when Adam had made an early surprise visit home from college. I was only in my bra and boy shorts panties when he had barged in to wake me up, and the look of horror that struck his face as he froze in the doorway told me he knew what I had been doing.

The fight that had erupted in the house was like a war. Adam's voice boomed so loud as he called out to Mum and Dad that I was sure the neighbours had heard him. He dragged me out by my arm to show them the bones protruding from my skin, demanding to know why they hadn't done anything about it to help me since he was gone.

Mum and Dad just stared shocked at me; they had no clue about any of it. It wasn't their fault, but that only made Adam more furious. He had packed my bags, and I moved in with him. I'll never forget the sight of my mother sobbing as we drove out. It was the right move. He helped and arranged for me to finish school early and from home. There were non-negotiable doctor appointments, and with the help of my brother, I was back to a healthy weight. I had never stepped foot on a set of scales since then.

Chris did know; I opened up and spoke to him about everything. That I had an eating disorder and that was a big part of why my brother and I were so close. Chris understood, and he never once made me feel anything less than sexy.

I stepped out of the shower and was met with nothing but silence. The whole house was dead quiet, and I knew that the tension was going to be thick once I went back out to them.

I changed into a pair of black yoga pants and a breastfeeding top. I made my way over to pick up Lucy but noticed she wasn't in her bed. Adam must have come and got her. I walked out and went back down towards the kitchen. Mum was cooking a feast for their breakfast, typical of her.

She was always trying to prove a point.

My bowl made a clunk sound as I dropped it into the water in the sink. I looked around and over to the sliding doors; Adam was outside with a bottle, feeding Lucy. He had even changed her clothing, dressing her in a floral-patterned summer suit.

"I can't wait until you have kids," I said, joining them.

"No kids for me. I'm just happy playing uncle." He laughed back, wiping a bit of spilt breast milk from her chin.

"You don't need to worry about me." I looked at them, sighing. "I'm eating properly. I'm not going to starve myself."

"I know. I just worry; we all do." He offered a smile. "Just make sure you take care of yourself."

I hesitated and bit my lip. "I sent a photo of Lucy to Chris last night. He called. We spoke very briefly, but he asked for a photo, and I sent one," I confessed, trying to ignore the swirl of emotions in my stomach.

He nodded, leaning back on the wicker chair and looking out at the ocean. "Did he say anything back to you?"

"Yes." The bubble of well-kept emotion was about to burst. "That she was perfect."

"Are you okay?" he asked with concern, his eyes shifted to mine.

With a shrug, I could easily lie and say yes. Or, I could be honest and say no. I just didn't know anymore. "I miss him." It was God's honest truth. I just really fucking missed him.

I was glad I had not bothered to put a full face of makeup on because it would have been ruined by the crying I was now doing again. I hated crying. I was doing my own head in with it. I thought I would have been well out of tears by now. After a couple weeks of constantly crying, it should have only gotten easier, but instead, it was getting harder.

Everything was becoming too much for me. I was slowly crumbling, falling in defeat over my mess of a so-called life. My parents being here was adding a new stress that I didn't need. I didn't need to listen to the nagging and complaining; they were still bickering in the kitchen. It was no wonder Adam was sitting out here on his own.

"Do you feel like going for a walk?" I suggested. A walk always cleared my mind.

"Sounds like an effing good idea." He blew out a long breath, placing the towel over his shoulder, and getting ready to burp Lucy.

We bolted out of the door, ignoring Mum's yelling to come back and eat the food she cooked before it went cold, both of us laughing as I pushed the pram down the pathway towards the beach.

It was going to be another beautiful day; the water was falling against the sand as it came to shore.

The beach was one of my favourite places to be.

We walked in nothing but complete silence. There was a pathway going right around the edge of the water, so we just kept on following it. I spotted Mum and Dad walking towards us, and I hit Adam in the side, making him turn around and groan as he ended the work call he had taken. "Fingers crossed Mum has calmed down."

"One can only hope." I chuckled as we reached them, both looking nervous yet happy. They were up to something.

"I have a wonderful idea." Mum smiled as she reached us. "Why don't you come back home and live with us? I can take care of you and Lucy when Adam goes back to work."

I looked at Adam, and he just shook his head and walked off. Mum acted as though Adam couldn't help me, and he was incapable of being able to look after Lucy as well. "Mum, thanks, and I really appreciate everything, but I am staying here for the time being. I like it here."

She nodded but didn't say anything. It was a telltale sign that she wasn't happy with my answer.

After we came back from the walk, Mum managed to force me to sit down and eat everything she piled up on my plate. There was so much food, and I had told her after eating both pancakes, I didn't want any more. She didn't listen and piled two more on, plus more eggs and three sausages.

I hated sausages with a passion. There was no way she would get me to eat them.

Feeding and changing a diaper that made me want to throw up, I put Lucy to bed and walked into the bedroom for a break. I

56

was done listening to the constant fighting. I had come here to relax and get away from all the tension. I wanted a new life and a new start, but instead, I was feeling suffocated.

Mum was trying to help, but it was making me feel like I couldn't take care of myself. I felt judged.

I stood up and walked out calmly, but I held my ground. "That's it," I said firmly. "This needs to stop. I am staying here until I sort something else out. For now, this is my home, and you can't come in and tell me how to live my life. I'm twenty-six for crying out loud; Adam is almost thirty-five. You treat him and me like incapable stupid children. I need some space," I seethed, my temper flaring as I shook my head. I heard Lucy wake again and let out a frustrated groan.

"Let me take her." Mum offered when I walked back out with her.

I shook my head, refusing. "No. I am her mother. I'm taking her for a walk. Alone."

"Don't you dare leave here; we haven't finished talking. Lucy needs a nap so put her to bed; let her cry to sleep. We need to sit and have a long talk about everything that's going on," Mum called out, following me.

I turned back, and if my expression didn't tell her to back up, then my words sure did. "Don't you dare tell me what to do with *my* daughter. I am her mother, and I will be taking her with me."

"Charlotte." I heard my name being called.

Not in the mood, I snapped back. "What?" I asked, placing her in her pram and tucking the blanket in.

But when I turned to see who was calling out to me, I was frozen to my spot.

My heart was racing, and my breathing faster as I gripped the handle of the pram. I just looked at Chris, unable to blink. *What was he doing here? What did he want? Had he come to deliver the divorce papers in person?*

I had so many questions to ask, but there were no words; nothing came out as I opened my mouth to speak. He hadn't shaved, and it was almost strange to see him without a clean-shaven face. He was dressed well: jeans, a polo shirt, and a pair of brown leather shoes. Almost rugged, sexy.

It was like seeing him for the first time all over again.

But then I remembered what he had done, and how he had left me and his daughter.

CHAPTER SEVEN

"Mum? Dad?" Chris called out as we entered his parents' home.

A big beautiful country house that he had spent his entire life growing up in. The family home he was raised in until he moved out almost ten years ago, living alone ever since then. Well, until now.

"In here, Christopher," a woman, who I assume was his mother, called out.

I heard Chris groan at being called his full name. It only made me giggle. "Ready to meet the parents?" He winked, placing a hand against my lower back and trying to sneak down to my ass as his fingers spread out to caress.

I squirmed, wiggling and sliding away. "Now is not the time to turn me on, Christopher," I murmured in a low voice, glancing up at him as he let out a quiet chuckle, and pulled a face at my reference to his name.

Walking through a wooden oak door to a large kitchen, I was met with an older greyer version of my boyfriend—his father. I had seen photos of his parents, but to meet and see them in the flesh was daunting. His mother, carrying a tray of biscuits as she walked out, greeted us both with a warm smile.

I spoke first, unafraid. "Hello, I'm Charlotte."

"Son?" Mr. Rivers spoke, looking from me to Chris, who stood beside me.

"Dad, meet my girlfriend." Chris wrapped his arm tighter around me "Charlotte, these are my parents, David and Cindy."

"Pigs must be flying if my big brother is finally in love." Another voice called out as a bubbly woman bounced out with eagerness, greeting us with a huge smile. *"Did he pay you?"*

"I wish." I winked.

"Shut up." He scoffed, rolling his eyes at then woman. *"Charlotte, this is my sister, Samantha."*

She walked right up and pulled me in for a hug *"Nice to meet you, Charlotte. If you can put up with my brother, then you must be one hell of a woman."*

"He's all right. I've got him tamed. Still, a little bossy and obsessed with neatness, but I'm almost on the verge of a breakthrough." I laughed, looking up at Chris, giving him a grin and nudge at the same time.

He rolled his eyes back at me. *"Well, at least I follow the 'leave the seat down' rule perfectly."*

Two gasps followed that revelation. Both came from the women. *"You two live together?"* Chris's mum asked, placing the tray down and removing her oven mitt.

"For about two months now," Chris said, making himself at home by going to the fridge, opening and taking a drink out.

"Wait, how long have you been together, and what the hell is on your finger?" Chris' father walked over, grabbing hold of his hand, and his sister did the same with me.

"Oh my god! Are you serious? A fucking tattoo?" Samantha screeched loudly; her eyes were full of humour, clearly loving the drama about to unfold.

"I know. We're crazy, aren't we?" I just smiled, slipping onto the bar stool opposite his mother. *"He talked me into it. I was ink-free until this man convinced me to spend the weekend with him."* I teased, as Chris let out a laugh.

"Bullshit. You had a tattoo before me." He smirked, running a finger over the nape of my neck. *"Birds of all things."*

I rolled my eyes. *"Birds are pretty; we should get one for the apartment,"* I teased, poking my tongue out at him.

"Don't hold your breath." He winked and went off talking to his father about a case he was currently working on.

Three months together, and I wouldn't change a thing; he was definitely the one for me.

*   *   *

My reality was like a bucket of ice water thrown in my face.

"Chris," I said, knowing he was really standing here, but not wanting to believe it.

He looked like he hadn't slept in days. His eyes were glazed over, appearing darker than they usually were.

"Charlotte." He stepped closer towards me. His voice wasn't what it used to be; he sounded as though his life was over. There was defeat in him. "I had to see you."

"Why? To drop off the divorce papers?" I couldn't stop myself from saying it.

"I don't . . . I just . . ." he trailed off with a murmur, his gaze dropped down to where he stood. Shuffling his feet, he looked like a lost child, standing there, waiting to be found.

It was only a matter of time before Adam, or worse, my parents walked out and spotted him.

In my mind, I wanted to punch him. I really did. I just wanted to hit him and scream at him. Curse his name under the sun about how much he had broken my heart. But my heart was yearning for him. My heart missed its soul mate. Part of me didn't want to care. I just didn't want to feel a thing for him. I wasn't the one who left after all. The strange thing was that I still loved him.

So instead of being a bitch and telling him to fuck right off, I took a step towards him, offering the kindness he didn't deserve without any emotion at all. "I'm going for a walk; would you like to join us?"

"Yes." His reply was so soft I almost didn't hear, but I didn't miss the glimmer of hope in his eyes that I hadn't written him off completely. I had a thousand questions for him, and a million more things to get off my chest.

We both fell into a slow pace; he stood beside me as I pushed the pram down the pavement, leading the way to nowhere in particular. But it was nice to just walk; it took the focus away from the anger I felt towards my mum at the moment with her intrusive questioning.

It would have to be the most awkward and uncomfortable silence I had ever been in. Chris didn't speak. His hands were in his pockets, as he looked ahead towards the ocean. I didn't know whether I should make the first move or wait until he spoke to me. So I stayed silent and just kept walking, holding my tongue as my mind raced with every thought possible.

Nearing a picnic table opposite the water, I broke the silence. "Do you mind if we sit for a moment?"

He nodded, cutting over the grass towards the table as I manoeuvred the pram to a stop. "Are you okay?" he asked, sitting but looking with concern.

"Just sore," I said quietly, because I was sore. My stomach was healing, but there was a reason I was on strict six-week–no-overdoing-it rules.

The awkward silence was there again; neither of us making any move to talk. I sat, rocking the pram back and forth so Lucy wouldn't wake up. It was minutes later when I decided to talk, not knowing what good it would have done, but it was worth a shot.

"She was born 4:32 PM the day I had gone into labour. The cord was wrapped around her neck and was choking her. I had to have an emergency C-section. She was blue when they pulled her from me. She didn't cry at first, not until after her cord was cut." I gazed down at Lucy, remembering how worried and scared I had been that she wasn't making a sound. "She was so perfect against my chest and eager for my breast. She was so small, but definitely has your height." I didn't dare look over at him, afraid my voice would waver, and my words would turn to cries. "I had no one. No one visited me in the hospital. My first baby and I were alone. I had to drive home against doctors' orders because I had no one to help me."

"Charlotte—"

I ignored him and kept talking. "Ness asked me to come here, and it was better than being alone back there. I didn't think; I just packed what I needed and left. Adam came a couple days later and had helped me a lot. My parents arrived yesterday morning, and you can imagine it's been hell." I bit my tongue, holding onto the emotions that were starting to break. "My brother is doing the job you're meant to do. He's up with me during the night, helping with feeding and soothing our daughter's cries. He holds her while I try and shower, or when I'm so exhausted, that I need an hour of sleep." I blew out a hard breath, calming myself. "You destroyed me." I didn't yell, nor did I scream or say all of that to make him feel bad, but to make him see that he has missed out on so much. "You know me. You know I would never do something so cruel and hurtful. You should know I would never cheat on you."

When I looked up, I realised he was crying. His whole body was shaking, and his cheeks were wet as he put his head in his hands and shook his head. I couldn't help but notice he was still wearing his wedding ring as I reached up, taking his hand in mine.

"What's her name?" he asked, still keeping his head down.

"Lucy Charlotte Rivers."

"Lucy?" he turned his attention on me, surprise evident.

Nodding, I pulled my hand back. "I knew you would have wanted to call her that."

"Wow, I don't deserve that at all." He sighed. "Thank you. It means a lot that you called her after my gran." He licked his lips, rubbing his eyes with his thumbs. "I was just angry—so fucking angry. I really believed that it was you in the photos. Then when you sent them back last night, I felt as if I had the wind knocked out of me. I had to come here." His voice was shaky. "I abandoned you. I abandoned our daughter. I hate myself. I fucking hate myself."

I felt the pram move for a brief second. Lucy was awake. I stared at him and said the only thing I could think of. "Would you like to hold your daughter?"

He shook his head. "I don't deserve to hold her after everything. I thought she wasn't mine, Charlotte. What type of dad am I? I believed you cheated on me," he said, cursing himself angrily.

I ignored him and stood up, leaning over the pram and unclipped Lucy's safety belt, pulling her out gently and sitting back down beside Chris. Lucy's eyes were wide open as she stared up at her dad; she just looked mesmerised by him as he looked back down at her.

"Hold your daughter because she loves you no matter what you've done, Chris. She's too young to understand the hurt you've caused me." I moved her closer to him. He looked afraid to hold her at first, but then he reached out and held her out in front of him, his hand behind her head and the other on her lower back as her legs lay on his thighs.

"She is better than the photo." Chris smiled weakly.

"Of course, she is. She's beautiful." I leaned closer towards him, resting my head against his shoulder.

Lucy made little bubbles with her bottom lip, her eyes still looking closely at her father. She was so contented just sitting there in his hold. Her arms and legs stretched out, moving up and down. Her legs kicked Chris's stomach, but he just stared at her, holding tightly with no intention of letting go.

He spoke, giving me a quick glance. "I do want to be a part of her life, if you will let me. I know you're mad and have every right to be. I'm begging for a second chance here, anything you're willing to allow. I don't deserve anything from you; I know that."

"What does that mean for us?" I asked hesitantly because I was unsure about it all.

"I love you. I've never stopped, and if you want to divorce me for what I put you through, then I will sign whatever you want and give you everything you ask for, but I don't want to miss out on our daughter's life any more than I have," he stated as he cleared his throat, bringing Lucy to his chest and kissing the top of her head. "I fucked up beyond words, and I have to live with this for the rest of my life."

"When do you have to leave?" I asked, pulling back from him, and running my hands over my thighs.

"Whenever you ask me to." He shrugged. "I will stay tonight in one of the other motels down the road."

"No," I said firmly, surprising myself. "You can stay with me."

He shook his head. "I will stay in a hotel room; it's no problem."

I didn't care what he had to say; I was going to make it clear to him what I wanted. "I don't want to get a divorce. You are my husband, and I love you. I want to be with you, and I want us to live together. I want the plan we had dreamed of and spent Sundays talking about. But I also think we need to learn to trust each other again. I am still so hurt that you left, and I know you're angry too, but you accused me of something so unspeakable. I can't forgive you for leaving me; it's going to take time. I need to trust that you won't leave again, that you will be here for me and Lucy, and not abandon us." I paused a moment, then continued. "I promise you that I won't use you leaving the day she was born against you. I am willing to put it aside if you can as well, and move forward and get back to how we were. I need to be able to trust again."

"I want you to bring it up every day," he started, but I cut in, not hearing a word of it.

"No, I know you're paying for it. You missed the birth of our daughter, and that is something you need to live with for the

65

rest of your life, but I don't want to be the type of person who would use it against you in a fight. I need time—time to heal and see if we can get past this."

"I don't deserve you," he muttered, sighing heavily.

I nodded, knowing that was true; he didn't deserve me. Our eyes were still locked. My heart was racing furiously as he leaned in closer, resting his forehead against mine. His warm breath was blowing against my face as he moved. I ran my hand up to the base of his neck, slowly tilting my face towards his, and placing a single kiss over his lips. His lips were wet yet warm, tasting of salty tears.

A simple kiss that felt like the first kiss of my life.

Sparks came back to life, the fire in my belly that I had longed for. The love I felt for him spilled throughout my body as if he was seeping into my veins, bringing me back to life. But, I also couldn't forget the hurt he had caused me—the deep pain and embarrassment of him accusing me of cheating.

"I want you to fire Katie," I said with seriousness. "I have never involved myself with your work because I don't believe in doing so, but I want her gone."

I would assume he was going to say no. However, his brows raised, and he gave a single nod. "Already done. She was the one who sent the photos. I even asked Joel, and he admitted it to be true."

My mouth fell open. "What?!" I was disgusted that he was in on it too.

"After I got that email yesterday, I went to his house to ask him again, and he admitted to lying. He said he had a thing for you and wanted you for himself, so I broke his jaw. I have never been so angry, Char. It's their fault, and I fucking believed them. I'm a lawyer for Christ's sake, and I was made a fucking fool."

I couldn't believe it; they were sick. "Wow. I'm blown away. I can't believe they would do something so horrible. This pretty much destroyed a family."

They had destroyed our family.

"How long are your parents still here for?" he questioned.

I had started to forget about them being here until he mentioned it. "Yeah, they were meant to leave today after lunch. I don't know if that will happen since mum is watching me like a hawk with my eating."

"Can I say something without you getting angry?" he asked hesitantly.

Raising a brow, I was curious as to what he had to say, but I nodded anyway. "Go ahead."

Chris and I were always able to talk to each other about anything. Now, it felt like we had to go back to the start all over again. "You need to stand up to them. Stop letting them get inside your head and making you feel as if you're doing something wrong."

He was right about that. "I know, I know." I stretched my legs out in front of me, crossing my feet over the other.

"Is Lucy up a lot during the night?" Chris asked as he smiled down at our daughter.

"Yeah. Although last night, she slept the whole time, but that was because she was up the whole time the previous night. Adam and I were walking her in the pram at 3 AM for a good hour." I groaned as I remembered her cheeky face as we pushed her.

Lucy started to grow restless, and I knew she was soon due for another feed and change. Chris placed her back in the pram after walking with her in his arms for a bit. I offered for him to push her, but he said he was all right. I knew he was still very nervous. He wasn't the confident man I married; he was now the complete opposite. I knew it was a huge deal for him to come back here to try and make us work—to try and fix everything that had happened over the past three weeks. He was a stubborn man—a man who never liked to admit it when he was wrong. But the fact he had apologised was a small step in the right direction.

I wanted him to be as involved as possible in his daughter's life. He should feel like any new father, and he really needed to have that bonding time with her.

Just as we were making our way back to the house, I was met with the angry looks of both my parents. Their anger was directed towards Chris. I knew that because my father stepped forward and clenched his fists as he angrily asked, "What the hell do you think you're doing here, son!?"

CHAPTER EIGHT

"I love you," he whispered.

"I love you." I smiled up at Chris.

We were now meeting my parents, and I was nervous. My parents were kind of strict; they would flip if they knew how much older Chris was than me, and I was slightly nervous about that. Hell, I was nervous for him.

"Just know when I'm nervous, I kind of speak without thinking, I blurt out random stuff," I warned him as my nerves picked up. I had never brought a boy home before.

Chris frowned as he noticed and placed his hand in mine. "I already know that, babe. Don't be nervous; we can just leave if they are that bad."

I nodded and opened the front door to my parents' house. Adam was here as well which was only because I begged him to be, that or I would tell Mum about the one-nighters he was having recently; I only found that out because I read his texts.

"Charlotte." Mum smiled as we walked into her view.

"Mum, Dad." I smiled back, holding Chris's hand slightly tighter than normal. He wasn't complaining though.

"Who's this?" Dad spoke just as Adam walked into the kitchen, sitting down at the dining table.

"This is my boyfriend, Chris."

"Oh?" Mum spoke, narrowing her eyes at me

"He's Adam's age," I replied, grinning.

"What?" Dad blinked, laughing. "He's in his early thirties?"

"Yeah. I guess he's my sugar daddy," I replied, then realised that wasn't the best thing to say.

Adam's drink went spraying out of his mouth and all over the cutlery. "I'm sure that's what they're going to be pleased about," he muttered. "Tell them where he works."

"He is Adam's boss, and I think when you go back to work, you may be fired," I spat as glared at him.

I heard Chris chuckle behind me as he stepped forward and held his hand out to my father. "It's nice to finally meet you both. Charlotte talks about you constantly."

I mouthed suck up. "Oh, do I?"

"Yes." He winked.

With that, my dad took hold of Chris's hand and shook it firmly, welcoming him into our family. "Scotch?"

*   *   *

I know I should have expected this.

The standoff between my parents and Chris—the extremely uneasy tension currently enveloping us. I mean, in my parent's eyes, they would loathe the man who abandoned their daughter and granddaughter.

"Dad. Please, don't," I said, warning my father. This wasn't the time or place to be getting into anything. With a hothead like him, there was no telling what was going to happen if he let loose.

"Darling, why don't we go inside? Lucy needs a feed, and we can let the men talk out here." Mum tried giving me a smile, but I wasn't having any of it.

I glanced from her to Chris as I held my daughter close to my chest, patting her bottom and giving her a soothing bounce as I stood by the door. "Chris is going to feed her."

"Char, go inside. I'll be in there soon." Chris knew what was coming, and now wasn't the time for a big man pissing contest.

I raised a brow, placing my lips on Lucy's soft head, and rocked her back and forth. "No. You're coming inside to feed your daughter for the first time," I said, surprising myself with how firm and demanding I was towards him.

I never bossed Chris around; he was the one who oozed authority and gave the usual orders. I liked that about him—him in control and taking charge. It went with his personality: dominant and strong.

My dad stepped forward, walking closer to him. Their height difference was noticeable as Chris towered over my dad by a good foot. I could tell by the way my dad's eyes narrowed, that I knew he wanted to hit Chris. I also knew that Chris wouldn't try and stop my dad, and as much as he deserved to have the possible shit beat out of him, it wasn't going to fix anything.

"Charlotte." Mum placed a hand on my elbow, trying to move me along.

I shrugged away, shaking my head. "No. Chris. Inside now." I didn't take my eyes off his.

Chris looked over, his shoulders slumping. "Okay. Let's go and feed her."

Dad's anger simmered even more, shaking his head angrily with both arms thrown in the air. "So, what? You're just going to take him back after that? After everything he's done to you and your daughter?!"

"Don't!" I snapped back, frustration filling me. Deep down, I knew he was right, but I just couldn't do this. Not here, not now. "Just drop it. I'm not going to kick him out and send him away."

"He left." Mum really didn't need to remind me of this. I damn well knew it. "What's to say he won't do it again? Jesus, don't ever fall pregnant again."

My face fell, and I tried to mask the hurt because I didn't want anyone to see or know just how badly that hurt to hear my mother say those words. Don't fall pregnant again? We had wanted

71

a big family, with at least three or four children. I'd never want my daughter to be an only child with no siblings to play with.

"Enough." Adam joined us, standing in the doorway, half asleep with a shirt inside out. "Just fucking stop. Leave them alone. Let them sort it out, and if you can't, then go back on another trip. You're not helping anyone by fighting."

"You can't be serious." Mum shook her head disapprovingly, watching Adam retreat inside until he was gone, and it was just us standing back out here.

Turning to my parents, I decided nothing was going to change when they held onto their disapprovingly looks. Groaning, I just turned into the house and slipped off my shoes, making my way to the bedroom, hoping today's fight was over and done with.

"I'm sorry." I sighed, falling down on the bed.

"Don't be," Chris said, propping himself up on the bed as he held Lucy in one hand, and a bottle in the other. "You should have let your father hit me. I deserve it."

I looked up, raising a brow with a half-smile and smirk. "If anyone is going to hit you, then it will be me."

He let out a laugh, smiling for a brief second, stretched out on his side as I turned and lay facing them both. Lucy was between us as Chris held the bottle to her mouth while she looked up at him, drinking. Her little mouth was sucking the bottle as if her life depended on it. She began to cry when there was none left.

"She's still hungry," I pointed out, lifting my camisole and propping my breast close to her mouth. Her head turned, and her mouth opened, eagerly taking more.

"Does she drink like this all the time?" he asked, looking at me.

"Clearly, she drinks like her father," I pointed out, winking playfully.

With a scoff, he rolled his eyes. "I don't drink that often."

"Only after every win at work." I smiled, sticking my tongue out. "Anyway, she's pretty much done." I noticed as my nipple fell from her mouth, and I looked down to see her fast asleep.

We both lay there, Chris tracing his long fingertip over Lucy's features, taking in her appearance and soaking up the bliss of her beauty. I was starting to drift off when he reached over and tucked a strand of hair behind my ear.

"Will you show me your stomach?" he finally asked.

Catching me off guard, I frowned, a crease forming between my brows. "Why? It's gross."

"I want to see where they cut you." He didn't take his eyes from mine, pleading with me. Silently, I nodded. It terrified me that he would see something no one else had done. It was daunting.

I watched as Chris picked Lucy up, carefully placing her in the bassinet and pulling her pink blanket over her small body. He moved back onto the bed, kneeling between my legs as he lifted my black top, lowering the yoga pants slightly with my panties so that he could look at the scar close up.

He didn't say anything at first; he just stared. My heart was racing with every possible thought he may be thinking about.

Then finally, he broke the silence. "You're still beautiful; the scar is beautiful. Does it hurt?" He looked up with pain filling his eyes.

"Not as much anymore, but it did hurt pretty bad. I found it hard to walk the first three days. I couldn't even dress myself; the midwife had to do it and help me shower," I admitted softly.

The pain that flashed across Chris's eyes was hard to miss. He shifted until he lay beside me, looking afraid to even touch me anymore. "I should have been there."

I didn't say anything; I knew it was true and I couldn't deny it.

Reaching out, his fingers found mine and interlaced our hands. He brought my hand to his lips and pressed a soft kiss against my skin gently. "Will you stay here tonight? In here with us?" I asked quietly.

"I don't mind getting a hotel. I won't make it uncomfortable for you and your family." He sounded nervous, unsure of whether to be here or not.

"Please," I begged, fighting the tears back. I bit my trembling lip, moving closer towards him.

His arm slid beneath my neck, wrapping around my shoulders as his other arm pulled me close against him. My eyes shut, and for the first time in weeks, I felt safe again. My heart was steadily beating, content to be here. He pressed his lips against my forehead as I started to doze off, finding a slight peace in knowing he wasn't going anywhere tonight.

*   *   *

I opened my eyes to find myself alone on the bed. A blanket was covering my body, and the blinds were drawn shut. I looked around, trying to see where Chris was, but I couldn't see him, and Lucy wasn't in her bed. I heard water running and knew he was taking a shower.

Peeking around the bathroom door, I smiled as I spotted Chris in the shower with Lucy; she was loving it. I ducked out, grabbing my camera. I couldn't miss an opportunity like this. Chris was just standing there as he held Lucy out under the water that was running over her tummy and her smiling up at him with beaming eyes.

"Hey," I spoke, making it known I was awake, and snapped a photo of them.

"Did I wake you up?" He smiled, giving me a quick glance. "I thought you could use the extra sleep."

"No, you didn't wake me. I'm good." I leaned back on the sink, watching them.

He nodded. "Do you want to get in? I'm finished."

"Maybe later. I had a shower this morning," I said quietly. Chris nodded and reached for the tap, turning the water off.

I felt bad. It wasn't as though I didn't want to shower with my husband and daughter, it was just after everything that had happened, I was still hurting, and I couldn't go back and pretend everything was normal. I couldn't jump into bed with him and act as if he didn't accuse me of cheating, and leave me, asking for a divorce.

I grabbed a towel for Chris, my eyes lingering over his body for a slow second, trying my hardest not to get caught perving, but I had definitely missed that body—running my fingers up and down his tight stomach down to the dark spread of hair above his thick cock that was kept neatly trimmed.

Ugh, I needed to think of something else. I needed a distraction big time.

"Would you want to see her room?" I offered; it was all I could come up with.

"She has her own room? Like a nursery here?" He wrapped the towel around his waist after drying the droplets from his body. There was a noticeable bulge in the groin region as the towel was flushed to his skin.

My words caught in my throat as I coughed. "Yeah, it's not like the one at home, but it's still nice."

"I need to talk to you about that as well." He ran another towel through his wet hair, drying it off.

I nodded, leaving him to clean up as I went down to the other bedroom. I had wrapped little Lucy in her towel and was busy blowing raspberries on her bare belly. She stuck her tongue out, squirming with big wide eyes, to which I mirrored her actions with a smile as I pulled silly faces.

I hadn't noticed Chris in the doorway until I spotted him out the corner of my eye. I looked up and gave him an uncertain look. He hadn't moved; he was watching with intent. When I went to question him, he broke out into a warm smile, which I then mirrored. "You know, I really do love you."

"I know. I love you, too," I answered honestly, as I stood back upright. "I haven't stopped loving you, Chris. Sometimes, I wish I could have done. It'd be easier, but I just can't switch my feelings off. That isn't me."

"You shouldn't love me. I've hurt you too much." He turned, facing me after he reached in and took a sleepsuit for Lucy to wear to bed. I ignored his statement. My mind was saying he was right.

"She needs another feed before bed. I might just sit in here and do it." I lifted Lucy up, then sat on the light grey fabric rocking chair beside the window.

My eyes closed as I fed; the relief soothing as she hungrily guzzled down her milk. Chris was on the floor, reading Lucy's hospital book, looking over everything to see what else he missed. His words, not mine. I let him be; there wasn't much more I could say about the birth. The only way he could see was through the photos and reading what the midwives wrote.

"What did you want to talk about earlier? You mentioned the apartment." I looked up, clipping my bra back on.

He frowned, biting his lip before kneeling and taking my hand in his. "Don't be mad, but I've already sold it."

If I weren't sitting down, I would have fallen to the floor or dropped Lucy. *He what?!* "Excuse me? So when did you have it on the market?" I asked again in slight disbelief.

"Look. I was mad and upset. I made a rash decision when I realised you had gone. I sold it the week after you left." His adam's apple bobbed up and down as he swallowed hard.

"Oh," I whispered, not knowing what else to say. Our home was gone.

"Don't look so disappointed; it wasn't suitable for children." His blue eyes rolled, and he brushed his thumb over mine. "I brought us a house with a yard like you wanted; it's a big

76

place," he spoke a little hesitantly. "It's safe for Lucy. She can grow up outdoors, and the neighbourhood is quiet."

I listened to him as he described the house; it sounded amazing, something I wasn't expecting. He had always loved living in the city. It was convenient for him because of his work. We had spoken about the suburbs before, but nothing ever came of that. I just didn't expect him to go out and buy us a home without me being there with him. To decide together.

"What if I don't like it?" Probably not the best thing to say to a man making a grand gesture.

When he pulled out his phone, he swiped through each photo. I was pretty much speechless. It was the big white modern farmhouse I had always dreamed of. There was land, and beautiful high ceilings with timber beams; a stunning large kitchen, wooden flooring, and marble benchtops; a swimming pool in the backyard, with plenty of room for chickens, and a swing set. It just blew me away.

"I want you both to come back with me. Please." He looked up at me, his brows dipped slightly. "Come home with me."

"But I'm here," I said quietly. "I can't just leave when I've made this a temporary home."

"Then I'll buy this place as well. I want you home, Char—where you belong, us as a family," he said firmly. "The three of us."

I knew he wouldn't hesitate to whip out his chequebook and buy this place. He probably already has brought it, but still, I wasn't sure if I was ready to leave. He may have come back this morning, but it was too soon to make my mind up. The pain I felt was still too raw and real. If I came back with him, that would mean all is forgiven, which definitely wasn't.

"I just need time." It was all I could manage to say.

He nodded, but I knew he was disappointed that I didn't say yes. He just needed to gain back the trust that was broken. I was scared of moving back, and then him leaving again. My heart couldn't take any more pain.

77

There was a quiet knock on the door. Adam popped his head in, giving me a smile as he walked in and closed the door behind him. "She's been quiet today."

"Yeah, she's good. Did you catch up on sleep?" I asked, noticing he seemed a lot more awake than before.

"Yeah, I don't feel like death anymore." He chuckled, sitting on the floor beside Chris.

The three of us spoke as if nothing had gone wrong. Adam wasn't rude to Chris, which I really was thankful for. I didn't want to listen to another dispute. I just wanted to have a quiet night where we could try and get back to normal. To find a normal that was enough for everyone to try and maintain some peace, to allow things to be worked out, and for us to work on our relationship. Fighting and arguing solved nothing at all.

"I need to warn you that when you step out of this room, Mum and Dad are holding an intervention for you," Adam told me, shaking his head while laughing.

"What!?" I groaned making both men chuckle as I stood and passed Lucy to her father. "Put her to bed, please. I'm going to see what my parents want."

CHAPTER NINE

"*Sam, I would like to introduce to you my girlfriend, Charlotte.*" *Chris beamed as he and the older man shook hands.*

"*Pleasure to meet you,*" *Sam greeted, leaning forward and offering me a handshake.*

Sam was a partner at their firm. They were having their annual Christmas dinner, and Chris asked me to come with him. Hell to the yes, I accepted. I wore a little white cocktail dress, nothing too revealing, but it held a hint of sexiness and class. Chris wore a black suit, and by the end of the night, I was going to have him half naked and screwing me in the back of the car.

"*Have I told you how beautiful you look tonight?*" *he whispered against my ear as his hand slid from the curve of my hip to my ass.*

"*Six times already, but I'm still listening.*" *I grinned, reaching behind my back and shooing his hand away.*

He laughed and placed a light kiss over my mouth, his hand still holding onto my waist. I looked up and saw a leggy brunette strutting across the room directly towards us, her eyes dancing with happiness as she kept her sight on Chris. I groaned when I realised who it was: his assistant.

"*Be nice,*" *he whispered in my ear with a smirk.*

"*I'll blow you on the drive home if you don't touch her,*" *I whispered, and he immediately closed his mouth.*

"*Chris, good to see you.*" *She went to lean in to kiss his cheek. He had suddenly stepped aside out of her reach, clearly wanting his evening blowjob. Unfortunately, her footing lost balance, and she tripped, spilling her glass of red wine.*

I bit my lip to stop the massive laugh that was trying to escape. Adam looked up and realised what had happened as she screamed out. He turned around, and I could see his body shaking as he laughed on the sly. I would have felt bad if she wasn't such a massive bitch.

"You pushed me!" She turned to me; her little red number was stained with alcohol.

Was she crazy?! "No, I didn't. You tripped."

"Chris!" She glared at him

Expecting Chris to back me up, he instead said nothing, passing over a napkin towel and helping the leggy brunette clean up the spilt liquid. She glanced at me with a victory smile.

Oh wow, just how I wanted to spend the evening. I walked off and left the party. I didn't say goodbye to Chris. I did text Adam and told him I was leaving if Chris asked; he should know the reason for my early departure.

About ten minutes after I had gotten into bed, freshly showered and in my pyjamas, Chris walked through the door, looking ready to blow, and not in the way I'd prefer. "What the fuck was that?" he half shouted. "You left me there alone."

Rolling my eyes, I scoffed with a sarcastic laugh. "Rule number one when in a relationship: always stand up for your girlfriend, not the fucking whore who's trying to screw you!" And with that, I threw him a pillow and left him to sleep on the couch.

That was our first fight.

The next morning, I woke up to thirty red roses by the bed and a note that said: "I'm sorry."

*   *   *

My parents were sitting at the small wooden table when I walked out of the bedroom and into the kitchen alone. Then I noticed what was on the dinner table.

I swear, Mum went and brought one of Nigella Lawson's cookbooks, making everything in it. There was food—more than enough. Even dessert, and I rarely ate dessert.

"Sit. Eat," she commanded. "There is enough for everyone. The boys can join us too, once Lucy is in bed, of course." Mum smiled. I looked at her warily because earlier, she was yelling about how Chris was here, ruining all our plans. But now, she had cooked a family dinner? I couldn't keep up with her.

I took a seat just as Chris walked out with Adam behind him, both talking about football. The two of them often went to watch a game, becoming more of brothers than co-workers. Sitting down next to me, Chris's hand went straight to my lap. It was instinct, and as he realised, he started to pull away, but I grabbed a hold, keeping it there. I had forgotten how nice that felt, the small comfort it gave me.

I needed to let him do the things he used to. I had to try as much as he was. We had to try.

Of course, Mum went straight to dishing my own plate up. I was obviously "incapable" of doing anything for myself. I knew she wanted to watch what I ate, and honestly, I was hungry, but not starving. I didn't need to eat as much as she was piling up. I loved her dearly, and clearly, she was just trying to help and make sure I was okay, but I wasn't a child anymore.

When she spun around to go back into the kitchen, Chris swapped plates with me. I noticed he had only placed half of what was on the other one. I smiled at him and he winked, knowing exactly what I was thinking.

"So, Chris. How's work been?" It was a usual question, but coming from my dad, it caught us off guard.

All of us stopped eating and looked at dad. This morning, he wanted to hit Chris, but now, he was acting normal. I really didn't get my family at all.

"Busy. I had court all this week," he answered before taking a bite of his scotch filet steak.

"That's good." Mum smiled as she came back from the kitchen. "And, did you win them?"

He nodded "Yes. One is going to trial, but the other two were quashed by the judge."

Adam cut in, asking about Ness, and I rolled my eyes. He needed to just ask her out and stop beating around the bush with these annoying questions. I could see right through him. Chris then asked my parents about their travels and the places they went to; they seemed to have really enjoyed their time away. But they were glad to be back home with us kids and Lucy.

"I want to visit Bali." I grinned. "I'd love to go there."

Chris smiled. "We could have gone for our honeymoon, but you chose the Maldives."

I looked at him like he was crazy. "Umm." I laughed, nudging him. "Well, yes, that's true. Next holiday then."

"Charlotte, have you decided on what to do?" Mum spoke with her soft voice, interrupting us. I knew the intervention my brother had warned me about had started.

I looked up at Mum and frowned; all eyes were on me which made me extremely uncomfortable. "What are you talking about?"

"Well, we have the room at our house."

I ran my hand through my hair and shrugged. I hated confrontation. "I don't know yet," I mumbled. "I'm fine here for the time being."

"But you can't do it alone," she pressed, her eyes glued to mine.

Opening my mouth to talk, it closed again as Chris cut in. "She won't be alone. I will be here."

"You have a job; your life is in the city. It's not like you cared about them before, just kicked her to the curb." Dad scoffed, brushing Chris off. "You're a fool of a man. You can't come back crying for forgiveness when you damn well fucked up."

82

Chris didn't say anything as he nodded. He stood up and walked down to the bedroom, closing the door without another word. I looked at Adam, urging him to help, but he just sat in silence. It wasn't his fight. This was my own, and I needed to nip it in the bud before they started anymore.

"Thanks a lot." I hissed, keeping my voice low. I didn't want Lucy to wake and scream. "Chris is trying. You were all for him being back here earlier on, and now that he is, you're telling him to piss off?"

"Well, I just want him to feel something. He can't just waltz in here and expect everything to go back to normal. He screwed up and hurt you, god damn it!" The volume of his voice increased like a thunder as his fist slammed to the table.

"Dad," Adam spoke with his own voice rising. "Clearly, you don't know the whole story, so just calm down."

"I don't care! Charlotte, either you come back with us tomorrow, or—"

"Or what?" I asked, standing up. "You'll throw me over your knee and hit me with your belt?"

Mum's eyes widened, and she frowned with disgust. "Charlotte, that wasn't very nice."

"And neither are you, making Chris feel worse than how he already feels!" I exclaimed, throwing my hands up. "You've been nothing but horrible to him. Jesus Christ."

"Why the hell are you standing up for him?" Dad stood, leaning over the table with both hands on the wood, glaring harshly at me.

"Why? Because he's my husband, and when I stood up there, I promised forever, not just until things got tough!" I hollered back at him. Standing with a jerk of my chair, I walked off towards the bedroom, feeling more pissed than I did at the start of dinner.

Chris was lying down when I came back in and slumped against the door. I was trying, but it was hard. Really fucking hard. I understood why they were mad, but it wasn't their right to be rude. They couldn't give Chris a chance to make things right. "You know, you shouldn't stick up for me, Char," he spoke, breaking my trance as I turned to him.

"Would you rather I didn't?" I asked, making my way to the bed and spotting Lucy fast asleep beside him, her dark lashes fanning out over the tops of her cheeks.

He didn't say anything to start with; he just pinched the bridge of his nose and inhaled. "I'd rather you hate me, tell me you didn't love me, and make me beg you each day to let me near our daughter."

"Christopher, don't. I can't deal with a pity party right now." I just couldn't listen to him hating himself, and my family hating him. "Does your family know that I've had the baby?" I asked, sitting down next to him.

"Yes." He sighed again. "They're pretty pissed off, angry, and hurt."

"I shouldn't have taken off, but they wouldn't talk to me." I felt myself starting to cry; the build-up of emotion was getting to me. "All my friends hate me. Your family stopped talking to me, and I was alone. God, so badly I want to hate you, Chris. I really do. So badly I want to divorce you and never see you again, never have to look at you, and just live a life where I hate you." I reached over, tilting my head to the side as I ran my fingers over the white duvet. "But I can't because I love you. I love you so fucking much it hurts. It hurts me to love you." My voice broke, and I sniffed back the tears.

I stood up, salty tears falling down my cheeks and walked towards the window as I broke down and started sobbing hard. I found myself being pulled into a chest, a set of strong arms wrapping around me as I gripped his shirt tightly, crying as all my emotions came out and let loose. The pain gripped my heart and just hurt.

"I'm so sorry, Charlotte." His words were soft, lips pressed to my head as he pulled me ever closer to him.

We stood there, holding each other until my legs grew tired. Chris pulled me down onto his lap as he sat on the sofa chair next to the window. I have no idea how long we were just sitting for; it had been well over an hour, the sunset and the sky grew dark.

I was tired, too exhausted to move.

When I yawned, he took the hint I needed sleep and helped me back up.

Undressing and changing into pyjamas, I pulled back the duvet and climbed in. "What are you doing?" I asked, with a crinkle of my nose.

"Char, I think I'll just go stay somewhere else," he whispered, walking back towards the door. "I don't want to hurt you by being around. I'm sorry."

"Chris, stay here, please. I promise it's okay." I scooted over and pulled the covers back more, patting the empty space beside me. "I want you here when I wake up." I let out a loud yawn and sleepily smiled at him as my head hit the pillow. "Please."

He came back to the bed and started to undress. I watched every muscle move as he raised his hands to pull his shirt off. Clad in tight boxer shorts alone, he came over to me. Normally, he would sleep naked. I moved closer as his arms hesitantly wrapped around me, bringing me close against his body. I felt the warmth of his lips as he kissed my forehead gently, resting my head against his chest.

This felt like my first time sharing a bed with him. I was nervous, my heart was racing faster. "Chris," I whispered.

"Hmm," he replied as his fingertips ran gently through my hair.

"Why did she answer the phone and say she was changing that day?" I asked, feeling the beat of my heart quicken even more. I had to ask, and more importantly, I needed to know.

He shifted slightly, so he was now facing me, his hand wrapped around my waist as our bodies pressed together. "I left my phone in the office, and she was on it when I walked in. Nothing has ever happened between us," he said seriously. "I swear."

I nodded. Usually, I could tell when he lied to me. But now, I wasn't so sure. "Okay. You should go to sleep. Lucy might wake up soon," I whispered quietly.

"I don't mind," he said back quietly, placing his soft lips to my forehead again. "I never touched her. I would never fuck anyone else, Char. Believe that."

Leaning forward, I pressed my lips to his and kissed him for a longing second. Snuggling down against his chest as my eyes closed, sleep finally overtook me.

*   *   *

Waking up with a startle, the sun beamed through the sheer curtains. I sat up in a panic. I was alone. Lucy was still in her bassinet, and it was morning. I had slept the entire night without her waking once? It was amazing.

"Good morning." I was greeted by Chris walking in, holding a tray of hot tea and toast.

"When did you wake up?" I asked, propping the pillows up behind my back to sit up comfortably.

He grinned, lying back on the bed. "Couple hours ago."

"Why? Why didn't you wake me up?" I asked, noticing my heavy chest. "My boobs are very full."

With a laugh, he shook his head. "Because you were passed out cold. I tried waking you, but you didn't budge. I just heated her a bottle and took her for a walk around the park instead. She's a night owl, that's for sure. It wasn't worth going back to sleep, so I made you breakfast."

"Well, thank you. I must have needed sleep." I then moaned, sipping on the tea. He knew how to make a damn good tea, that's for sure.

I was able to take a shower alone, dress and put some effort into my appearance while Lucy slept for another hour. Chris tended to her when she woke and passed her over when I came out to feed her.

Adam was watching the morning news, raising a brow. "Did Mummy and Daddy behave last night with the baby in the room?"

I rolled my eyes. "You're disgusting. Nothing happened."

"I know. Ears like a hawk remember." He winked back with a smirk. "We used to live in the same apartment. I'm not deaf."

Chris sat beside him with the paper, laughing. "Ahh, yes. Good old days, you being a peeping Tom while I slept over."

"Bullshit. You were just showing off" Adam defended.

I glanced around, noting it was quiet. "Where's Mum and Dad?" I asked, bringing that to a stop. "I thought they would be here this morning."

Adam's head fell back against the sofa, and he yawned sleepily while Chris went to take a shower. "They went into town for a little bit, and I think they want to have another talk with both Chris and you. Mum's hell-bent on having you go back with them this afternoon."

"Why would I leave when I've got this place? Chris also bought a home for us, he said."

"He told me. It's a nice place, and the price was pretty good. Pays to be a rich lawyer, I guess." Adam looked at me as his eyes studied my face.

I scoffed, rolling my eyes. "Is there anything he hasn't told you?" Adam seemed to know everything else.

"Not really. But I do know he's planning on moving here and quitting the firm if you don't come back. He's serious about

87

making things work, and I kinda feel bad for the guy; he was tricked. To be honest, when I first saw the photos, I really thought it was you, but you're my sister, and I know you wouldn't do that to him. But with him, just remember his previous girlfriend constantly cheated on him, and that fucks with your mind a bit. I know what it's like to come home and find the girl you're dating being taken in ways she wouldn't let you. Chris was fed bullshit, and as a lawyer, he just looked at the evidence and believed it. It all came back to you being guilty, and if I were him, I probably would have done the exact same thing." He sighed. "I'll tell Mum and Dad to back off, but don't string Chris along if you don't want to go back with him. He came here the day after you sent the photos, and that's saying something," Adam said in a slightly hushed voice as the water in the bathroom had now stopped. "I know you're hurt. He's never going to live this down; just don't do something you might regret in years to come."

I sat there for a moment, unable to think of what to say. My brother had just defended Chris completely. I knew my brother wouldn't say any of that if he didn't believe him. Still, it made me rethink everything. I got up from the chair and passed Lucy to him. She was sleeping with her rosy cheeks and little plump lips puffed out as she breathed heavily.

"Wait here," I said, making my way down to the bedroom. When I opened the door, I was met with a very naked man in my full view. "Oh . . . uh, sorry." I blushed slightly as I looked away, biting my lip as he dressed. Christ.

"Charlotte, you've seen me naked before, but it's nice to see you blushing again." Chris chuckled. "I'm decent now," he added a few moments later.

I turned around, stepping closer towards him. I reached out to cup his face in both hands, his unshaven face rough in my hands, and I couldn't help but wonder what it felt like elsewhere. "Chris."

"Yes?" His hands slid to my waist, pulling me hard against him.

I leaned closer, my lips almost brushing against his, skimming as my words came out softly. "You don't need to stay here." I kissed him when he went to object. Pulling away all too quickly, I smiled, staring up into his eyes. "We will come back home with you."

CHAPTER TEN

"*What do I have to do again?*" I asked, slightly nervous as everyone was looking at me.

Chris let out a laugh and wrapped his arms around my waist tighter. "*Shake the can, open it, and empty it as fast as you can.*"

We were at one of his old college friend's place, Jordan. Unfortunately, his age was just a number, and he was proving that he could still be young and fun; that he knew how to do something other than work. It was only because I had told him he was a workaholic and boring.

I rolled my eyes and cocked my head to the side. "*What happens after I drink it all?*"

Jordan burst out into loud laughter. "*Sweetheart, there is no way you could finish that can. You're too innocent for these types of games.*"

"*Let her have a go,*" Chris answered before I could speak.

"*I might surprise you.*" I smirked at Jordan, and he laughed.

He quickly shook the can for a few seconds, and Chris stepped back, either not wanting to get thrown up on or soaked in beer. "*You can try, darlin, but this is a man's game.*"

"*Oh, god. Don't even start on what only men can do.*" I stuck my tongue out and laughed.

I had never done this before, but what the hell, it seemed pretty straightforward. I grabbed the drink and pulled the tab open. The foam from the beer started to spray up as I quickly placed my mouth over it and began to drink quickly.

Squeezing the can until nothing came out, I dropped it in the bin and spun around to look at Chris who was grinning widely as he pulled me into his chest.

"You. Me. Car. Now!" He throatily groaned and started pulling me along with him.

Straddling him in the back seat of his car that was parked down a deserted road, we made out heavily like a couple of sixteen-year-old school kids, his hands hurrying to pull his jeans down as I moved up and pulled my underwear to the side.

"God, I love you." He groaned over my mouth.

"Love you more," I cried out, moving back down over him, his hands roughly gripping my hips as he moved with me. I fucked him hard and fast, the need primal. It was a race to come with him; he always came second.

The next morning, I had woken with a headache from hell. Chris sunk back in the bed and groaned loudly as he rubbed his own temples, turning to look at me with his half-closed eyes. "I feel sick," he muttered.

"Maybe you should listen to your body when it says you're too old." I lightly laughed, keeping my face into the pillow and away from any form of sunlight.

He wrapped both arms around me, and I looked up as he raised a brow. His hair stuck up in all directions. "If I weren't so tired, I'd have my cock down your throat for that." I see the small smirk appearing across his face.

"You know what the best cure for a headache is?" I sat up letting the black sheet fall to my naked waist. "What would that be?" he whispered with a yawn, eyes going straight to my breasts.

"Lots and lots of sex!" I lazily moved over on top of him.

He rolled, pinning me down. I could already feel his arousal pressing into me as he raised his hips and sunk in with a slow, deep thrust.

*   *   *

"What are you thinking about?" Chris asked as he joined me outside on the balcony. I had been out here enjoying the sun and listening to the sound of the waves; it was very calming. The ocean was just magical.

"That time we fell asleep in the middle of sex." I shook my head as I laughed.

A light laugh came out from his lips as he lay down on the lounge chair. "That was a hell of a night. I hadn't drunk that much in years."

"I barely remember it. I know you were dancing and singing as we walked to the apartment," I said as I grinned over at him.

"You gave me a lap dance." He winked, and I rolled my eyes. Of course, that's what he remembered.

It had only been a couple of hours since I told Chris I would come back home with him. He had pulled me into his chest and hugged me so tightly that I thought my ribs were going to crack.

It felt like the right thing to do. I knew it was the right thing to do.

"So, how do I get out of this lease then?" I asked hesitantly. I really liked being here. "I signed for it."

"We'll buy it, come down when we want to get away, and relax."

"Chris, isn't that a little much? I mean, it probably isn't even up for sale and would you really take time off to relax?" I didn't believe that.

"Everything is for sale, Char. You just need to make the right offer for them to sell it."

I half scoffed. "Alright, money bags. I forgot you could talk your way into anything you want."

"No. I can just see how much you love being here, so I'll buy it and we'll come up at least once a month for a weekend or a few days." He sat up and leaned over towards my chair, taking my hands in his and rubbing them softly, "I just want you to be happy."

"You don't need to buy my happiness," I reminded. "But you're right, I do love it here. It's calming, and I love being able to see Vanessa when I want. This place gave me comfort when you weren't there. I just don't think they'll sell it." I stopped talking when I heard a commotion coming from inside and grew worried.

"Charlotte!" Mum called in a panic.

I jumped up, worried something had happened. "What's happened? I'm out here," I called out. Chris went to stand up to leave, but I grabbed his hands and shook my head. "You don't need to leave whenever they come out here. Stay," I whispered.

"Only if you're sure." He sat back when I nodded that I was sure.

Mum came out, standing by the door in confusion. "Where is Lucy?"

"She's in the bedroom, asleep," Chris answered, and I couldn't help but grin as she hadn't expected to see him out here.

"Sorry, I thought you'd left, Christopher." She took a seat beside me, looking anywhere but at him.

"Actually, Chris is staying here for a couple more days," I spoke up, and Chris eyed me as if to say "I am?"

"Then back to the big city?" she asked suddenly, looking a little more than happy, which ground my gears big time. When Dad walked out, she took no time in filling him in. "Chris is heading back to the city in a couple of days."

"Oh, he is, isn't he?" Dad grumbled, taking his seat beside Mum.

"Yes, I am," Chris answered.

Dad then spoke as he and Mum nodded at each other, like having telepathic communication. "Well then Charlotte, we'll stick around for a little while longer if you want us to."

"You can stay as long as you like, but you should know that Adam will be here too." I smiled. "Umm, but I'm going back with Chris."

"For how long?" Dad asked gruffly.

93

"For good. Lucy and I are going back with him," I said firmly, letting them know it was my decision, and was final.

"I won't allow it." Dad stood, shaking his head. "I won't."

This is what I wanted to avoid—the harsh conflict and confrontation. I bit my lip, sighing as I ran a hand through my long blonde hair. "Dad, are you seriously saying that you want me to divorce him?"

"I do." He nodded. "You're making a big mistake."

Chris had stood up in a flash, towering over my father as he narrowed his eyes at him. "I don't care if you don't allow it. I never asked your permission to marry Charlotte, and I sure as hell don't need your permission now. If you don't like it, then I suggest you get your ass out of this house before I do it for." It was easy to forget how sexy Chris could be when defending me.

The way his whole demeanour changed, becoming the strong and dominant man that I adored.

He never once raised his voice at my father, always showing respect towards my parents. Hell, right now, even Dad was clearly shocked; his mouth was half-open and half-closing. It was definitely a nice sight to see him stunned.

"Chris, there is no need to get angry." Mum tried to cut in, but it only made him angrier.

"No need?" he spat, shifting his attention, "You're filling Charlotte's head with nothing but negativity. I know I fucked up, but so have you both. You're coming in here and treating her like a child; you're telling her she needs to come back and live with you both. Why? So you can raise Lucy the way you see fit?"

"And you honestly think you're a better parent than we are?" Dad shoved a finger against Chris's chest, and I felt my heart pounding faster by the second.

"I know I fucked up!" Chris retorted and stepped closer to dad, his breathing heavy and fists clenched at his side. "I fucking know this."

"Chris," Adam's deep voice cut in placing a hand on his shoulder. "Don't. It's not worth it."

"You're right, because Charlotte and Lucy are coming back home with me, and that's final. I don't give a flying fuck what you both think!" Chris shouted at my parents, and I felt my insides melting, smiling at him taking control, not backing down.

This was the Chris I knew; this was him being possessive and caring.

I could hear a faint scream coming from the bedroom, and Chris immediately pushed past Adam and stalked inside. I couldn't believe Dad had dropped that low to make remarks about his parenting skills. To call Chris unfit to be a parent was uncalled for, not even I would call him that.

"What happened?" Adam stepped in and took Chris's place. "I don't understand why you can't just talk without yelling."

Mum scoffed, sitting down and sighing. "He thinks Charlotte and Lucy are going back with him. He can't come gallivanting back and make everything fine again."

"God, just shut up!" I exclaimed, standing up. I was horrified at myself, speaking to her like that. But I can't just sit here and listen to her bitch and moan about Chris again. "Ever since you both came back, you've been nothing but a headache. Chris is my husband and Lucy's father; nothing is going to change that. We might divorce, but we will still be connected for the rest of our lives."

"You could go through with the divorce. Leave him and come with us," Mum spoke softly, trying to convince me. I snapped my head to her. "Ask for full custody. I know you asked him for that."

I shot a glance at Adam. *Had he told her that?* "Excuse me?" Adam spoke, looking completely and utterly stunned. "Don't try and use my words against me."

I didn't even hear what they had to say. I was pissed off, and I just walked out of the room. This was getting us nowhere. I knew that Chris had screwed up and asked for the divorce in the first place, but I wasn't going to just give up. If he never bothered to come here and try to make things right, then yes, I would easily have left. But he was here, and he was begging for a chance to fix everything.

I was going to give him that, at the very least.

"Chris?" I called out when I walked into the bedroom. Looking around, I couldn't see him or Lucy anywhere. I went to the other room down from mine where her little nursery was to see if he was in there. They were there; Chris sat on the rocking chair with Lucy against his chest as he read her a story.

"I'm sorry." He sighed, putting the book down. "I shouldn't have gotten so angry."

"It's okay. I would have hit someone if they spoke to me that way."

"Stop it, Charlotte." He sighed heavily. "Just stop."

Already fired up, this was not the time to tell me to be quiet. I walked closer, both hands on my hips. "No, you stop it. Stop putting yourself down. You fucked up; I get it, okay? So, if you want us to try and move on and be a family, then I suggest you start acting like that man I just saw out there. I know you're kicking yourself for what happened, but you're here now, so let's just try and get back to the same old us. The couple who stayed in and ate take out most nights because I can't cook anything other than pizza, or how we would spend all day Sundays in bed doing nothing but talking about our future. That's the man I need you to be. Otherwise, they're right; we're not going to work." I stopped talking and took a breath, groaning. "I need you to be the man I fell in love with because this version really sucks."

"Sucks?" Both of his brows rose, and he just chuckled. "Fine. And I love your pizzas."

"Of course, you do. I make the best pizzas." I smiled lightly as I walked over, sitting down on his lap as he shifted Lucy.

"I can't promise it's going to be easy for us, but I can promise I will try."

"Me too. I won't ever hurt you, Charlotte. I won't allow myself to."

"I know. It's just going to take some time for me to believe it." I leaned against his chest as his arm wrapped around me, pulling me into a comforting embrace, and he continued to read Peter Rabbit until Lucy began to cry. She wasn't settled after her feed, and we decided to take a walk again.

Ness was in the living room, throwing daggers at the man next to me when we walked out. She didn't hold back, nor has she ever done. "I go to work for a couple of days, and this is what happens? Charlotte, what the fuck is he doing here?"

"We're working it out," I spoke, giving her an eye glare, and she did the best friend thing and nodded, not saying another word. I couldn't handle her having a go at him too.

"Cool, you're both going for a walk?" Adam asked, pulling on his runners. "Mind if I tag along? Kind of miss the noisy girl." He grinned, and I knew he was making an excuse to get away from Mum and Dad.

The four, or well I should say five of us, headed down to the beach for a walk. Chris and Adam jogged ahead of us while Ness and I stayed behind with the steady pace of the pram.

"So, spill." Ness nudged me. "You're sleeping with him again, aren't you? I can feel the sexual tension whenever he looks at you." She winked.

"Oh, god." I laughed, rolling my eyes. "Yes, I'm dying to tear his clothes off, but no. We're not having sex." I rolled my eyes, sexual heat my ass. It's more like burning desire heat. "As much as I would love to rip his clothes off and explore every inch of his amazing taut body," I said, watching Chris run, his shirt clinging to his back.

Ness slapped my arm, laughing. "You've got it so bad. You're practically screaming come fuck me."

I giggled, blushing for a split second. "Am not! Anyway, it's not that easy. He's making up for the mistakes he made. He's hurt, and so am I, but we're going to try and work things out." I pulled her to a stop, "I'm leaving in a few days to go back with him."

"To the apartment?" she asked.

"No, he sold it," I confessed. "He bought us an actual home. He said he's going to buy the place here, so we can still visit here whenever we want, which will be nice."

"God." She let out a long-winded groan. "Damn, I need to marry a rich guy," she said and wiggled her brows. "So, Mr. City Lover bought a house with a yard?" she asked, raising her brows, looking slightly impressed. "That's a big move for him."

Don't I know it. "Yeah, he feels bad, and I feel bad that he got played like that. Chris' friend told him we were having sex. They even edited some photos to make it look like we were having an affair. How sick is that?" I scoffed keeping my voice low from the guys.

"Photos of you and another man . . . that's why Chris left?" she asked, and I nodded, "Shit. Now, I kind of feel bad for him."

"I know, but it still doesn't excuse what he has done. The best I can do is try and forgive him, but it's hard. His whole family and our friends hate me," I muttered, remembering that when we go back, I would be facing them also.

"Don't worry about them; fuck them all." She laughed loudly and made the guys glance over their shoulders at us.

She was right in a way. I didn't have to take their crap. I knew the truth, and so did Chris. Well, he finally knew the truth now, so he was able to back me up. All I could do was hope for the best and have him stand up for me as I do for him.

We ended up right down near the water; the ocean breeze blowing lightly against our faces as the wind picked up. Ness and Adam took off down to the lower rocks while Chris and I stayed back, his arms around me and held me to his side as I leaned into him. It felt like home, that nothing had gone wrong.

"Does this house have furniture?" I asked, spotting a dolphin out in the water, and pointing.

"No. I thought you would like to buy that together?" Chris kissed the top of my head, and I felt my eyes starting to water. Call me emotional or whatever, but my mind was filled with fears of this not working out.

"I'm scared," I admitted.

"I know, and I promise I will make it up to you—you both," he corrected and turned me to face him, his hands cupping my cheeks gently as he pressed his lips against mine—a long lingering kiss, no tongue or parting our mouths, just his lips on mine. It felt nice.

The kiss felt really nice, but it was also playing on other emotions I had been feeling of late.

Pulling away, I cocked my head to the side and ran my hands up and down his chest. "Let's head back to the house. Maybe we can take a shower since it's getting a little cold?" I suggested.

"What?" he asked, looking at me slightly confused as I continued feeling a little embarrassed to want a shower with my husband and needing to ask him to join me.

"Little steps, like when we first dated. I need to make things easier as well, and we always showered together. I want to take a shower with you."

"My cock will get hard; you know this, right?" He looked embarrassed, but a slight grin played on his lips.

Eyes rolling, I groaned. "I'd be offended if it didn't."

With a laugh, he grinned wider. "Oh, really?"

"Little steps, remember? I just want to shower, and have you hold me."

"Little steps," he repeated and brought his lips back to mine.

CHAPTER ELEVEN

"Do you like it?" Chris looked at me hesitantly.

"Chris! I love it. It's so cosy and romantic." I smiled up at him and threw my arms around his neck.

He had surprised me with a trip to the woods. Well, more like rainforest, a relaxing long weekend away since we both had been busy with work this week. I had worn a blindfold for the last half hour of the drive, and he only just peeled it off as he carried me through the doors.

There were no clues given as I kept asking where he was taking me. He replied, "Shut up and enjoy the drive."

"It'll be good to get away, no phones or emails, just us," he said as rubbed his hands up and down my waist.

"Making love a lot?" I wiggled my brows as I bumped my lower waist to his.

"Sex freak," he muttered, holding in his dying-to-break-out grin.

"You love it," I sang slowly, shaking my hips side to side and pulling my shirt up.

I ended up giving him a sexy slow dance, but only lasted until I went to unclasp my bra. Chris and his rather visible friend decided that they wanted in on the action and I was tossed over his shoulder and carried to the bed. He dropped me down and hovered over me.

"You're sexy," he whispered huskily.

"You're hot," I replied.

"I love you." He pulled back eyeing me.

"I love you more." I smiled wide at his annoying face.

"Can't you just let me give you a compliment and not have you respond in kind?" He groaned and laughed loudly.

"Okay," I said and made a zipping-my-lips-shut motion with my fingers.

"I love you so much, Charlotte. You're the most beautiful woman I know, and I can't believe how lucky I am to be with you," he whispered and kissed me, a deep passionate kiss that had my knees buckling even though they were flat on the bed.

My hands stripped his shirt off and threw it to the floor. "Make love to me, handsome, charming, and best boyfriend ever."

"As you wish, sweetheart." He grinned as he lowered his body to mine, kissing and caressing every single inch of skin with his lips or fingertips.

"Charlotte." He pulled back and stared down at me, his body looking amazing in the light glow of the fire.

"Yeah?" I whispered back trying to find my voice.

"I really do love you, more than you'll ever know." He then lowered his head back to mine and kissed me. We made slow, passionate love that night, and it was more incredible each time we did.

The trip proved to be just what we needed. Our love grew stronger, if not, more solid as we spent those three full days together just doing nothing but loving, exploring, and just enjoying being together.

* * *

"Charlotte?" His words sounded unsure. "We don't have to do this. We can wait."

I turned around and pulled my top off over my head. "It's fine, Chris. I want us to take a shower together as a family, and as you said before, it's not like I haven't seen you naked."

"Okay then, I'll go and undress Lucy." He walked out of the bathroom, and I carried on with undressing myself. Of course, I was completely nervous. He hadn't seen me fully naked now. Well, my body isn't what it used to be anymore. I have bigger breasts, curvier hips, and stretch marks on my stomach.

I turned the shower tap on, adjusting the temperature when the water sprayed out. I stepped in, hoping the steam would block his sight when he entered. It felt like when we had our first shower together. Mind you, that was way before we slept together. Sure we had done other things, but I was still shy when it came to undressing in front of him.

I heard the door open and the footsteps nearing. Chris handed over Lucy, so he could undress. God, I had to look away. Otherwise, I would want to jump him.

"After this, I might go see the owners and make him an offer to buy the place. What do you think?" he asked over the water.

"That sounds good," I said, smiling down at Lucy who was just blinking sleepily as the water ran over her tummy. I moved my arms, so she was lying over my chest. I looked up and saw Chris staring right at me. My eyes skimmed over his body, and I wanted to smack myself hard.

"Like what you see?" He winked, walking in and in front of us.

"You know I do," I replied, looking up at him, my cheeks flaming red as a grin spread over his face.

"What's wrong? You're not embarrassed, are you?" He looked down at me, his dimples slowly fading.

"Of course, I am," I muttered, "You're all hot, and I'm . . ." I trailed off.

"Perfect," he finished. "You're still as beautiful as the day I met you outside that supermarket, if not, even more now. You've given me a daughter; your body is only a reminder of giving me something so amazing, and I love you for that, so stop thinking anything else negative. You're beautiful to me, and that is all that matters."

"Why do you have to be so sweet all the time?" I whispered and felt all my insecurities wash down the drain. He had a knack for making me feel beautiful, and he's just done that again.

"Not all the time. I can be a grade A jerk as we both know," he retorted and moved behind me. "Now, let me wash your hair because I know how much you love head massages." He laughed lightly, reaching for the shampoo.

It was nice to have this together—the bonding between the three of us as we washed together. Chris washed my hair, something I always got him to do back in the apartment, and his fingers were almost good enough to put me to sleep.

Well, good enough to put me to sleep, and drive me completely wild.

"We should get out. Lucy looks ready to fall asleep," he whispered, kissing the side of my neck softly.

"Mm, she loves the shower. It always puts her to sleep." I tilted my head, looking up at him, my heart racing as he stared back down. He had the same lust he always had when he looked at me. My heart was beating a million times an hour as he brought his lips to mine and kissed me softly.

Pulling back, he smirked, and without a word, he reached and took Lucy from my arms. "Wait here," he spoke and walked out, leaving me in the shower alone.

He soon returned and dropped the towel, water trickling down the front of his toned chest as he stepped back into the shower, looking at me with that hungry and lustful look he always got before we had sex.

"No," I blurted out as I realised what he was thinking.

His hands ran down my hips as the water spilled over the top of us, his mouth coming closer as he pulled me flush against his chest. "Oh, yes."

His bent his head, placing little kisses all the way down my neck, sucking gently as he reached my collarbone, his teeth grazing over my breast as he nipped and licked lightly. I wanted to say no, but the desire in my body was saying yes.

"Chris," I breathed out a soft moan as his mouth reached over my hips. His lips were sucking my skin as he ran his hands easily down the curve of my ass, lifting my thigh over his shoulder and his mouth bit down hard on my butt cheek.

"Ouch!" I laughed, squirming. "What was that for?"

He chuckled, kissing my bottom and coming back to the inside of my thigh "Well, baby, I do have a lot of ass-kissing to do. May as well start at the bottom." He winked, and without warning, he took my core into his mouth, licking and teasing me as he always did so well.

If there was one thing he knew how to do, then it was this; always so generous and giving. Never once has he gone down on me and expected me to do the same; it was always my pleasure over his own.

"Oh god," I moaned loudly as he pushed his fingers inside and curled them, running over the sensitive spot and pushing harder.

I looked down at him, my back against the wall. He looked up at me, giving me a flirty grin like he always does. He then sucked harder on my clit, sending me into a definite knee-buckling orgasm as he pushed his tongue deep inside me and removed his fingers. His hands went up, gripping my breasts and going to a slower pace to draw out the unbelievable bliss I was in right now. My hands which were gripping his hair tightly, slowly loosened as I came down from the high.

"Keep the beard," was all I could say at this moment. *Fuck me. That was staying.*

He kissed his way back up; his hardened dick was pressing into my stomach as his mouth crashed over mine. I went to touch him, but he pulled my hand away. "No," he breathed out.

"Why?" I pulled back.

"Char, I can wait," he groaned as I ran my fingers down his chest, my hand reaching down and fisting around his hardness.

"Okay, then stud." I smiled and pushed him off me, grabbing the towel and running into the bedroom as I left him there half-shocked and very hard.

I checked to see if Lucy was in her bed, but she wasn't. I figured Chris must have put her into the big cot to sleep and get used to it during the day more.

I didn't know whether it was the hormones acting up or the fact that Chris walked out completely naked with his cock bobbing, but I wanted him.

He was looking at me in the same way: desire, want, and hunger as his body moved over mine, his mouth kissing me as I wrapped my legs around him. His hands held mine out, and I don't know if that was because I kept trying to touch him, or he just wanted to hold hands.

"Let me," I spoke over his mouth as I tried to pull away.

"No," he groaned. "We're not having sex until you trust me again." He pulled back, looking slightly annoyed.

I raised my brows. "Who mentioned sex?"

"What do you want then? Because I won't fuck you." He sighed, lying down beside me.

My hand did the talking as it slowly skimmed down his chest and reached the area I wanted. It was only fair that I gave him what he gave me. I stroked his dick, lying by his side and watching his reaction. My hand moved up and down, twisting around as we continued to kiss, his hand running over my bare body as he gently caressed me.

"Char, I'm going to . . ." he breathed out. A low husky groan came from his mouth as he tilted his head back. His breathing quickened from his parting lips as he blew over his chest while I stroked faster, wanting him to come hard.

My hands ached as I let him go and grabbed the towel to clean him up, but stopped and leaned forward, knowing he was still watching as I licked the white fluid from his chest and trailed my tongue lower, down to his flaccid cock that still had semen around. I cleaned him with my mouth, not because he had just eaten my pussy like a king at the buffet, but because I wanted to.

"You didn't have to do that." He sat up and reached for some underwear.

"I know I didn't have to, but I wanted to." I shrugged, pulling my shirt over my head.

"I'm sorry." His face softened. "I shouldn't say that."

"I just want us to be how we were. We had sex all the time, and I could barely keep my hands off you. Now, I'm too nervous to touch you." I sighed, sitting beside him.

"Me too. I think you're right when you said we need to start over. I love you, and I will do anything to prove it to you. Just remember I fell in love with you long before we had sex. We did other things before that," he said as he pulled me close to his chest and held me.

"You're right, but I do enjoy seeing your face when you get off." I smiled.

"And I love seeing you the same way." Chris stood up and walked over to the bassinet. "Where's Lucy?"

"Didn't you put her in the big cot?" I questioned, panic setting in. One, because I couldn't believe I had just done that with her in the room.

"No." He frowned, standing up as he threw his clothes on quickly.

I felt my stomach drop as we both raced out of the bedroom and into the hallway. There, Adam was standing with his arms crossed and shaking his head at us. "Really?" He smirked. "Not while my beautiful niece is in that room, you don't."

"We just took a shower. Where is she?" I asked him, breathing out a relief that she hadn't been kidnapped.

106

"In her cot. I didn't want her to be scared of the disgusting noises coming from that shower. You couldn't keep your legs shut."

"We didn't have sex." Chris scoffed and went to the kitchen to grab both of us a cold drink.

"I don't want to know what you did. You're my boss, and Charlotte is still my innocent little sister in my eyes." Adam shuddered then walked away. "Keep it zipped up. or else . . ."

"Well, that was embarrassing," I muttered, feeling uncomfortable.

"You were kind of loud." Chris handed me a Coke and grinned as we went to the living room.

I slumped down on the couch next to Adam who held Lucy in his arms, running his fingertips over her small nose and dark brows. Chris had gone to talk to the owner of the villa. I told him not to go crazy and spend a lot, but he insisted money wasn't a problem. It never was with him.

"So, you and Chris are obviously doing better then," Adam broke the silence.

"We're good," I answered.

"Don't let him seduce you into forgiving him, Charlotte," he warned. "Sure, he might be good in the sack, but that doesn't make up for anything."

"Adam, we weren't having sex. We're just doing what we did when we dated." I shrugged, then cringed realising I told my brother that we were giving each other oral.

"Sick. I didn't need to know that," he grumbled.

"Well, stop it. If I want to forgive Chris and have that trust again, then we need to do things we used to do. Hell, I still love him; he was my husband, and we both had needs. I would prefer to pull him off than him go elsewhere," I spat back at him. Chris and I were married, and I didn't see what the big deal was.

"Okay. Gee, I get it!" he muttered, giving me an eye roll before changing the subject. "So, when are you heading back home?"

"In a couple of days. What about you?"

"Think I will join you. Do you reckon there is a spare room in that mansion Chris bought for you?" Adam winked and gave me the old puppy dog eye trick.

"Of course, there is, big bro. Nothing like mooching off your little sis, is there?" I winked and laughed.

He scoffed. "Yeah, I'm the lawyer here, and just remember who used to live off me all those years ago."

I smiled and kissed him on the cheek. "You're right, and I love you for that. So, when's Mum and Dad coming back?" I asked, curious as to why I hadn't seen them around all afternoon.

Chris walked in the door and tossed his keys to the table. "Bought it."

"Seriously?" I asked.

"Course, I am. You wanted it, so it's yours." He shrugged and sat beside me, his arm slung over my back as he pulled me closer to him.

"It's ours," I corrected Chris before I realised Adam didn't answer my question. "Where are they?" I asked, reaching over and taking my child from him. Seems as if when he's about to never hold her.

I leaned into Chris more; Lucy was now in his arms and he took her off me as soon as I picked her up from Adam. I didn't mind that he was getting more comfortable around her. My brother finally decided to answer me. "Charlotte, they left hours ago. I thought they would have said goodbye to you?"

CHAPTER TWELVE

"Chris!" I hissed quietly, as I tried to pry him off my body.

He winked and slid his hands further up my thighs. "Come on, Char. Just a quick one."

I giggled. "Isn't that the usual for you?"

His brows shot up as he laughed hard while he tugged on my legs, pulling me down in a swift movement until I lay underneath his body. "You want to take that back?"

I rolled my eyes trying to push him off me but failed. "I'm sorry, babe." I winked and gave in to him, realising that I was losing this fight already. I wasn't going to appear weak though.

"Did you bring your camera?"

I nodded. "Yes, I'm going to take lots of photos of you and us and put them on the wall in our home—big black and white ones. What do you think?"

He chuckled and lowered his mouth just over mine. "Sounds perfect. I love you, Charlotte, but please put me out of my misery and let me stick it in you."

"Go and do that in the shower. We're not having sex in your parents' home." Yes, that's right. We were staying with his family for the weekend. Apparently, we didn't spend enough time with them as it was, so Chris planned our weekend with them without telling me. I was looking forward to doing nothing, but he was determined to teach me how to fish and then gut one. Yes, I wasn't looking forward to that part.

"What if they hear us? We're not that quiet," I whispered, wrapping my legs around his waist.

He kissed me passionately and ran his hand up and down my body lightly until he pulled back. "Please, baby. I'll buy you anything you want." He bargained.

The words slipped from my mouth before I could stop them. "A diamond ring?"

He smirked, running his hand down between my thighs. "Would you like a diamond ring?"

I moaned; this conversation had just gotten serious quickly. "I love you."

He frowned. "Charlotte, are you telling me I need to up my game and go shopping for a rock?"

"Chris, I have you. I don't need a ring; all I want is you. You've got me hook, line, and sinker."

He fell beside me and clutched his stomach as he laughed loudly, I loved it when he laughed. So carefree and happy. He leaned closer and cupped my cheek. "I love you, Charlotte. You've got me too, hook, line, and sinker as I am, completely in love with you."

His mouth claimed mine, and we stripped off our underwear as he made love to me, forgetting all about his parents who were down the hall as we rolled around in the sheets more than once that night.

The weekend turned out to be the most fun one we had. Chris had pushed me into the lake, and I grabbed him as I fell backwards. That soon turned to making out in the freezing cold water as the rods next to us were bending to let us know we had each caught fish. He did teach me how to gut them, and I watched with my eyes closed, and then we cooked them for dinner.

*   *   *

I looked out the window, watching as the ocean slowly faded into the background. There was nothing left to see other than trees, buildings, and mountains. We were on our way back to the

110

reality of city life—going home to face the music of things and deal with it all. *Together*.

Adam was driving Chris' car behind us while Chris, Lucy, and I travelled together in the SUV. It was nerve-wracking to be heading back, knowing his family was mad at me. That was the worst part—they all still thought Lucy wasn't Chris' daughter.

I turned my head, looking over at Chris as he drove—one hand on the wheel and the other resting against the window seal of the door, rubbing his temples. I could only imagine the headaches he was getting from it all. He suffered migraines badly, and the stress of everything was eating him up inside.

He could try to say he was okay, but I knew he was barely holding on. I knew him, and that's what he needed to remember.

I heard the little noise in the back and hoped Lucy wasn't hungry again. We had stopped twice already so that I could feed her. The last one was half an hour ago. Luckily, she stayed asleep even though Chris let out a light breath of relief. I think he just wanted to get home.

Mum and Dad weren't talking to me. I called them when Adam told me that they had left and headed back to their home. I was so hurt and upset that they couldn't even say goodbye to Lucy or me. Even a note to say they were going. But they said nothing.

Chris and I were good. Well, I think we were. He was helping a lot through the nights. It was amazing that he woke each time Lucy cried, and got up to pass her to me and watch me feed our daughter. We talked on and off, but mostly, we were just silent. It was the same comfortable silence we always had together.

I reached over and slid my hand over his thigh. He hadn't touched me much since we fooled around in the bed and shower. We kissed, but that was it. But then again, it had only been a few days, so I couldn't complain. I just hoped it hadn't ruined things between us.

"Can you hold my hand?" I asked quietly.

He looked down at my hand before his eyes darted to mine. He changed hands on the wheel, using his left to drive, and dropped his right over my hands, lacing our fingers together and squeezing tightly. "I love you, Char," he said. It was like he was too afraid to even hold my hands.

I leant over in my seat and kissed his cheek. "I love you too. Are you feeling okay?" I asked.

He shook his head and squeezed my hand tighter. "I wish you would hate me; it would make this easier."

This is what was hurting the most—him hating himself. He wanted me to hate him and tell him I wanted a divorce and would be taking Lucy away from him. He didn't think he deserved us in his life, and it was killing me so badly that he wanted us to leave him.

I felt the tears as I pulled my hand from his and shifted, facing the window and letting the tears fall down my cheeks. I felt the car slowing down and pulling onto the side of the road, finally stopping. Chris opened his door swiftly and walked around to open mine. He stood in front of me and pulled my belt off, swivelling my legs around. The next thing I knew, he was kissing me.

He was kissing me in a way he had not touched me since being here, his hands holding me tightly, grabbing and squeezing my ass as I kissed him back, sliding my hands in his back pockets, clutching onto his back, and pulling him closer over me. Our tongues found each other, and twisted together, lips moving in perfect sync as we made out on the highway. A couple of cars passing us honked their horns, but Chris ignored them. His lips moved to my neck, sucking it before they were back in my mouth as his fingers gripped my hair lightly.

He broke the kiss and cupped my cheeks, brushing the tears away with his thumbs as he rested his forehead on mine. "Please don't cry. I hate it when you cry, Char."

"Have you changed your mind? Do you not want me anymore?" I asked quietly.

He shook his head. "No, I love you so much. It's just I don't deserve to have you coming back with me, Char. You are too fucking nice to me."

"I love you. I'm trying to move forward, but you're pushing me away, and it's making me doubt coming back with you. Do you really want me to forget about you and have Lucy grow up without a dad? Or worse, have someone else be her dad? Just bloody decide what you want; I'm not going to be strung along," I explained, knowing it might be the push he needed to realise that was a big possibility if he kept pushing me like this.

His brows hardened as if he had not thought that far into it. "You're mine, Char. Lucy is mine, and I will not let someone else take you both away from me. I will not lose you again. I love you both, and I'm sorry. I just thought if I push you away, it'll just give me what I deserve."

"I know you are, but please stop pushing us away, Chris. I want us to work." I leant up and kissed him lightly, brushing the hair from his face and running my fingers over his cheek. "Help me make us work. I need your help." I pulled him back towards me for another steamy kiss.

Finally getting back on the road, we soon fell into an easy conversation about his work. I loved listening to him talk about the cases he was on. It was fascinating to me, and he was never one to bring up work at home. I was the one to always ask him and make him tell me all about his day. It went on for about twenty minutes until Lucy decided to start screaming her lungs out and had us pulled over for the third time.

"Is she not well?" Chris asked, sliding in the back seat with me and running his hands over Lucy's forehead gently as she sucked but squirmed, grunting almost.

I shrugged. "I don't know. She's so cranky today." I looked up at Chris and gave an exhausted smile. "I love you. You know that, right?"

He leaned forward, resting his forehead against mine. "I know, and I love you too. Both of you."

I tilted my head up and planted my lips on his, kissing him lightly. I proceeded with feeding Lucy for twenty minutes, and the rate we were going was we wouldn't be back until dark.

We went through the drive-through, and Chris still cringed at me when I ate my fries, by dipping them into the ice cream. It was something I had done the entire pregnancy, and he thought it was gross.

"You should try one; they're so good." I held one up, teasing him with it.

"I don't see how anyone could enjoy them like that." A grin spread over his face while he kept his eyes on the road, but still lent over and opened his mouth to try it. His face scrunched, and I knew he didn't want another. "I can't wait until you see the house."

"Me either. I'm looking forward to it." I really was.

"I should have listened when you asked to move months ago. You wanted a big home in the suburbs, and I want you happy."

*   *   *

I must have dozed off. The next thing I knew I was waking up as Chris was pulling into a driveway; the sun was slowly starting to set. My eyes were glued to the stunning house, or should I say the *massive* two-storey home. It looked better than he had described, and definitely more perfect than the photos I had seen from his phone.

"Chris, is this really it?" I asked, getting out of the car while he grabbed Lucy from her seat.

"Yes, it's really it." He laughed coming up behind me. "Come on, Lucy. Let's go find your new room to put all those clothes in." He wrapped his free arm around my waist as we walked up the cobblestone pathway.

Each room felt like this was where we would spend our lives, growing old with our children and grandchildren. Rustic but still modern. There was a hint of country life in this place, and that's what I loved. It was new, unlived in, but felt as if it had been here for years.

Now, we just had to fill it with furniture. There was no bedding, so we spent the night in a hotel and went shopping the next morning for furniture. Nothing too fancy or crazy. Our style was similar: simple and comfortable. We both liked nice things and had the money to afford to splurge on more costly things. Everything was going to be delivered that afternoon, and all we needed were groceries to fill our butler's walk-in pantry.

I grabbed the basics, so we could at least eat and drink and would do proper shopping online after we were settled in.

Adam had arrived not long ago the furniture was delivered and was walking outside with Chris. I made us all a hot drink while the guys spoke about work; those two could bond over that subject all day if they had the chance to.

Adam walked in first and went straight to the rocker on the living room floor while Chris flashed me a smile and sat beside me, watching as my brother unclipped Lucy and held her close to his chest. He was obviously missing his niece.

"So, what's the go with Ness and you?" I asked Adam. Those two really needed to get together.

He looked at me and laughed. "Nothing. We're just friends."

"Yeah, that wasn't convincing at all." Chris laughed, reaching over and taking hold of my hand.

Adam just smirked at me, a look telling me to stop asking questions and let him see where it leads. I could do that for him. I'll let him try to get serious and just hope they work out.

"So, do I get to pick my room out?" he asked and stood up, walking back to pass Lucy to Chris. It was as if I didn't exist when those two were around with her, not that I minded. I loved seeing Chris holding our daughter.

Chris stood up as well and nodded. "Upstairs and down the hall. Pick whichever one you want."

I walked over, giving my brother a goodnight hug. "Good night, Adam. Thanks so much for helping me these past few days. For helping make the flat packs too."

"No problem, sis. Behave, and remember my ears are like a hawk's. No kinky sex, please." He winked over at Chris, and I blushed; he just had to embarrass me, didn't he?

We headed towards our room, and Chris closed the door. "So, Mama, would you want to go take a bath? I'll put Lucy to bed. Do you want her in our room again?" he asked and walked into the bedroom. Lucy was dressed in a dark purple pair of PJs, and I pouted. They were so cute on her.

"Do you want her in our room, or hers?" I asked, knowing what he wanted.

"Yeah, I want her in here too." He grinned, laying her on the bed and pulling the cot bedding back. "Did you want to feed her? She's stopped being cranky, but I'm not too sure if she'll wake up again soon."

I nodded "Okay, I'll feed her, and you run us a bath that is definitely bigger than our last one."

I fed Lucy, and when I say fed, she guzzled on both boobs and was now lying in her bassinet fast asleep. Chris and I were relaxing in the tub. Chris was behind me, spreading the body scrub over my back, kneading it into my skin which felt amazing.

"Chris," I breathed out, tilting my head back to get a glimpse of him.

"Yeah, you ready to get out of the bath and into bed?" he asked, and I nodded. I was more than ready to get into that bed with him.

116

I moaned over his mouth as I straddled him and kissed him deeply, his hands running up and down my back, resting on my hip as I ground into him. His deep breathing became huskier as he flipped us and pushed me into the mattress of softness. His hand was now running up and down my thigh, grabbing my ass as he ground himself against me, which made us both moan loudly into one another's mouth.

It had been far too long since we were like this.

"God, I love you," he said, kissing down my neck, sucking and nipping at my soft skin.

I bumped my hips up and arched into him as he kissed further down, kissing down past my stomach, and hiding away beneath the covers; his tongue working slowly as he licked me, kissing and sucking at my clit with hunger. I was enjoying this; I loved the way he made me feel as he did this. I wanted him. I wanted more.

With my eyes rolling backwards, my hands gripped into the sheets as I rocked my hips up and down, gasping for air with each stroke of his tongue.

"I'm coming!" I breathed out, grabbing a handful of his hair, and pushing my hips up against his mouth more. His own groaning only increased my pleasure as he licked me until I had come and was twitching from being overly sensitive. I tried prying his face away, but he wasn't having it and kept sucking until my legs fell beside him.

"I love your taste." He kissed back up my chest, his hardness pressed into my core again, but I pushed him on his back. "No, Char," he uttered, but his voice failed him. He wanted this as much as I wanted to give it. There's nothing to stop me.

"You want it. Let me show you how much I've missed you, Chris. I know you want it too," I said.

"Yes, but I don't need it. Like I said before, I am fine without it." He cupped my cheeks and ran his thumb over my lower lip.

I ignored him as I moved back over him. "Let me love you, baby." I kissed him and sucked his lower lip, kissing down his neck and giving him a mark just above his collarbone while I slid my hand down his chest and touched his growing shaft. The deep sexy groan that escaped from his lips had me moving quickly underneath the covers to finally touch him.

I licked his cock up and down, using my hand to pull up and down as he held my head while I took him all the way in and sucked slowly. I wanted him to enjoy this, and it had been a while for him. I could tell he was itching to take it further, but he was holding off pretty damn well.

"Fuck." A guttural groan escaped from his mouth as his hips began thrusting up faster.

I swallowed his release when he blew and came back up. "I love you," I said, smiling lazily and ran my hands up and down his chest.

His hands moved up my thighs and towards my breasts. "I love you too. That was amazing, sweetheart."

"You were amazing as well." I kissed him softly and lay down beside him, "I missed that," I admitted.

He was silent for a while as he held me close to his chest. "Mum called earlier," he finally spoke. "She wants us to go there tomorrow for lunch. Only if you're up to it, that is. I don't want to force you to rush back there."

It was then my turn to be silent for a little while as I thought about it. I wanted to go, and I guess it was only fair, but I was still worried. "Umm, promise that you will stay with me and not let them go off at me. I don't want to fight, especially if Lucy is around." I looked up at him.

"I promise, Char. They won't say anything to hurt you or Lucy. You did nothing wrong. It was all my fault, and they know that. Mum said it would be something quiet, and just us and them there. No big dinner or anything. Adam can come as well if that would help." He caressed my cheek and kissed my forehead lightly

118

as I turned to my side, facing him as our bodies pressed together like old times.

Everything in this moment was perfect; nothing could wipe the smile from my face as I lay in my husband's arms with our daughter sleeping peacefully beside us in her bed. I felt loved, safe, and happy.

Nothing could wreck the feeling I had.

Nothing apart from the hell that was unleashed the next day when the so-called small lunch had happened.

CHAPTER THIRTEEN

"Just stand there and look pretty," I said, grinning as I checked out the camera settings.

"What? No," he responded with an eye roll. "I'm not a puppet."

I looked up and gave him a smug smirk. "Oh, but you're my boyfriend. You will do as you're told. Remember, my dear. You may be the boss in the bedroom, but out of there, it's me."

He scoffed. "You can't make me do this. I'm a businessman, not your model. I have work to do and important calls to make."

"Christopher, don't you dare pull the work excuse on me. Now, take that top off, get your jeans on the floor, and stand there until I'm ready. You promised me you would do it," I growled, narrowing my eyes at him and showing him that I meant business.

"You asked me when I was about to blow. It doesn't count since you tricked me into this!" He threw his arms up, exasperated, and then pulled the black top off. Oh, he was so doing it.

"See? It's not so bad, is it? And by the way, you've tricked me during sex as well. If I remember correctly, you went down on me just before you asked me to let you go on that boys' weekend, which I let you go to," I reminded him with a raised brow.

"Charlotte!" Chris snapped angrily undoing his jeans, kicking them off and tossing them across the room. "Just hurry up and do it then. I won't be smiling either."

I rolled my eyes at him and scoffed, putting the camera down and placing my hands over my hips as I walked towards him more. "You will do it because you love me. Now, shut up and stand there until I'm ready."

He was pissed because I was taking photos of him in nothing but his underwear. I wanted to do a full-on naked shoot, but he said no to that, so boxers were the next best thing.

He let out a loud sigh as he sat down, crossing his arms over his chest and scowling. "How about you stand there naked, and I will take photos of you?"

"Spoken like a true pervert." I winked and smiled, pulling my shirt up over my head and throwing it at him.

His eyes widened in shock as he stood "What are you doing?"

"Getting naked. We'll take photos together naked from the chest up." I put the camera back on the tripod and set the timer and picture frame settings.

"I don't want your tits out!"

"God. We'll have our chests pressed together. Plus, these photos are just for us when we're old, and I want to show our kids what we were like young."

He laughed and pulled me towards him. "Fine, let's do this, and maybe if they're good, then we can put them on the wall."

I wrapped my arms around his lower waist as he held me back; our bare chests pressing together as we looked into each other's eyes. "Oh, I know they'll be good." I smiled widely at him.

He laughed. "Char, you're lucky I love you because I would never normally agree to this. I'm not the type of man to take pictures of myself."

I leant forward. "Think of these as our family portraits or your new business cards. We both know you wanted a nice photo for that." I winked as I pressed my chest harder into him and hooked my arms around his neck "Kiss me," I asked quietly.

The photos turned out amazing. I couldn't have tried to take more of a perfect shot if I tried. Chris was stunned when I showed him the photos. He couldn't believe that we had taken such amazing pictures, and in the end, he chose five photos, which he had hung in the apartment.

The black and white shots of us looking so lovingly at each other, the ones of us kissing and holding, and there was one adorable one of him pouting and me laughing—they all hung in the open.

*   *   *

"Charlotte?" I heard my name being called. I looked to my left and saw Chris walking towards me with his morning messed up bed hair.

"Morning," I greeted and let out a yawn, covering my mouth and looking back at the wall of photos of Chris and me when we were dating. All of them were splayed out, telling a story of us when we first dated up until I was nine months pregnant. We had done the whole pregnancy reveal and a maternity shoot. We had even stripped off naked with Chris standing behind me, his hands wrapped around my swollen stomach and covering my breasts.

His body came behind mine as he wrapped his arms around me, kissing the top of my head. "You've been quiet all morning. Are you okay?" he asked softly.

I nodded and took a sip of the hot tea in my hands. "Yeah. Just nervous, I guess. Plus, I was going to ask if you would want to take photos with Lucy like we planned to do?" I asked, a little more nervously.

"I would love to take photos with our daughter. I told you I would do it and I haven't changed my mind." He ran his hands up and down my arms as he kissed my cheek. "You're nervous about lunch, aren't you?"

I nodded again. "Yeah, I don't know what to expect."

"Expect a small lunch like she said it would be. I don't want a bunch of people around Lucy and having her passed from person to person. If it gets out of hand, then we'll leave and come home." He slowly turned me around to face him, and I gave him a weak smile.

He was trying.

"Okay, that sounds good."

"Good. Now, come and eat something. I've made you breakfast, and Lucy will be up shortly. I'd like to have some alone time with my wife first." He wiggled both brows. "Without your brother, I mean."

I cocked my head to the side and smirked a little. "You didn't get enough of that last night?"

His eyes darkened slightly. "Baby, I loved last night, but I'm talking about us eating breakfast outside until Lucy wakes up, and then I'll hear her." He held the baby monitor up and wiggled it in his palm. "Come on. Do you still love pancakes with strawberries and maple syrup?"

I nodded. "If you're making them, then I definitely do!"

We sat outside in our pyjamas under the morning sun and shared a plate of pancakes. Chris always made the best ones and often cooked breakfast for us every morning. When I first found out I was pregnant, I wanted them all the time. He had made a fresh batter each morning, so I could cook them during the day while he was at work. To this day, I still have no idea what he puts in them.

I moved from the wicker chair and sat down on his lap, my arms loosely resting over his shoulders as he placed his on my hips. "Thank you for breakfast." I leaned forward and pressed my lips to his.

The cry of a baby had us pulling apart to catch our breath as what was meant to be a simple kiss had turned into something hot and steamy. Making out at the outdoor dining table when my brother was in the building was a big risk to take.

"I'll get her." Chris kissed me once more and I stood up to let him move.

"Okay. I'll clean up and meet you in the shower," I suggested, and his brows shot up, not believing if I was serious or not. I was being serious. "Be up in five."

I cleaned up and put the tea towel on the table when Adam strolled over, looking like he was rested and well. His hand went to my hair, tousling it up. "Morning, little sister. How's your sleep?"

I slept amazingly after what Chris had done to me. "Good," I replied simply.

He gave a slight frown, but then covered it up with a smile. "So, in-laws today huh?"

"You want to come with us?" I begged. He wouldn't let me go on my own, would he? I had to have him there for backup, to help me if things went from good to sour immediately.

When he shook his head, my heart dropped. "Charlotte, I would go any other time, but this is something you and Chris need to do. On your own," he spoke in a firm lawyer voice, and I gave him the finger as I walked off. I understood what he said, but still. I was annoyed slightly. If you couldn't tell, I really didn't want to do lunch today. Adam laughed, even more so when I stalked off.

"Here's Mama." Chris grinned as I stepped into the shower and was sprayed with a splash of warm water when Lucy's hands jerked out as she made a loud squeal noise.

"Someone's excited to have a shower." I kissed Lucy's little cheek and felt her fist going right to my boob.

"Actually, she's hungry. Her mouth was going crazy when I held her to my chest, and she tried to look for milk."

"I wish I could have seen that." I laughed and quickly started to wash my hair and body.

An hour later, we were in the car on our way to his parents' home. It was a thirty-minute drive to their large mansion in a gated community, of course, since they were more upper-class type of people. I was still nervous, and I had begged Adam to come along with us. Even Chris asked him to join us, and he still said no.

Lucy was fast asleep in the backseat. I had dressed her in a little light pink outfit that Chris picked out. He even put the dark purple crochet beanie hat over her head. I really think he loved dressing her more than I did.

"It'll be okay," he spoke as he pulled up in their driveway.

I went to agree with him until I spotted all the cars, more than what the immediate family was meant to have. "Chris," I spoke in a warning tone.

He let out a sigh and rubbed his temples. I didn't want to fight, so I just unfastened my belt and made my way out of the car. Chris was still standing there as I pulled Lucy out and grabbed her changing bag. She didn't wake once I held her in my arms. Chris went to the backseat, pulling out the baby sling. "Put this on," he said.

I looked at him, slightly confused. "Why?"

"She's asleep. I won't have her being passed around like a doll. Nobody touches her while she is asleep other than you or me, okay? Especially strangers." I could tell now wasn't the time to argue with him.

He was going all papa bear, and he was sexy as hell like this. I nodded as he helped me place the sling on, carefully moving Lucy into it, and finally covering her up with the little pink blanket. I didn't expect that from him at all.

"Are you okay to carry her?" he asked me.

I nodded. "Yeah, if she gets too heavy we can swap."

"Yes, but we won't be here for long if she's done something crazy."

Crazy was the operative word. When we walked into that house, it was filled with people; it was basically a dinner party. I was already feeling overwhelmed. I normally never minded coming to these things, but I, for one, was underdressed, and another, we now had a baby, and I thought his parents would like to meet her on their own without all their friends and families around.

125

"I should have worn a tux," Chris noted, glancing down at his jeans and polo shirt.

"Incoming," I whispered, nodding ahead at the person making a beeline for us both.

"Charlotte, oh my, you're a welcome sight." I squeezed Chris's hand tighter as his sister walked towards us, a massive smile plastered on her face as her eyes zoomed in on Lucy's covered-up body.

"Hi." I smiled at her feeling the nerves slowly vanish.

"Chris wouldn't tell us anything other than the baby was perfect. Boy or girl?" She rolled her eyes and peered at the blanket.

I let out a soft laugh and pulled the blanket back. "Little girl, Lucy," I answered her as Chris's arm went around my shoulder.

His sister broke out into tears as she looked down at our sleeping baby, and then punched her brother in the chest. "You're a fucking moron, Chris. She's a spitting image of you."

"Don't," I spoke to cut her off. "I didn't come here so we can all fight. He's here now, and that's what matters."

Her eyes widened as if to say "you're kidding me" but she shook her head. "You don't deserve her, Chris. If that were me, I wouldn't be so forgiving. But who am I to judge? She's perfect, and you both look good with a baby."

Chris muttered something under his breath, and I shot him a look; I wasn't in the mood to listen to him put himself down today. "Chris, do you think we could put this bag in your old room?" I asked.

"Sure." He looked at his sister and pulled me closer to his chest as we made our way to his bedroom.

He closed his bedroom door and took the bag from my hands with a sigh. "Fuck, we should just leave. You want to go get junk food and have a movie marathon?"

I nodded, sitting on the edge of his bed and laughed. "Yes. She won't notice if we leave quickly."

"Let's just go home. I'm done with this shit, and just want to focus on you and Lucy this afternoon." He leant forward and pressed his lips against mine, being careful not to bump the sleeping baby between us.

"Sounds like a great day to spend the day," I said honestly as I broke away from his touch. The smile that he gave me had tugged my heart. It was infectious not to smile back at him.

Opening the door, I was pretty sure he had just about had a heart attack as much as I did when I spotted the woman dressed to the nines standing in front of us, tapping her nails as she stared right at me. That was until Chris stood in front of me and blocked her off from sight.

"You come back home, but don't bother coming to say hello?" she uttered, the drama clear in her words. It shocked me because they were always a loving and happy family supporting each other. I hadn't ever seen them fight or be this rude.

Chris's flat palm went straight to the door and pushed it open with a louder thud. It banged loudly into the wall, the noise jerking Lucy from her sleep but not enough to wake her. Thank god for that, "You said family dinner. This is a fucking circus," he sneered. "What the hell, Mum!?"

"You didn't think that we were really having a small get-together, did you? You just had your first child, so we need to celebrate. Charlotte, good to see you. Although, I would have appreciated a phone call to say my granddaughter was born." She eyed me, looking down at me as if to say I was the worst person in the world. "Oh well, better late than never, I suppose."

"I did call when I was in labour and gave birth to my daughter alone," I muttered sarcastically. "You all cut me off first, so remember that."

She looked shocked at my sudden slight outburst and gave a brow raise and half an eye roll. "Well then, if you're not mad at him, I will put it aside and ask if I can please have a hold of my granddaughter. I believe you named her Lucy?" she asked. "You should have asked for permission first."

"Mother, she's asleep," Chris spoke, stepping towards us.

"I don't care. Babies always sleep." And before I knew what she was doing, she had reached into the sling and pulled Lucy out, waking her up in a screaming fit and taking off down the hallway with a pat on the bottom.

Chris and I stared at each other in shock. "Did she just do that?" I asked him.

He nodded. "Fuck."

My maternal instincts were to go and hunt her down, get my baby back, and leave. Grandmother or not, no one snatches my child and takes off without a word.

We could hear Lucy's little cries as we walked down the stairs, and both of us moved faster. I didn't like my daughter just being snatched from my arms like that. Family or not, she should ask first. Chris was caught up by his father and his group of men's club friends. He gave me a sympathetic smile. I simply nodded and went to take my child back alone.

I was walking around, being stopped by random people and asking where Lucy was. My response each time was "That's what I'd like to know." I could see Chris talking to his dad heatedly by the bar. I couldn't make out the words, but he was pointing inside, so I could only guess that it had to do with this whole lunch thing. I didn't blame him for being furious.

I was about to walk into the kitchen when I heard some hushed whispering that had me stopping and listening in. "Didn't you hear? The baby is not even Chris'. That woman just took off when he found out, so she didn't get caught in a bigger lie."

"I heard that she's blackmailing him, that's why he's staying with her. She threatened his career and to take all his money," another woman said in a hushed voice.

I couldn't believe these women were holding my daughter and talking about me as if I was some kind of scheming con artist just after his money and law firm.

"Charlotte," Chris called out. "What are you doing standing here?"

I jumped, startled by being caught. "Just listening to people saying that I'm a gold-digging whore who left you with a child that isn't yours." I shrugged and kept my eyes on the floor while another woman spoke.

"I heard that she tricked him into marrying her. Funny how they were pregnant so soon, especially after being married not long after meeting. I think she set him up, charmed her way into his bed, and got pregnant on purpose!"

Chris walked, well, I should say he brushed past me abruptly into the room where the women continued to make snide comments. "There's my baby girl," he uttered before taking Lucy in his arms and turned to the gossiping women. "Slander—it's a case I've often dealt with, but I never thought I would have to file my own suit."

"Christopher, we weren't doing anything," one of them defended.

I scoffed, finally moving from the corner and making myself known to them. All the women's faces were pricelessly shocked.

"Excuse me," I said, realising Chris' mother was standing there too. "Don't you dare hold or take off with my daughter without our permission again. And just so you know, Lucy is Chris' daughter, so don't spread gossip when you don't know the truth about anything." I hissed, causing her to gasp, looking embarrassed for being caught out.

"Charlotte, you're not leaving, are you? We've barely spent any time with you." Chris' mum chased after us in a panic.

I went to talk, but Chris cut me off, "Yes, we've had enough, and maybe, if this was more intimate, then we could have had a better afternoon. Obviously not."

"I didn't mean to upset anyone," she defended herself.

She could say that all she wanted, but I didn't believe her. "Yes, you did. You knew better."

We left the house. Chris was fuming, but not saying a word until we pulled up at the house and just sat there, standing out the window at the garage "So . . ." Chris started as he sighed and clicked his tongue. "That went well."

I leaned over in the seat and kissed his lips. "Indeed. How about we go and take some family photos of the three of us? Then we can all get into our bed, watch movies, and eat junk food?"

He smiled into the kiss and spoke over my mouth between the kissing that had turned into passionate kisses. "Sounds perfect, sweetheart!"

CHAPTER FOURTEEN

"Happy birthday, handsome," I whispered as I removed my hands from his covered eyes.

His face broke out into a wide grin, and he turned in his leather chair to look at me. "No way! You're kidding me. You seriously got me this?"

I nodded. "Of course, I did. I'm not going to have my boyfriend working all day without having a birthday cake, now am I?"

"Char, you're incredible."

I laughed. "Just blow the candles out. I made it, so even if it isn't nice, just say it is." I passed him a lighter and hesitated. "Your office won't get flooded by water, will it?" I asked, a little worried that the smoke detectors would go off.

He ignored me and lit the candle. "I want to make a birthday wish," he spoke and lit the candle, leaning forward and blowing it out in a quick puff. "Done, and no alarms went off." He winked and walked to his window and opened it, letting the fresh air come in.

"Are you ready for your present?" I asked him with a devious smile.

"Charlotte, what are you up to?" He grabbed the fork, digging eagerly into the side of the thick, rich mud cake, taking a bite, and then looking up at me curiously.

I had gotten the nerve to put on some sexy red lingerie—since that was his favourite colour—and wear it underneath a wrap dress. Now, I was standing in a pair of heels, the lingerie, and nothing else. "You better cancel any meetings you have after lunch, my hot lawyer. The only case you're going to win is this one. I plan on fucking you on every piece of furniture in this office—the

131

couch, the desk, against the wall, on the floor. Then you're going to push me into the window and screw me harder."

"Charlotte." His eyes ran over my body. "Fuck," he groaned, his hand loosening his tie as he gulped again, his dick was firm, and the bulge became completely noticeable as he walked towards me.

I wasn't normally like this. I was a good, innocent girl, Charlotte. But today, my boyfriend was going to see me as the bad girl who gave him anything he wanted. "Do you like?"

"Like?" He smiled wide as his hands reached and ran his fingertips over the laced push-up bra. "I fucking love it. But why?"

"This is birthday sex. God, for a smart lawyer, you're really thick at times."

He grabbed my wrists as I went to cover up. "Oh, no, you don't! Mistress, you're going to fuck me the way you just promised. Can't turn me on and leave me stiff."

"Mistress?" I laughed a little.

He nodded, pulling the dress completely off me. "Birthday sex is fantasy sex, and you've just made my fantasy come true: being dominated in my office by a hot woman. Now, I want to taste the sweetness hiding in between your thighs, my love. Then I'm going to clear my afternoon and have you any way I want."

"Clear away because tonight, you're only in for more of this. You may want to take the day off tomorrow," I whispered as I slowly started to unbutton his white shirt.

He groaned as I pushed him down in the leather chair by the window and crawled up in his lap, kissing him, teasing him, and grinding myself into him. "Happy birthday, handsome."

"Fuck, you're incredible," he groaned as his hands wrapped around my waist. I kissed him deeply, kissing down his chest whilst kneeling and unbuttoning his pants.

Giving him his most memorable present ever!

*   *   *

I looked at the man in front of me and smiled. Oh, how I loved him in a suit. He wore them so well.

We had spent three days at home doing nothing but being a family. Lucy was getting into a better routine; she was waking once a night while Chris and I just kept on making out and doing everything but sex. Last night, we had nearly done it. We were naked in the bedroom alone, and he was right on top of me. His cock was pushed against me, and it was so tempting to say, *"Do it."*

The only thing to stop us was Adam knocking on the door, asking if he could take Lucy into the yard for a walk. Talk about bad timing, but it really was *good* timing. It was good that we didn't go the whole way. It would have been too soon, and when we had both calmed down, we agreed that it was too rushed. Chris wanted to take it slower, wait until I was sure, and he wasn't feeling guilty still.

But damn, the waiting was starting to suck.

It was like he was teasing me—naked showers and walking past in a suit with his hair combed over to the side. I damn hated waiting.

"Do you have everything?" I asked as he picked his briefcase up and opened it, looking through his papers.

"No," he replied, turning to face me.

I was confused, glancing around to see what was missing. "What do you need to get? You're going to be late for your meeting at 10 AM."

He shrugged, giving me a cute little pout. "I don't have you two coming with me. I don't want to go to work."

I laughed; he was acting like a toddler on the first day of school. "Sweetheart, you have us at home. How about Lucy and I come to have lunch with you?" I asked nervously, thinking that maybe he didn't want me to come and have lunch with him.

His hand went to my cheek, his fingers stroking it. "I'd love that."

I nodded. "Good, because we want to see Daddy, don't we, little girl?" I smiled, holding Lucy up and taking her little arm, giving a little fist pump. "Maybe he's got some more candy stashed away in the drawer." I would usually raid his office for them.

A million-dollar smile spread across his face as he let out a laugh. "The stash is well and truly empty. My teeth are getting too old for them." He winked and walked towards us. "Can you pick up some more for me?"

"Sure, go to work. Lucy and I will come in around lunch once we get organized. Did you want me to pick you up something to eat other than your sweets?"

"No, I'll take you out on a lunch date; wine and dine you, but without the wine."

"Like an actual date?" I laughed "Won't that be weird?"

He shook his head. "Not unless you think it is." He laughed and placed a kiss on my cheek. "See you in a few hours. I love you both."

I was still standing in the kitchen after he left, holding Lucy and slightly stunned, my heart racing from his words. A date? I wasn't expecting that. I was thinking maybe a sandwich in his office, not going out for lunch. I rolled my eyes, realising that I now had to get the pram in the car and pack a bottle just in case Lucy got grumpy.

I went to our room and laid Lucy on the bed, climbing back in it and feeding until she fell back asleep so that I could slip into the shower. If Chris was making an effort, then I would do the same. I wanted to look nice for him; I wanted to show him that even though he thinks it's just him who needs to make things better, it's me as well who needs to fight to save what we had. I need this to work just as much as he did, and I have to try to move on.

The only problem was I couldn't stop thinking about it. In the back of my mind, all I could think about was how my husband left me the day our daughter was born. The guilt was eating me up, trying so hard to make sure everything was okay, and I desperately needed it to be okay.

I drove into town, cleaning up the already spotless house and dressing Lucy in a little pink-and-white striped romper suit. I was nervous; the last time I was here was a week before I gave birth. I was nervous to see how they would react. More importantly, I was anxious to see his new secretary. I wanted to make it clear to whoever was working for him that he was off limits and mine. I won't play nice and bite my tongue this time.

I pushed the pram into the large office building and made my way towards the elevator. Pressing Chris' floor number, I made my way up to the top floor. I was getting looks; people were obviously shocked to see me coming in, probably expecting a war of divorce to break out.

Seeing Chris's portrait on the wall after coming out of the elevator always made me feel lucky to have such an accomplished husband. I couldn't be prouder that he had strived to work hard and fairly. Chris took pride in his job, and his employees were notably happy to work for him.

"Charlotte," I spun around to see Adam, his smile wide as he peered into the pram, peeking behind the blanket that covered a sleeping Lucy up. "Aw, I wanted cuddles."

"Where is she?" I asked him. "His new assistant."

His brows shot up, and he scratched the base of his neck, laughing a little. "Maybe you should talk to Chris first. His new assistant is different, and he's fucking pissed. Everyone is avoiding him today."

"Why?" I asked confused.

He didn't speak; he let out a low cough, and I spun around when I heard footsteps nearing us. "Oh, you must be Charlotte. I'm Tilly, Chris' new woman." The girl looked no older than sixteen;

135

her hair was tied in pigtails, and a lot of makeup was on her face. She let out a giggle and went to pull the cover off the pram.

My hand reached out and stopped her first. "Don't you mean, Mr. Rivers?" I raised a brow at her. I couldn't even get jealous of this girl.

"Who?" she asked, giggling again. I rolled my eyes; she couldn't be serious. No wonder Chris was pissed off; she was basically a child just out of school with no experience. I was all for learning, but this was just stupid to give a man someone so inexperienced.

"Your boss. You better call him Mr. Rivers if you want to keep your job," Adam spoke with humour laced behind his voice.

"Oh, you mean Chris." She stared at us both, and I turned back to Adam, eyes rolling. She was going to be fired by the end of the day. I knew it.

I said goodbye to my brother, promising to come and say goodbye before I head back home. I made my way behind the little brat and waited as she knocked on Chris's door. "Your wife's here, Chris." She peeked in, and I felt my stomach knot up at what she called him again.

I could hear a groan and a loud thump. "Mr. Rivers as I told you this morning!" he barked. God, he was in a bad mood.

Chris came out, and his eyes lit up as he spotted us, walking over and placing a kiss on my lips. "Hey, you ready for lunch?"

"Yes," I answered calmly, "Can I feed Lucy in your office first, please?"

"Sure." He opened the door back up and held it open as I pushed the pram in. Once the door was closed, he locked it and lent back against the door. "Have you seen the fucking child they sent me?" he growled and shook his head.

"Tilly?" I laughed. "Or should I say your new woman as she introduced herself to me, *Chris*," I added with a change in voice, mocking her.

He looked at me and walked over, pulling Lucy from her pram and passing her to me. "I can't get a replacement until tomorrow. I'm so fucking pissed that they sent someone so fucking incompetent." He sat down, stretching out his long legs and my eyes went directly to his crotch. I had it so bad for him right now.

However, I had bigger things to deal with. Like him in a suit. It was like me in lingerie for him. Completely and utterly sexy.

"I've changed my mind about lunch; we're going to go somewhere else," he stated, placing his hand on his thigh, brushing a piece of cotton from the material.

"Okay. Where?" I asked him, a little confused by the sudden change.

"Nope. It's a small walk, but it's a nice day, and I'm in no rush to get back. I don't have court anymore, so I can take a longer lunch." He kept his eyes to mine, his dark eyes that were looking over my face. "You're wearing makeup. You haven't worn that for ages."

"I know. I wanted to look nice for you," I admitted, liking that he did notice, but also wondering if I had been lacking in that area.

He smiled. "You look beautiful."

*   *   *

Lunch was different; we went to the park across the street—a massive park with people walking, running, and eating. Chris pushed the pram while keeping his other arm around my shoulder.

"Apart from your new woman, has your day been okay?" I asked, leaning into his side as we continued to walk.

"Yes. I would prefer to be home, but it was good. I'm going to be very busy in the coming weeks; a case came up that's just giving me a headache thinking about it." He sighed and kissed the top of my head.

I pulled him to a stop and sighed. "Can you go get checked, please? Your headaches scare me, Chris."

He smiled, brushing me off. "It's called stress. I promise I'm fine, and after a couple of aspirin, they're gone."

I groaned and narrowed my eyes. "You get a migraine far too often. Please, get a check-up."

I found myself being pulled into his arms. "I will go get checked; we'll go do it together if it's worrying you that much."

"I'm sorry. I'm scared of losing you again, Chris. I can't lose you; you've had a headache every day since we've been together, and not all those days were stressful." I clung to him tighter, panic set in as the idea of something happening to him played out in my mind. I needed him still.

He kissed the top of my head, and I leant back in his arms. He reached up, using his thumb to brush away the tear trailing down my cheek. "I'm not leaving you, Charlotte. I promise I won't ever leave again. We're going to grow old together and have the life I promised you."

I reached up to my tippy toes and cupped his cheeks hard, his lips squishing up a little as I kissed him passionately, not giving a damn that people could see us making out in on the middle of a footpath.

At that moment, he was my husband, and I loved him.

"Take the day off and come home with us," I whispered between kisses. "I need you, Chris. I want you more than ever."

"Same, Char. God, I fucking need you so badly. I can't fucking breathe without you around me." He then took over and dominated the kiss, hungrily and greedily kissing me, our bodies tightly pressed together.

The only thing that parted us was a cough and scowl of an elder woman. Well, she was in her forties. "Don't you think that's inappropriate, especially with a child right next to you?"

"Not at all. How do you think this baby was made? If you don't want to see me kiss my wife, I suggest you keep running along and get yourself laid into happiness." My face buried into Chris's chest as he spoke to her that way. He would always tell people what they thought, but I didn't think he would say that to her.

I held in the giggle until I heard the elder woman running off. Chris looked down at me, a boyish grin spread over his face, and my heart fluttered. "I love you," I whispered to him, meaning every breath of it.

"I love you too. Now, let's eat before we get arrested for public indecency." He laughed, resuming our position of walking with me under his arm.

"Lucky I'll have the best lawyer in town to get me off the charges." I winked and smiled wide at him as we walked to the picnic seat right in front of the pond.

We ate, talked, kissed, and flirted. Chris filled me in on his caseload before we made our way back to his office, walking slowly and ignoring everyone else around us—ignoring the constant stares of the women in the office looking at me as if I had done the worst thing in the world. I then decided to shut them all up for good.

"I'm going to take Lucy over to Adam. I'll just leave the pram here."

"Okay. I'll meet you over there. I'll finish up and make sure I've got a replacement coming in tomorrow who knows how to work and take calls." He smirked and picked Lucy up, handing her to me and fixing her leg that had the trousers pulled up halfway.

I walked past the group of snickering women and glared back at them. I swear to god, if Katie was here then I would probably have thrown her out a window. It was obvious that she was the one who started the gossip in the workplace.

I knocked on Adam's door, well aware they were still watching me. When my brother opened it, he looked behind me and frowned as he took Lucy from my arms. "Charlotte, about time you got here. I was getting worried you were keeping her from me."

I let out a laugh at his manner. "Sorry, Chris and I got a little over sexual at lunch. He's on his way here, and we're going home." I winked.

"Yuck. You're both sick," he groaned, and I laughed. He glanced over my shoulder, then looked back at the girls behind us. "She's the spitting image of Chris, don't you think? Oh, that's right. You prefer to listen to office gossip than do your actual work. I'm still waiting on the case files for Walter," he said harshly. "Someone get me a coffee."

"Sorry," they all muttered and took off. It was amusing to see how fast these powerful men could make the women swoon, but at the same time have them completely frightened.

"Since when do you get someone to make your coffee?" I asked, crossing my arms over my chest.

"Never. Until now." He grinned.

Chris came over and took Lucy from Adam's hands. "I'm off for the day; have important matters to attend to." He winked looking down at me, and I blushed. God, he was such a flirt at times.

"If that important matter meant my sister, then I don't want to know about it." He held his hands up and walked back into his office, closing his door on us.

We both laughed as we walked back to Chris' office and grabbed the pram to head home. When we arrived at the house, we went to Lucy's bedroom and put her in her big cot, testing it out and seeing how she liked having naps in there during the daytime. I walked out of Lucy's nursery to see Chris looking at me, his suit half undone and chest on display. My eyes were scanning over him as I stepped closer towards him.

We kissed furiously as he carried me up towards our room, his fingers digging into my ass as I moaned over his mouth and tightened my legs around him. I nuzzled down his neck, and he let out a deep, sexy growl. "Char, god, baby."

"God, I love you." I kissed from his neck to his mouth as he pushed me back on the bed, his body lying over mine as our clothes started to strip apart. Both of us wore nothing but underwear as he pulled back, kissing down my stomach and licking me teasingly over my red silk panties. Coming back up, he stopped just above my mouth.

His heavy breathing was fanning my face. "You're mine, Char. You belong to me, and I won't give up that easily anymore."

He went to lower his head when I pushed my hands to his chest to stop him. "Chris," I whispered out, a little huskier than normal as I started pulling him back down towards me. "Make love to me."

CHAPTER FIFTEEN

I couldn't stop giggling; it would have to be the funniest thing ever.

Chris lay flat on his ass after he slipped and fell down the stairs. Unfortunately, he didn't seem to share my sense of humour.

"Don't laugh at me," he grumbled, still sitting.

I walked over to him and smiled as my laughter died down. "Baby, I'm sorry, but seeing a grown man fall and slip was just too funny. How about I kiss it better?" I knelt between his open thighs and cupped his face.

"You could kiss something better," he mumbled with a sad pout and wiggled his brows.

I rolled my eyes at him. Of course, he would want to get lucky. The man falls down six steps from the stairs, and now he's after a blow job. "How sore is your ass?" I asked, "And don't lie either!" I warned him.

"Fine! My ass feels like it was fucked by a fist."

"Oh god." I snorted. That did it for me again. I couldn't help but laugh even harder as I fell forward onto his body, his arms pulling me into him and he finally laughed with me.

He grumbled something under his breath as he kissed my nose and ran his hand over mine that was still on his cheek. "Can you help me up?" he asked quietly.

I bit my lip to hold in the laugh. "Okay, sweetheart. I'll pick you up and throw you over my shoulder as you do to me, but don't blame me if I fall from your heavy weight." I smirked and kissed him again as I stood up and held my hands out for him to hold.

"I can walk, Charlotte." He laughed as he held my hands. The problem was when he pulled on me, my feet started to slide over the flooring. He laughed as I gave him a hard pull and up he came. I actually don't think I helped much at all, but he didn't say anything; he made me feel like I did all the work. But I knew there was no way I could have lifted him; it was him just playing with me.

I watched him limp to the living room and lay down on the large couch face first. I climbed on his legs and started to pull his sweats down. "Char, what you are doing?" I heard him ask into the cushions.

"Just making sure you didn't break your arse." I went to reach for his fitted boxers when his hand stopped mine. "I'm looking for a bruise, Chris. If you want me to play doctor, then you need to let me inspect your cute butt."

His hand loosened, and I pulled the black material down. "Is it bad?" he asked. I could tell he was smiling though.

"No, just a red mark, but it doesn't look too damaged." I leaned down and kissed the small mark before pulling his underwear back up. "I'm horny."

"Same," he responded. "Get on all fours; my ass is killing me."

I laughed and moved as he rolled over, pulling our bottoms off as I bent down, kneeling with my ass in the air. He gave my ass a swift spank before he lowered his boxers.

*   *   *

Chris pulled back, looking at me with intent. My heart was racing, but not in panic. I knew I wanted him to make love to me. I loved him, and at the end of the day, that was all that mattered.

"Do you forgive me?" he asked, barely a whisper but I still heard him.

I didn't know what to say. I ran my hands up from his arms to his face and held him. "I don't know, but I know I want you. I know that I love you and that I want to make this work with you. I know that you're my husband and I won't be leaving you. I know that I want to make love to my husband. I'm sure of it."

He shook his head, and my heart dropped. "I can't. Char, not like this. I'm sorry." And with that, he stood up and got off the bed, leaving me there feeling embarrassed and rejected.

I should have known. I shouldn't have pushed him. I didn't want to cry, but I couldn't help it. I felt humiliated for asking that. I knew I wouldn't have regretted it. I went to the bathroom and stayed there for some time. Chris didn't come in, but I knew he was in the bedroom, getting changed, and then I heard the door close and a car starting up.

I had pushed him away again.

I walked out of the bathroom and pulled on some leggings and a long-sleeved shirt. I looked at the bed, and he had made it again. I wiped more tears away and headed to the room across from ours. Lucy wasn't in her bed, and I found a note in the cot. *'Will be back soon.'*

I had the house to myself, and it felt strange. I walked to the kitchen and opened up the fridge to find another note. *'Don't bother cooking dinner!'*

What was he up to?

Making myself a hot drink, I curled up on the couch and turned on Netflix. Onto the third episode of *The Good Fight*, I heard the back door open. Chris walked in with Lucy in one arm, and three bags in the other.

"She needs a feed," he called out. I stood, making my way to meet him halfway. I couldn't look at him. I felt stupid.

"About earlier," he began.

I shut that conversation down as quickly as he brought it up. "Don't. Please don't say anything."

He sounded pained. "I didn't mean to upset you."

Looking up, I shrugged. "Yeah. Well, you did. Making me cry is nothing new, Chris," I uttered before I could even register what I had said. "Sorry. Please, can we not do this? You don't want to sleep with me, I get it. You made your point loud and clear."

He didn't say anything, but I knew I hit a nerve. He stood back up and walked out of the room, leaving me to feed Lucy while he went to the kitchen to do whatever it was that he was doing. Lucy fed for a little over half an hour before I stripped her off naked, so she could have a lay about on the couch beside me. She soon fell asleep after re-dressing her, and I left her in the swing to sleep.

Too focused on my show, I didn't hear Chris come back over until he was sitting beside me and his hand was turning my head to face him. His lips passionately claimed mine as he pulled me up onto his lap. His hips flexed up, digging his fingers into the curve of my ass and gripping my thighs as I kissed him back. Enjoying this unexpected kiss from him, his hands slowly ran up my back; his fingertips grazing over my bare skin as I kissed him back just as hungrily.

I don't know what was coming over him, but whatever it was, I loved it.

When he pulled away, he was breathing heavily—we both were. "I love you," was all he said, and he moved me back to where I was sitting earlier just moments ago before he stood up, leaving the room and leaving me speechless.

Lucy was still sleeping, and I sighed. "Your daddy is a little crazy," I whispered to her and smiled. I had no idea what came over him to do that, but I loved it.

By the time it was 5 PM, the back door opened, and Adam walked in. He gave us a wave and then headed into Chris who was still in the kitchen. I had been instructed to stay out of there; to just relax and finish my TV show. I wasn't going to complain. I had eight more episodes to watch, and I had seven other shows to start on. I could hear the hushed whispers from my brother and husband, but I stopped trying to listen; it was pointless, and I lost cause trying to do so.

"So, how're my favourite girls?" Adam's cheery voice came over to us as he sat down on the couch, picking Lucy up from my chest and laying her on his.

"Umm, could you please ask permission to touch my daughter?" I laughed a little.

He flashed me a grin. "Never." He laughed and kissed Lucy on the head.

I lay back on the couch and ended up dozing off. I had no idea how long I was asleep, but it was long enough to know that it was late and dark outside. I shot up off the couch and realised Lucy wasn't around.

"Chris?" I called out, a little panicked, yawning as I stood up.

He came running out of the kitchen with a worried look on his face. "What's wrong?"

"Where is Lucy?" I walked over towards him.

"I bathed and fed her. She's tucked in her big bed, fast asleep."

I looked at him, stunned. "She's in her own room?" I asked warily.

"Yes, she's in her own room tonight. Are you hungry? Because dinner is almost done."

I nodded, and my stomach grumbled a little. "Yes, I'm starving. Did you cook?"

He took my hand and led me into the dining room. My eyes adjusted to the darkness as the glow of candles flickered around the room, and the table had two plate settings made up. I looked back up at him, and he was looking down at me, my stomach getting butterflies. "You did this?"

"Yes, I cooked you dinner for our date tonight."

I laughed a little. "Date?"

He nodded, rubbing the base of his neck, looking embarrassed. "Lunch wasn't much of a date. Even I knew that. Today was a bit of a fuck up."

146

"Well, I look forward to it. Something smells really good, Chris. I wasn't expecting this at all," I admitted. I felt a little bad for what I said to him earlier. I knew he was trying hard, and I owed it to him to treat him better.

"Good. Now sit down, my love. I have cooked you something different to try." He kissed my cheek and led me to my seat, pulling my chair out and tucking it in as I sat. He would always do this, even when we were dating. He really is a gentleman.

I tilted my head backward; his smile grew as he lent down and kissed my lips lightly. My eyes closed briefly, relishing his touch.

He came back in after a few more minutes with a bowl of something; the pleasant smell was filling my nose as he placed it between us. "I don't know what it will taste like, but it's Thai Chicken Risotto, if you can't tell."

I grinned. "You made this? I'm really impressed. It smells really delicious and looks amazing." I reached over and held his hand. "Thank you."

It was nice having our little date night. It reminded me of what our first date felt like—the flutters in my stomach and the giddy feeling whenever he would look at me and smile. The best moment was when I looked up at him and found him staring right back at me, his eyes looking at me with so much love. He had a knack for making me feel like the only girl in the world.

By the time we finished eating, we were both full, and the candles were almost burnt out. We'd both had a couple glasses of wine, and our flirting had increased. Increased to a point where I was sitting on his lap as he kissed down my neck, his hand cupping my breast, as I ran my fingertips through his jet-black hair.

"Let's clean up." I moaned slightly, as he sucked on my collarbone.

He groaned and kissed back up my neck towards my mouth. "I'll do it. Go get in bed, and I'll be up soon." He kissed me one last time and then helped me up off him.

147

I went into Lucy's room to check on her. I wasn't sure if Chris was serious about her sleeping the whole night in here; I would need to ask him once he came back upstairs. I lent down and kissed her forehead. "Mama loves you, beautiful," I whispered then left the bedroom.

I was putting my pyjamas on when I heard the door closing behind me. Chris' voice caught me off guard to the point I almost tripped over, trying to put my feet in the bottoms. "You won't need them on," he spoke huskily, walking up behind me and running his hands down my sides, spinning me around to face him without warning. "Not when I plan on having you naked for a good few hours."

"Chris," I breathed out, shocked and turned on by the way he was looking at me. "What?" I was confused.

"Get on the bed; lie down, and spread your legs," he instructed, his voice husky and clear.

I stepped backwards until my feet hit the bed and sat down. I lay down on the mattress, keeping my eyes on him while he undressed in front of me; his body outlined by the dim lamp beside me had me breathing heavier.

He stepped forward, his hands on either side of my waist as he pulled me down. My core was firmly over his face as he began to lick and suck my clit. My hips bucked upright as he kept moving faster, slowing down when he had me breathing heavier and closer to my orgasm. "Not yet, baby," he whispered, and I looked down at him, confused.

"What?" I asked. *He wasn't going to let me come?*

He smirked as he moved up between my legs, his body lowering to mine as he kissed me slowly for a short few seconds. "I want you to come when I'm inside you."

I didn't realize what he was saying until he was pushing against my entrance, slowly sliding in. My hands shot out and gripped his back; the pain was intense as he moved slowly. I bit into his shoulder, and he stopped moving.

148

"Char, are you okay?" he asked, staying completely still, but his cock throbbed inside of me.

I nodded, taking a steady breath. "It feels like I'm losing my virginity; just keep going slow," I breathed out, and he kissed my nose as he continued to push in.

Stopping and letting me get used to the feeling again, it had been so long since we had last made love, His kisses were picking up as I wrapped my legs around his thighs and locked him in. Kissing him back, my hands roamed his skin as the slight discomfort disappeared and the pleasure picked up as his thrusting began.

"I love you, Chris," I whispered against his mouth.

"Not as much as I love you, Char. I love you so much," he spoke as he moved a little quicker, soon rolling us, so I was on top of him. Moving at the same speed as he was earlier on and keeping my body down to his, his hands were on my hips as he helped me move up and down. I loved how close I felt to him at this moment; the love between us, and the fact there was no big stomach in our way. I could ride him hard and enjoy every inch of his thick cock.

I was being rolled back over as he came back on top of me; his tongue slipped inside my mouth, exploring my hot cavern and taking his dominance back. I was coming undone beneath him as he kept his steady movements up, thrusting in and out, slowly and deeply. His hands clenched mine that were outstretched above my head while our fingers laced together. His breathing grew faster, hips rocking back and forth faster.

I moaned, my body trembling as he fucked me right into an orgasm. My legs locked tight as I fucked him back, the pleasure almost blinding me. "Ohhh." I cried out. "Faster!"

Not stopping, he kept going through my shattering orgasm, getting faster with each stroke. His own grunts and heavy breathing were only driving me crazy. I squeezed his fingers tighter as he slowed back down and kissed down my neck. I could tell he was trying to hold out, that he was trying to last longer as it had been so long for him as well.

"Come in me," I begged, and that's when he let go, his thrusts hitting me deeper as he came, slowing down until he stopped, but still kept kissing me.

"You're incredible." He smiled lifting his head. "Christ, I missed that."

I smiled, nodding. "Me too. It was amazing."

Placing feathered kisses, he smiled. "I love you," he said, and before I could respond, his mouth was back on mine and cock was firming up inside of me.

When we woke the next morning, we were still tangled up beside each other. Chris's fingertips were grazing softly up and down my naked stomach as I looked up to find him staring right back at me. I held him back, feeling content for once in my life.

"Did Lucy sleep all night?" I asked, still tired and sore. Very sore, but in an incredible way.

He nodded. "I checked on her not long ago. She's fast asleep and snoring."

"All night? I can't believe that." I was expecting her to scream and wake up constantly.

"She's a good baby. I think she likes her room." He grinned sleepily, I loved how he looked in the mornings; his deep sleepy voice was husky and so sexy.

I pouted. "She's too little to be on her own."

Chris chuckled. "I'm sure she's okay. How are you feeling about last night?" he then asked a little more seriously. I could only think that he thought I was regretting it.

I reached up and ran a hand through his black hair. "I feel amazing, it was incredible, and you were perfect. Why? Do you regret it?"

"No, not at all." He leaned forward and kissed me.

I felt my insides melting as he kissed me harder than he did last night. He was turned on, and I didn't mind the slightest. I pulled him closer to me, raising my hips as he thrust deep inside me.

I needed him as much as he needed me.

A knock on the door pulled us apart from each other's sweaty bodies. "Lucy is up!" Adam spoke with a laugh.

Chris and I groaned until he called out to Adam with humour in his voice. "There's a bottle in the fridge, and you know how to change her."

I held in my giggle as Adam groaned, scoffing and calling us sick people, warning Chris that he better not be naked with his sister. Chris' lips then came back to mine. "Daddy is a bit busy right now."

"Oh, is he just?" I wiggled my brows and pulled him back down to me, kissing him and picking up where we left off.

CHAPTER SIXTEEN

"Babe, does this look okay?" I called out as I fixed the shoulder on my red clinging-very-well-to-my-body cocktail dress that just sat mid-thigh. It was seriously a hot-to-kill look.

I could hear him chuckling. "If we weren't late, I'd be fucking you again right now. I promise you look beautiful."

I rolled my eyes as I met him. He was wearing a pair of navy-fitted jeans and a fitted grey V-neck shirt. I groaned at how hot he was. "You know, you have to say that I'm the prettier one. You traded up," I warned.

Chris sighed, shaking his head. "She's got nothing on you. Stop worrying, please?"

We were going out for dinner. Unfortunately, his ex-girlfriend was going to be there, and I had yet to see what she looked like. I was super jealous, like madly and insanely jealous. This bitch had seen my man naked.

"Fine." I huffed and grabbed my purse only for Chris to put his hand over mine.

Shaking his head as he spoke and lifted my hand up, "You don't need that, Char."

I laughed, rolling my eyes. "You always do this. I have money you know."

His brows shot up as I rolled my eyes. "I don't give a fuck. I'm paying, and that's the end of it. Save your money for when we go on a holiday or something. You can buy the dinners then."

"You said that last time and still didn't let me pay!" I grumbled, and he shut me up with a kiss.

Running half an hour late as kissing turned into sex on the bench, we finally made it to the restaurant. The place was packed, and I spotted his friend, Cary, right away. Chris pulled my chair out after we reached them and then took a seat beside me.

"So, what took you so long?" a dark-haired woman asked. If I had known better, I would have said she was pissed or jealous.

Chris ignored her, and I went to ask why until it hit me. She was the ex.

I had warned him not to talk to her tonight. If he did, then he would be on the couch for a month. He knew I was being completely serious. Hell, I wasn't going to watch him and his ex be all chatty. It actually relieved me that he ignored her. She was very pretty, but I was hotter. Well, I had to tell myself that.

"Charlotte, is it?" she spoke again, and Chris's hand slid on my thigh, rubbing me gently.

I nodded. "Yes."

"So, how long have you two been together for?" she asked again, the whole table grew silent as they watched this encounter between us.

"Almost six months," I answered her.

She smiled, licking her lips and tossing her long hair over her shoulder. "I bet he hasn't given you a key to his penthouse. I was with him for over a year, and I never stepped inside it."

I grinned wide as I looked at Chris and lent over to kiss him. I looked back at her and couldn't believe I was jealous of her. "We moved in together after four weeks of dating. He's a keeper, so thanks for cheating on him. Although, I'm sure you would have fucked it up some other way. But still, he and I are happy and in love. You can't come between us, so don't even try," I spoke calmly and politely. If an outsider had seen her and me talking, it would have looked normal and not me being a complete bitch to her.

"I love you," Chris spoke after we had eaten our entrée. We had managed to avoid any further discussion with the ex. She didn't speak much to anyone. Chris leaned closer to me after the normal conversation had picked back up. "I need you. Now."

I turned to face him, "Want to fuck in a bathroom?"

153

"Yes." He laughed and excused himself from the table.

Sitting there a couple of minutes, I was eager to run off and go find him. When I did, he was hard and ready for me.

*   *   *

This morning, I was an emotional mess. Chris had his appointment, which I was getting ready for, but then he told me he didn't want me to come. I couldn't understand why. *Why wouldn't he want me there?* Even if it was just for support. I wanted to know what was going on.

"Char, don't cry." He sighed, wrapping the towel around his toned waist and grabbing another to dry his dark hair.

I refused to talk to him. I just turned around in the shower and let more tears spill out, jumping as I felt a set of arms wrapping back around me. "Please don't cry, baby. If it means that much, then you can come. I just didn't think you'd want to wait around all day, and well, I didn't think you'd want to leave Lucy."

He had a point, but today, my husband came first. I needed to be there for him and show him I was still in this. I wasn't giving up.

"I want to come, Chris. I want to hear this all because I know you'll sugarcoat it and say you're okay, even when you're not. Clearly, it's serious if they have asked you to come back in." I turned in his arms; his thumb reached and rubbed the salty tears from my eyes.

"Okay. You can come with me, sweetheart. I want you to come."

"Again?" I asked with a seductive voice.

He laughed. "You're not getting away that easy." He wrapped his arms around me and lifted me up, leading us back into the water and getting us both wet all over again. Joined as one.

The feeling of being so close, was a feeling that had me going crazy for him.

After our lovemaking, Chris finished getting ready as I tended to Lucy. When he came in, he headed straight over to Lucy and lifting her up from her rocker swing. "Hey, baby girl. Daddy missed you," he spoke, kissing her forehead.

He was amazing with her. I knew he was going to be an amazing father, but to see him in action, to see him changing her nappy and feeding her . . . not once had he complained about any father duty he was asked to do.

I made us both a coffee and one for my brother who was sitting at the dining table, hard at work. "Thanks." He took a sip and groaned. "Oh, Mum and Dad called."

"Did they ask to speak to me?" I asked hopefully.

He sighed as I handed him the coffee, "Nah, don't worry about them. They will come around eventually."

I scoffed. They hadn't responded to my texts, nor did they answer the phone when I called. "Yeah, right. Anyway, I have a favour to ask you, favourite brother of mine."

"If it involves being your puppet while you photograph me, the answer is no."

Rolling my eyes, I ignored him. "Can you watch over Lucy while we go to Chris's appointment? I really want to go and be there for him. I'm really worried, Adam," I said, my voice a little quieter.

He nodded. "First off, don't worry. Second, you know I will watch over my niece. Lastly, Chris will be fine. It's just all the stress from work. He's doing a tougher job than I am. He's got a lot of shit coming down on him from the other partners for taking off, and then all that shit you both went through. It wouldn't be a surprise if he had a heart attack."

I slapped his arm hard. "Don't say that!" I warned and stalked off towards the kitchen.

Two hours later, I bid a tearful goodbye to my little girl. I didn't want to be that kind of mum, but I couldn't help it. Chris laughed it off, but the fact he had texted Adam three times already told me he was just as worried as I was.

I let out a yawn, unfastening the belt as Chris pulled up in the car park. "We need an early night tonight."

"Yeah, an early night sounds good. I was thinking the three of us should go to the zoo one day; it could be fun, and we haven't been there for a while. What do you think?"

I smiled. "First family outing. She's too little to remember anything, but it will be fun to go there together again."

We walked hand in hand towards the front of the entrance, and I clung to him tighter. My nerves were picking back up. I was willing myself not to panic. There was going to be nothing wrong. It was all stress and from work, just like Adam told me.

Checking in and taking a seat next to each other in the packed waiting room, Chris reached over and took hold of my hand. "Do you want to come in?" he asked.

My eyes looked at him. "Yes, if you want me in there. I can wait out here if you like?" I asked quietly as the man across from us looked at me. I realised what I was saying and shook my head. "Yes, of course, I will come in. I didn't come to sit and wait."

Chris smiled and kissed my hand. "Okay. Good."

When the doctor came back out, I became more nervous. "Christopher Rivers?"

Chris and I stood up, following her and then making our way towards the small room. Everything was white and stark-looking. It was all so cold-feeling and very medical-like. At least, when I was pregnant, the room was a little pretty.

"Christopher, tell us what's been bothering you?" Dr. Hallow asked, her face giving a warm smile, reaching for her blood pressure equipment as Chris rolled up his sleeve.

Chris filled her in, mentioning the shortness of breath and swelling in his legs at times, always feeling tired and rarely hungry.

To be honest, the way he described what was happening scared me. I knew nothing of this, only that he suffered from bad migraines.

The more frightening part was when the doctor rushed around on her chair and reached for a needle and six little tubes.

"Okay, I'm going to do blood tests, check for everything. You're going to get a full medical check-up. I am concerned, and I will get you into neurology for a brain scan, as well as a body scan. I understand you're a busy man, so I will get a rush on these and make sure you have your results by the end of the day. I will make it happen just to give you both peace of mind." She patted Chris's leg, and he kept his poker face on. He didn't give anything away at all.

I, on the other hand, had to bite the insides of my cheeks and hold onto the tears that wanted to rush out like a frantic waterfall.

Half an hour later, we were heading to the X-ray lab. Neither of us had spoken to each other. I didn't really know what to say, and I don't think Chris did either. It was a comfortable silence, but the looming gloom hanging over us made it a little bit uncomfortable.

Chris pulled me to a stop as I reached for the doors, pulling me back from the passing people and cupping my cheeks. "Please don't come in here. I can't have you in there when all you're doing is trying not to cry."

I nodded as more tears formed. He didn't want me around.

"Okay," I whispered out.

Uttering that simple word was killing me.

He kissed my lips softly, but then more forceful. "I will meet you in the car. I'm sorry, I just can't do this with you around me, baby. It's killing me to see you so upset when I may be completely fine. You're making me nervous."

I nodded. I did understand where he was coming from. "Okay. I will meet you in the car. I love you, Chris."

He smiled and kissed me once more, letting me go and walking into another office.

I was probably overreacting, but I saw the look of worry in the doctor's eyes. I couldn't lose him. I loved him, but an ache in my stomach was still there. It had been there since he left me in that hospital and it's still there now. It's telling me I haven't forgiven him yet. I wished it would go away. I wished it would leave me alone and just let me be happy for an hour with that day burning into my mind.

I let out a yawn and wiped my eyes. I didn't know how long I had cried in the car, but when Chris opened the door, he was holding a bag full of what I was guessing was lunch. He had brought something to eat for us. He looked at me like I was crazy. "Char, how long have you been crying?"

"Since I sat down," I admitted, taking the bag as he passed it over. I peered in and pulled out the mixed sandwiches and drinks. The hot deep-fried food smelled so good, making my mouth water.

He slid in beside me, chuckling but still shook his head. "Baby, fuck, I don't know what to say to even make you feel better. I know the food helps, but my words are useless. Tell me what's wrong."

"Nothing, Chris. Maybe it's me being over hormonal still. It's just my body going stupid." That was a lie. "I'm sorry."

He looked at me, and I should know better than to lie to a lawyer. He knew my signs, and my giveaway was not making eye contact.

"I'm going to ask again; this time, don't bullshit me."

I sighed and blew out a hard breath. "I just want you to be okay. I'm worried."

"Well, don't be. Everything is going to be okay." He smiled, but it didn't reach his eyes.

Silence.

All that filled the car was silence as we sat there after eating. Sure, we spoke and called Adam to see how Lucy was going on. He said she was sleeping, and to stop worrying.

Unexpectedly, Chris reached over and took my hand. "Can you do something for me? I'm being serious. I need to know something," Chris spoke quietly.

I nodded, my throat hurting as I swallowed. "Anything. I will do anything for you," I spoke honestly.

"Don't leave, Charlotte. I need you. I will always need you, and I know you deserve better, but I can get us back to how we were. I can make you look at me the way you used to. I can get that feeling back you feel each morning when you wake up. Please let me show you just how much you need me, just like I will always need you."

I looked at him and smiled quietly. "I'm not going anywhere, Chris. I'm not going anywhere."

I let out a squeal as he grabbed me and pulled me onto his lap. "I'm not going anywhere either."

Leaning forward, the window fogged up as I traced a finger over his jaw, his hands both placed on my waist as he leant in. His phone rang just as our lips were about to touch. The call blared through our ears as he slid his hand in his pocket and pulled out his iPhone.

"It's the doctor," he said quietly.

"Already?" I asked, that was a lot quicker than I expected.

Chris nodded. "We've been sitting in here for a couple hours. You've been crying for most of that time." He winked and answered the call. It was true. Damn hormones.

I zoned the conversation out, not wanting to hear anything at all. I wanted the conversation to come to an end. I wanted to hear the words 'you're fine.'

But I didn't.

Chris hung up and looked at me, letting out a sigh as he, instead, crashed his lips to mine. Kissing me deep and desperately. A loving kiss with all the hunger coming into it. My hands were running through his hair, tugging as he squeezed my ass, pushing me down into his growing middle.

"Chris." I breathed out, needing to catch my breath. "I love you."

He looked at me and smiled. "I love you too."

We kissed a little more. Kissing and rubbing up against each other's bodies. I moaned over his mouth and pulled back again. His lips kissed down my neck, sucking lightly.

In the end, our makeout had fogged up the tinted windows, and I was growing restless. Pulling away abruptly, I groaned. "Tell me. Just say it." I just needed to hear it. I needed to have the Band-Aid ripped off and just be told the news.

He sighed and shook his head. "I'm good. I'm all good, baby."

I smiled and held him close, wrapping my arms around his neck and holding him tightly. I was so relieved. I was so happy and felt a sudden wave of nausea escape my body. I felt better than I did hours ago. I couldn't believe I was so worried over nothing.

Or so I thought.

CHAPTER SEVENTEEN

"Chris, why are we out in the middle of the woods?" I asked as he took my blindfold off of my head and wrapped his arms around my waist.

His lips kissed the base of my neck as he leaned down. "We're camping. You said you've never been and it's meant to be a perfect weekend weather-wise."

That was true, but what this man had done was more than camping. This was romantic camping. He had a tent set up for us and a fire pit with a blazing heated fire roaring to life in the middle of the ground. I looked up at him as I turned slightly. "I love it, Chris, but when did you decide to do this?" I asked.

I had come home from groceries after Chris sent me on a shopping spree for snacks to find him waiting beside the SUV with a massive smile on his face. I was then ordered to sit in the car and place a blindfold over my head while he drove us. Then I had to wait for another however long it took for him to set this all up. It was perfect.

"Well, I wanted to do something different. We always go out for dinner and those lodge places, but I like camping and thought we could do it together." He smiled and shuffled on his feet as he looked at me nervously.

I didn't take any notice of him. I walked over to the tent and pulled the zip down, thanking him mentally as he had brought the warm blankets and not sleeping bags. I wanted to snuggle my man.

"Babe, how long are we staying here for?" I asked as I turned around and looked at him.

He was sitting down on a log near the fire. Our dinner he had picked up along the way was beside him. "Just two nights. That's okay with you, right?" he asked, again looking nervous.

I nodded and took a seat beside him. "Sounds good."

He, however, moved, and I was confused at first until he knelt in front of me and took hold of my hand. "Charlotte," he started. "You know how much I love you, right?"

I felt my whole body tense up as goosebumps spread throughout my skin. "Yes," I replied in a whisper.

He smiled. "You told me I had to level up my game last month, and I haven't been able to stop thinking about this. I want to spend the rest of my life loving you, Char. I know you're the one for me. I have never loved anyone as much as I do you, and I would do anything for you. So, Charlotte, will you marry me, spend the rest of your life with me, and make me even happier than I am right now?"

I then knew why he was so nervous-looking. I felt the tears running down my cheeks as he opened his palm, revealing a stunning diamond ring. A ring so perfect and glittering with an incredibly large diamond. It looked so expensive, but the ring didn't matter because if he had asked me to marry him with a plastic ring, then he would still get the same answer. "Yes. Yes, I will marry you!"

"Yes?" he repeated as he slid the white gold ring on my finger. A perfect fit. "God, I love you!"

"Chris, I love you so much!" I kissed him so hard, wrapping our arms around each other as we kissed passionately in the darkness surrounded by stars and a fire. Unfortunately, the weather forecast was wrong, and a bucket of pouring rain came down hard over us.

Neither of us cared though. We were engaged and in love.

Chris pulled away, a brief moment only to lift me up and carry me inside the tent where we spent a lot of our weekend away.

*   *   *

I woke up and yawned, moving to wrap my arms around Chris, but, instead, met with a cold empty spot. I grumbled into the pillows. All this week he had been up and almost out the door before I was even dressed.

This case he was taking had a major toll on us. Well, mainly our sex life.

"Adam!" I called out sleepily. I knew he had my daughter; he would get up and play with her before he went to work as well.

The bedroom door opened, and Adam strolled in with Lucy, a smile plastered on his face as my daughter held her head up on her own. At two months, she was doing so well. "What's up?"

"Do you know what this case Chris is working on is about?" I asked quietly.

He looked at me and shook his head. "You've asked me this at least twenty times already. No, I don't. He's been flat out at work though, so stop giving him a hard time."

I threw the covers off me and put my feet on the floor. "Give me Lucy. Go have your own baby if you want her so much."

"Shut up. I have a date tonight actually." He grinned.

I rolled my eyes, knowing that when he said date, he was actually referring to getting laid. "You're disgusting," I muttered.

He laughed. "Yeah. Well, it's not like you two aren't screwing each night, and I'm a man with needs."

I laughed it off, but for the past two weeks, Chris and I hadn't made love once. We hadn't even made out or kissed with tongue. It was a peck on the mouth, and that was it. Ever since that doctor's appointment, he'd been closed off, and I thought it was just anxiety about maybe something being wrong, but it wasn't that at all.

I had tried touching him, and he'd told me he wasn't up for it.

I was rejected most nights, and it fucking hurt.

It didn't help that I fell asleep before him most nights as well. He said his workload was busy for the next few months, so I just had to bear with it.

But I'd seen him at his busiest, working a high-profile case that had him only getting four to five hours sleep a night and he'd still fucked me senseless each night. Something else was up. I could feel it in my bones.

I made my way down the stairs and found him in the kitchen, dressed in a suit, looking completely handsome as he filled his travel mug with coffee. "Morning," he spoke quietly.

"Morning," I replied. "Off again so early?" I asked.

He nodded but didn't say anything.

I didn't know what to say, so I didn't bother speaking either. I just left the kitchen and went into the living room, taking a seat beside the window that overlooked the large yard and started to feed Lucy. I could feel him watching me, like he did every morning just before he left.

Adam came in and looked at us both and shook his head. It was hard not to want to cry when I felt as if this was starting to end for us. Something wasn't right, and I had racked my brains trying to think of what it was.

I let out a yawn and looked up at Chris. "Are you coming home for dinner or not?" I asked.

He came and took a seat in front of me, reaching over and took hold of my hand. "I don't know. I will let you know what my day is like. I'll be in the office all day, but it's flat out, so I can't promise anything."

I nodded. "So, no then."

"I'm not up for a fight, Char." He sighed, dropping my hand and standing up. "I have to go. I've got an early appointment."

"When don't you?" I muttered. Yes, I was now feeling a little more bitchy than usual.

He didn't respond; he just kissed the top of my forehead and bent down to do same to Lucy. He was more affectionate to her lately: he fed, bathed, and changed her then put her down each night, reading to her and then going back to work. I wanted to know why things were different between us.

I was sick of sitting at home. All the thoughts were playing over and over in my mind. *What if Chris felt like I wasn't showing him enough attention?* I read some males felt like the third wheel after a new baby, so I decided to surprise him and go to his work for lunch. Plus, I hadn't been in there for ages.

"Let's go see Daddy, little blossom." I picked Lucy up and put her in the baby sling. She was asleep after screaming the entire drive from home into the city.

I rode the elevator up and had my bag with lunch in it. I hoped he wasn't in a meeting. Well, I guess I could always have lunch with my brother and listen to him going on and on about this hot date he had. Maybe I could talk him into settling down.

As I reached his floor, I made my way towards his office. A young man sitting at the desk stood and smiled. "Mrs. Rivers, pleased to meet you finally. I'm Kevin. Did Chris forget something?" he asked, walking towards me.

I gave him a slightly confused look. "Nice to meet you, and no. What do you mean?"

"He left an hour ago. He said he was working from home and not to tell anyone so they didn't hassle him there," he said as my expression turned to confusion. "Umm."

I felt my entire inside churn. He lied to me.

I played along, not wanting to look a fool as I had no idea where my husband was. "Yes, sorry. He said he left his phone on his desk and asked me to grab it." I laughed it off as I opened his office door.

I wanted to snoop so badly, go through everything to find out what the hell was going on. I was sick to my stomach at the thoughts running through my mind; the worst one was that he was with another woman.

I left the office in a hurry, not bothering to look around the office. I didn't want to be hurt any worse than he had hurt me. I didn't say goodbye to anyone as I blinked back the tears while rushing to the elevator. I cried the entire way home, and as I pulled into the drive, I still kept crying. Lucy cried on and off; she was due for a feed.

Lucy and I sat and watched as it started to rain outside, the pitter-patter of droplets hitting the window as I fed and then soothed her to sleep. I tried not to cry. I had even tried to call him, and the phone was turned off.

If that wasn't a sign of cheating, then I had no idea what the hell was.

I called Ness after putting Lucy down. We chatted, but only for a few minutes. I put on a fake happiness and told her everything was great. I think she knew I was lying though. I missed her so much.

When the front door opened at 7 PM, I was in the kitchen, staring into the fridge and fuming, trying to keep my cool.

"Hey, how was work?" I asked as I slammed the fridge shut.

He set his briefcase on the bench and frowned. "What's the matter with you?"

"How was work?" I asked a little louder. "Busy day? Well, I guess it was for you to be walking in the door after I put your daughter to bed, or were you busy with your other family?" I hissed, walking past him.

His hands shot out and pulled me to a stop. "What's the fuck is that supposed to mean?" he asked, his voice rising slightly.

I tried to push him off me, but he was too strong. "Who is she, Chris? Don't fucking lie to me this time!"

"Who the fuck is who? What the hell are you on about?" He scoffed as he pushed me against the wall. His body pressed to

166

mine wasn't doing me any favours as I could feel his hardened cock against my stomach.

My eyes were watering, and I couldn't help it. Chris looked at me, and his whole face looked as guilty as I used to look when I tried to tell him I hadn't eaten the last of his ice cream. I could easily spot when he was lying to me. His grip on me loosened, and he let me go completely and stepped away as I broke down crying.

"Char, you need to let me explain," he started.

I shook my head. "Explain why you left work at 11 AM and told Kevin you were home with me?" I asked through a cry of sobs. It was a good thing Adam wasn't home.

"Fuck," he muttered, running a hand through his hair and pacing the kitchen. "Fuck, fuck, fuck!" He hissed louder.

My crying was slowly dying down, watching as he paced back and forth and looked more than sick with himself. My eyes went to his hand and noticed he wasn't wearing his ring. Oh god, he was with another woman.

I couldn't breathe.

"I'm done," I spoke, surprising myself at how calm I sounded.

His feet stopped moving, and he stared at me, panic washing over his handsome face. Those blue eyes could have me falling in love with him all over again. Instead, they did nothing but tear at my heart even more.

"What do you mean you're done?" he asked, stepping closer as I backed away from him, my back hitting the kitchen counter bench putting me to a stop.

I lifted my hand and pointed to the rings on it. "Obviously, this means more to me than you, so go back to your woman and tell her you're all hers, because you and I are obviously over, Chris. You lied to me, won't have sex with me, or touch me. You're working more and more, and now you're leaving work, lying to me and telling me you're on some big case!" I yelled loudly at him, pushing him against his chest hard.

He cut me off from yelling any further, leaving me a little speechless as he pulled his ring from his pocket and slid it back on his finger. I went to talk, but his lips started roaming my body as he lifted me up and sat me on the countertop, pulling away and pulling his belt off and he threw it to the floor, unzipping his pants and pulling out his thick, stiff cock.

"Is this what you want, Char? You want this?" He growled out, pushing my thighs apart as he grabbed my leggings, pulling them down hurriedly and grabbing my panties, pulling them to the side as he thrust deep inside me.

It hurt, but I didn't care. I needed him to fuck me.

I wanted to feel something other than a fury for him. We were passionately kissing and grabbing each other tightly. "Harder!" I cried, my hands gripping his ass as he thrust deeper and faster.

"Is this what you want? You fucking accuse me of cheating. I should fucking throw you over my knee and spank the hell out of your ass!" He grabbed my ponytail and jerked my head back, so I was looking up at him.

This was a whole new side to him that I hadn't seen. He was completely in charge, and his whole attitude changed. I had never seen him so angry in our entire relationship. Sure, he had been pissed off, but not to the point of fucking me like he hated me. *Mind you, I didn't care.*

I, however, slapped his face. It didn't faze him as he wrapped his hand around my throat, and I almost came. The pleasure that shot through my body was insane right now as he brought his mouth back over to mine and sucked over my lower lip as he kissed me heatedly.

Our breathing and screaming at each other only became louder as we fucked our way through a fight, both of us reaching the peak of our climax as we cried out. I let out a moan of pleasure as he groaned, kissing me softer as he fell over me, leaning on his elbows as I held him by the face.

"I'm not cheating on you, nor would I ever do that. But we need to talk," he said quietly as he pulled out and helped me up.

I was worried, relieved as hell, but still worried and confused. "What's going on? We don't lie to each other, Chris. We don't even fuck like that. I'm . . . just talk to me."

I didn't know what to think, but I knew it wasn't good as his face paled, leaning over the kitchen sink and throwing up. Spewing up was something he never did, and I grew more worried.

"Chris," I started, my stomach turning with knots as he looked at me, tears brimming in his eyes as he rinsed his mouth. Sliding to the floor and shaking his head as he cried. I was right in front of him in a hurry, my hands shaking as I knelt down, running my hands through his hair and cupping his cheeks, wiping the warm tears away. "Just tell me what's going on. Please?" I asked, my heart breaking as his body shook.

Never have I seen him cry like this. I thought when he cried at the beach was bad, but he was a sobbing mess.

"I'm getting what I deserved for leaving you. This is my own fucking punishment for walking out on you and Lucy." He let out a deep breath, "I need you more than ever, baby. I need you to help me get through this because I can't win this fight without you. I need you to help me."

CHAPTER EIGHTEEN

We had been engaged for nine days, and his mother had already planned an engagement party for us. Mind you, it was done without our knowledge.

Chris looked down at me and smiled as he gave my bum a slight squeeze. "I can't wait until we're married."

"Same. I want to be Mrs. Rivers so badly," I replied and met him halfway for a kiss.

Being hugged, kissed, and asked the same question over and over again was what we'd heard from everyone at the party. Adam came over and smirked. "So, when's the wedding?"

"Shut up; you know when it is." I rolled my eyes at my brother and nudged him in the side as he pulled me into him.

He kissed the side of my head and sighed. "So, in six months, huh? You think you'll be organised by then?"

I nodded. "Of course. Chris and I have already picked out the spot we want to get married. Well, it's down to a top three, so we have to go check them out," I answered him. Chris and I had come home from the camping trip and got right into wedding ideas. More so, me, but he sat down and looked through ideas with me.

I looked around the room and smiled as I saw Chris. He looked up at me, and our eyes locked on each other. He was truly handsome dressed in a suit with his hair slicked to the side. I loved the comb-over on him.

"Where is Mum and Dad?" I asked Adam as I looked back at him.

He ran a hand through his blonde hair and sighed. "They wanted to come, but you know them."

I nodded. My parents were amazing but weren't too thrilled about our sudden engagement. Not too happy that Chris proposed without Dad's permission or that we had only been dating for six months. I told them I knew Chris was the one for me. He was my one and only, but they weren't having it. Mum thought it was a shotgun wedding. As much as we wanted to start a family, we both wanted to be married first.

Adam had been with me through everything, and I loved him for that. I turned and slapped his hand as he went to bite his nail—a bad habit of his that he did a lot. "Do you think they'll come around and be happy?" I asked.

He shrugged. "I'd love to say yes, but I just don't know, Charlotte. You know how they were when I got married. I'd been with that bitch for six years, and she was cheating on me for three, so fuck what mum and dad think because, at the end of the day, it doesn't matter. If you want to marry him, then go marry him."

I threw my arms around him and hugged him tightly. He was right. "What would I do without you? You've gotten me through so much, Adam."

He smiled. "Just keep being you. Plus, I'm the best man. I've got to make sure you turn up, or that fella over there will have my balls." He laughed just as Chris walked back over and took me by the hand.

Chris led us towards where people were dancing and pulled me to his chest. "You're amazing, Char. I'm so lucky you said yes."

"I'm the lucky one, Chris. I love you so much." I smiled as I wrapped my hands around his neck right before he dipped me low and kissed me in front of everyone.

*　　*　　*

I stared at him in heartbreaking shock at what he just told me. "What do you mean? You told me you were okay. I was sitting on your lap when you looked me in the eye and told me you were fine, and now you're telling me you've been lying this whole time?"

171

I felt sick, but I didn't know what to do. It was like time had stood still, and I was frozen—too frozen to move. My hands fell back from his as I felt back to the floor and felt as if I was going to have a panic attack as the word sunk in further.

What the hell was wrong with him?

"I have an acute kidney injury," he said. "It's . . . gotten severe enough that I will need surgery, and even then, it isn't guaranteed that I'll live." He used both hands to dry the rain of tears as he wiped his eyes. "I'm sorry, Char. I wanted to get all the tests before you get worried," he spoke shakily.

I snapped my eyes open. "How many more tests have you had done, Christopher?" I asked in a louder voice. My heart was racing as I tried to keep the anger and hurt in but failed.

"Every day. I've been in the hospital having blood tests and scans. I was going to tell you tonight when I got the results," he said.

I felt even more hurt, tears running down both my cheeks as he reached out to take my hand, but I flinched backward and let out a loud, strangled cry. "I thought you were having an affair. You shut me out and didn't touch me. How could you do this to me? To us!" I asked, standing up and grabbing the glass beside me and throwing it to the floor. I think I did that more to let some fury out.

He just sat there, his whole body shaking as he buried his head in his hands and cried.

So, I did what he did to me. I left.

I didn't leave the house; I just made my way to the backyard, so he couldn't see me breaking down and crying.

I was crying because I was afraid. I was afraid of losing Chris to a disease that kills, and he didn't deserve that. He had a family and a goddamn daughter; he needed to live. Not only for our daughter, but for me too. I needed him in my life to grow old with.

I sat down on the wooden seat and looked out at our yard lit by lights. It was so beautiful up here; I couldn't wait until Lucy was old enough to play outside.

The silence was only filled with cries coming from my mouth. A hand touched my shoulder, and I looked up. Adam was looking at me sullenly, his eyes filled with regret. Then I knew that he didn't really have a date. He was giving Chris time to tell me the news.

"You knew," I spoke through cries.

He nodded. "I promised him not to tell you—I wanted to—but you needed to hear it from him, Char. I'm sorry."

Adam sat beside me, and I threw my arms around him. I needed my brother more than ever right now. "I don't want him to die, Adam," I spoke into his chest, gripping his shirt tightly. "I don't want him to get sick."

My brother then broke down as well. Chris was the closest thing he had to a brother; they'd become best friends. It was cute to see the BFF relationship they had together, so I knew this was hurting him deeply. I hadn't seen my brother cry since he came to me after he walked in on Emily and his best friend.

He was so broken that day, and he looks just that now.

I pulled away and wiped my eyes. "I'm not mad. I'm just hurt he didn't trust me enough to let me in. I wanted to be there for him, Adam."

"I know. He knows that, and a big part of him not telling you is that he didn't know how to tell you, not after everything he'd done to you. He was worried you would leave him, fuck him off to die . . . and I think deep down, he wanted you to do it. He wants to give you a life you deserve and doesn't think you need to be at home looking after a man who's sick."

I looked at my brother and realised then and there, that as mad as I was, I was going to let it go. "I need to go to him. Can you keep an ear out for Lucy if she wakes up? I need to talk to Chris."

Adam checked his watch and scratched the base of his neck. "You better hurry; he's leaving."

I frowned. "What do you mean leaving?"

173

"He's leaving for his parents. He thought you wanted him to leave." Adam frowned and looked at me confused.

"No," I spoke quietly and stood up.

I raced up the stairs of our home. I was out of breath, but didn't care. He wasn't going anywhere. I opened the bedroom to see Chris grabbing the suitcase he used for business trips out of town.

"Put it away," I spoke up and closed the bedroom door, flicking the lock over and walking towards him.

"Char, I'll give you some space. I've fucked your life up so much lately." He sighed after speaking quietly.

I wasn't having it. I marched towards him, reached for the bag, and put it back in the walk-in closet. Chris just stood, looking helpless at me. "You don't get to decide that on your own. You're my husband, so start acting like it and sit on the fucking bed and tell me everything. Or I will leave and won't come back, Chris. No more secrets from me. I can't take the hiding and lying."

He just nodded and backed away from me until his feet hit the bed and he sat down. His dark hair was messed up, his eyes red, and his beard thicker, needing another trim. I loved his unshaven growth.

"I wanted to tell you, and I know I should have done, but I was afraid. I couldn't say the words. Adam walked in on me the other day at work and knew something was up, so I had to tell him. I'm sorry, baby. I never wanted you to think I would cheat. You know I would never do that to us." He grabbed me by the hand and pulled me towards his body.

Pulling me down on his lap, I cupped his cheek, and the other hand went to the back of his head, my fingers running through the thickness of his hair as he let out a low groan. "Chris, just tell me how bad it is. I mean, they can fix this, right? It has to be in the early stages, right?" I asked full of hope.

He blinked down hard, and more tears escaped. "No . . . I've been ignoring the signs for a while it seems. I didn't think they

were that bad until recently when you told me to get it checked."
My heart broke even more. "Besides, I don't think it's that easy."
He swallowed after speaking, looking at me as he waited for my
reaction.

"Okay, so what about the migraines?" I asked again, trying
to keep my hopes up.

He shook his head and ran his hand up to my cheek. "Just
a poor bastard who suffers from them. The MRI scan was clear."

"No. Chris, you're healthy. You don't party or smoke."

"I used to smoke, Char." He shook his head, "Look, what's
done is done, and I can't change things. All I know is this is fucking
karma for leaving you when you needed me the most. I fucked this
up, and now I'm hurting you more again."

I wasn't going to be a part of his pity party. "We are going
to fight this together. You're going to be fine, Chris, so don't think
anything else and never say that you got this out of karma because
that isn't true. You're going to be fine."

"Can you let me finish talking? I need to tell you some
other things too, and it's hard, Char. I'm struggling to get the words
out as it is. I'm fucking crying like a weak pathetic man. You should
never see me this way." He sniffed back a nose full of water and
held me tighter. I remained silent to let him talk. "They said I can
go on a transplant list, but I have to wait for a suitable donor, and
the list is long. I just don't know." His hand ran over his face. "I
won't sit and hope for the best when I'm probably going to end up
in and out of hospital."

"Chris," I whispered, not liking where this was going. "No,
you have to try."

"Do the surgery and then what happens? Will you be okay
after that?" I asked, god I wished I could have been at the doctor's
office with him to ask all this to them.

He shrugged, "The best outcome is yes. That's if I have a
match."

"I could give you mine. We both have the same blood type, so that's good, yeah?"

"No," he said firmly.

"Chris, if I can save your life, then I will do anything possible to do it. Give me one good reason you won't let me help you," I asked, pulling back slightly.

He just looked at me and gave a weak—a very weak—smile as he loosened his hold on me and moved his hand to my stomach. "I won't let you do this. You need to be strong for Lucy. There's a good chance I'm going to be infertile. I won't be able to give you a house full of babies . . . I want to give you more babies, Char."

"So, we get you to cum in a cup and freeze your sperm or whatever it is that they do. We'll have babies other ways, Chris. I don't necessarily need more children from you. We have Lucy. We have each other. That is all that matters." I leaned forward until our noses were almost touching, the heat radiating from our bodies was insane. I didn't care if I couldn't have another child with him; there were plenty of other ways to have a child.

The main priority was getting him healthy again.

"You're incredible, you know that? That makes me feel so much better, Char," he whispered.

There were no more words needed after that.

Our lips slowly neared each other, and our hands gently cupped each other's faces. He kissed me first, beating me to his mouth and pulling me down on top of him as he lay back on the bed. I straddled him, still lying down.

I didn't want this to end. I didn't want to stop kissing him, but he pulled away and shuffled, so he was now lying over my body, his hands running smoothly up and down my sides.

"I don't want to tell everyone I'm sick. I'm also thinking about quitting work," Chris admitted.

"Quitting? But you love your job. You love being a lawyer," I said, trying to talk normally, but I couldn't do more than a whisper.

"No, I love you and Lucy. Work isn't important, and I will always be a lawyer. I just won't be at the firm anymore. I'm not happy there anymore, Char." He sighed. "It's fucking too much. I just need to know if you can support me on that decision?" Chris looked at me as he caressed my bare skin, his hand sliding up underneath my top.

At the end of the day, I wasn't going to tell him no. "Of course, you know I will support you no matter what you decide, just as long as you let me come with you to your appointments, you let me ask questions and be as involved in this as you are. I won't say anything to anyone, but you should at least tell your family. It's between us like everything else."

I was giving him a hard bargain, but it was nothing compared to what he was dealing with.

"Deal. We do this together."

"And we never give up. Never *ever* giving up." I smiled as I looked him in the eyes and kissed him gently.

"Never give up," he repeated, leaning down to kiss me gently again.

Our bodies intertwined as we lay naked under the sheets, making love slowly and passionately. I hadn't told Chris to stop. I wanted this feeling to last forever, the feeling that everything was going to be okay. I know things were going to change tomorrow, but for now, I wanted us to just be in love and make love.

As Chris came, he fell to my bare chest, our sweaty bodies stuck together and saltiness tasted on our tongues as we kissed one last time. My hands ran up and down his back, gripping his bum and pushing him deeper into me as he started to slip out. I moaned as he sucked my lower lip and finally pulled away.

"Let's get showered, I want to go see Lucy." Chris pulled out completely and I ran my hands up and down his chest. I was just staring at him with worry. "Hey, I'm going to be okay."

I really hoped he was right. I couldn't take any more heartache. We quickly showered and changed into our PJs. Lucy hadn't cried, so Adam must have fed her before she screamed the house down. I was so lucky to have a brother like him who was willing to do anything to help us.

Chris sat on the chair as I sat on his lap with Lucy in my arms, snuggling her tiny body as Chris wrapped his arms around us both. He's kissing spots over my body every now and then.

A thought popped into my head, and I sighed. "You'll go on the waiting list and hope to Christ there's a match."

He nodded. "Yes. The doctors said it was rare to have the surgery, but it is an option. It's my preferred option, but I do have to wait. I don't want to be on tablets every day."

"What are the other options to fix this? Tablets for a couple of months and then you're all better?" I asked hopeful.

"Well, there's medicine to increase the blood flow to my kidneys and protect them. It also decreases inflammation. I'll need to go into hospital for IV fluids, and worst case, dialysis." He sighed heavily. "Surgery is my best option now."

"And what will the risks be with that? I wished you would let me do this for you; I don't want you to wait for one, Chris," I spoke leaning into his side.

Adam walked into the bedroom, showered, and ready for bed. He looked tired, his eyes also bloodshot. I was completely unaware that he had been listening to our conversation, but judging by how he looked at us both, he had been. "He doesn't need to wait for one."

"Adam, how is he going to get a kidney in time?" I asked confused.

He crossed his arms, narrowing his brows and leaning against the door frame. He looked like he was ready to speak business. "Because I'm going to give him mine. I've been tested and I'm a match. Lucy needs her dad around and you need your husband. If I can help, then I'm going to do everything possible to keep him here."

CHAPTER NINETEEN

My stomach hurt so bad from laughing so loudly. Chris and I were lying on the couch, watching the movie Grown Ups, *and I just couldn't stop laughing.*

"Baby, I can't hear the movie," Chris complained lightly, sitting up and placing the picture on pause.

I smiled. "I'm sorry, it's so funny though."

He rolled over so he was now leaning over me, his legs pinning me down and smiling brightly at me. "Char," he said quieter, running his fingers up and down my bare thigh. Yes. We were naked and snuggling. "I love you."

How was it possible for someone to make me feel so much love? "I love you too."

He shook his head. "Say it to me, not at me."

"Christopher Rivers, I love you truly, madly, deeply," I said as I held his cheeks and lifted my head to kiss him gently. I loved him more than words could express.

He grinned wider. "I feel it, and I feel the love you give to me."

Could this man get any more sweeter? I shook my head and tried not to let my emotions get the best of me. "I can't wait to be your wife."

"Now that's an image that makes me hard. Make sure your dress is tight and easy to get off. I may want to start our honeymoon early." He winked as his mouth kissed me lightly near my earlobe.

I laughed, laughing loudly again as he blew his breath over me, sending me a shiver but tickling me at the same time. "Baby, stop it! I mean it,

Chris. You know I hate to be tickled." And I was too eager to go back and watch the movie.

He slowly stopped and looked at me as he still lay half over me. "Charlotte, I want to ask something."

I smiled through my eyes; that man could melt anyone's heart. "Yes?"

"When can we start making babies?" he asked, looking at me like an overexcited puppy before turning back to a serious face.

That was something I hadn't expected at all. I didn't expect him to come right out and just ask that. "Uh, you want to make babies sooner or later?" My voice gave away my nervousness.

"Sooner, I want a family, a big family before I'm old and can't chase them around," He slightly grinned. "I'm older than you, remember? I want to get you pregnant easily and soon."

I rolled my eyes, only because he was looking at me so seriously. "Chris, you are not old. Far from it, and let's try after we're married. You're not going to have any problems getting me knocked up. I have a feeling you have rapid swimmers."

His smile grew wider. "Want to go get married next weekend?"

I groaned as I felt him harden underneath me. "Stop it. You're just horny and not thinking. We've got plans and bookings. Soon, we will be married, and then we can make as many babies as our hearts desire."

*   *   *

The dim glow of the lamp beside the bed told me my husband wasn't in the room. He got so worked up when Adam suggested helping that he took off after a loud thunderous 'no fucking way.'

A 'no' that had woken Lucy with a scream, but she fell back asleep almost instantly. Adam suggested it again, and Chris said no again, quieter this time. I knew Chris felt bad; he hated feeling useless. But I also felt like there was something else going on with them, something that they both weren't telling me.

I sighed and sat up, remembering the news he had told me earlier. Tears filled my eyes again as I started to get worked up at the thought of losing him. I could have handled a divorce if he wanted one, but him dying? That was something that would kill me on the inside.

"Chris!" I called out through a choked sob as I made my way down the hallway.

My husband came barrelling through the sliding doors, rushing over and cupping my cheeks. "Baby, what's wrong?" His finger slid up and down my cheek, wiping away salty tears as more fell.

I sniffed them back hard and my shoulders slumped. "I woke up alone and panicked. I just had a bad dream," I lied. "I couldn't find you."

He pulled me into his chest and kissed my forehead. "Babe, I'm here. I'm sorry. I came up and you were asleep. I didn't think you'd wake up."

"Do you want to come to bed?" I asked, my heart thudding against my chest. I just didn't want to leave his side anymore. I wanted to take care of him and be around him all the time.

"Can you give me another ten?" he pleaded, checking his watch, "Adam just needs some help with a case coming up and we've almost finished."

I smiled, wrapping my arms around his body, squeezing tightly, and kissing him, "We need to talk as well, Chris. Don't shut me out."

He looked down at me, and I hoped he didn't take off again. I cried so hard after Adam offered to do the surgery, and Chris walked off. I had no idea my brother would have done something like that. That was truly out of the blue, but it was just like Adam to help. He would give his life to save someone he loved.

That was my brother, thinking of others before him.

I went into the bedroom and waited. Lucy was fast asleep, so I reached over and flicked the bedside table lamp off, and snuggled down under the covers. I wanted to forget everything. Why did this have to happen to us? We were getting back on track, and now . . . well now, Chris was basically given a possible death sentence.

Ten minutes turned into half an hour. Half an hour turned into an hour. An hour turned into two. By the time I was dozing off, the bedroom door opened, and Chris quietly walked in. I think he was hoping I'd have passed out, so he didn't have to deal with talking to me about everything.

I had news for him. He was damn well going to talk.

"Tomorrow, I'm not going into the office. We'll talk tomorrow, I promise you." He sighed as he sat on the edge of the bed and took his shirt off. I reached up, brushing my hand over his toned back.

I didn't get to speak because Lucy started stirring, and I went to get out to her, Chris stood before me and walked towards her, lifting her up and holding her out in the air. "Ah, Mummy. Someone's soaked and needed a change."

I smiled, laughing as I tossed the covers off me. "Well, Daddy, you know where her room is." I went up behind him and kissed his shoulder blade then reached around and took hold of our wet daughter who was now starting to cry loudly.

"Ahh, someone definitely needs a change." I walked Lucy to her room while Chris followed behind us. He went and got her a new romper suit and passed it to me as I powdered her. Noticing she was getting a rash, I put some cream on her bottom as well.

Chris just stood and watched, his eyes only leaving mine to look at Lucy. "You're a wonderful mum."

I smiled. "You're a wonderful dad."

Back in bed with our little munchkin joining us as I fed her, Chris was on his phone checking emails, doing more work things, and then sitting the phone beside him before turning his attention to us, running his fingers through the dark mop of hair our daughter had.

"I don't want you to worry about anything, okay?" he said quietly.

I wanted to scoff. Yeah, because not worrying is going to be easy. I shook my head at him and moved Lucy as she lay against my chest while I clipped my top up. I laid down a little and reached over to hold his hand. "I'm always going to worry, Chris. You can't tell me not to do that. We've got a child together; we're still trying to make our relationship work and get that back on track. There's just so much to worry about. What happens when you have treatment and you can't work, or you spend your days in bed because you don't have the strength to get out?"

He looked at me, and I knew that he hadn't considered any of that. His blue eyes started to glass over with a film of water. "I don't know. I don't know what to do."

"What did Adam and you really talk about?" I asked, my tone firm and trying to let him know that I wasn't in the mood to listen to lies or cover-ups of the cold hard truth.

He swallowed hard. "I don't want him to give me his kidney, but he said he doesn't give a fuck of what I think, so he and I are going to the doctors this week and see what the next move is."

I loved my brother dearly, but I needed him and my husband around. "Let's get some sleep. We've got all day tomorrow to talk about this," I spoke through a yawn. It was late, and I knew I'd barely be able to get any sleep at all, not with all this running through my mind.

The night seemed to take forever to get through. Lucy didn't wake up, thankfully. But I barely slept a wink; I couldn't stop thinking about everything. So, I got up at 5 AM after watching Chris sleep for what felt like seconds when really it was hours.

Making my way down to the kitchen, I turned the kettle on and grabbed a large cup from the drawer. Taking myself to Chris's office, I sat behind the large desk and turned the computer on. I wanted to search Acute Kidney disease, but instead, I loaded all the photos taken the other day and started editing, but the nagging in

183

the back of my mind got the better of me and I Googled the surgery procedure.

I didn't hear the door open or see Chris coming up towards me until he kissed my cheek and looked at the screen. "You will go crazy if you read all that, baby. Trust me, I know."

"You need to tell your parents, Chris. Your sister needs to know too. I just think it's the right thing to do," I said quietly. This wasn't some minor thing; he needed their support and help.

He let out a hard breath. "Just let me do it in my own time."

"Chris, time is one thing you probably don't have. I need you around. I need you to get better," I snapped back at him, surprising myself at my annoyance.

He stood up, giving me a look and crossing his arms over his grey t-shirt. God, why on earth would he wear a tight shirt in the morning? I think he purposely tries to seduce me. "Don't tell me what to do, Charlotte. I need fucking time to think about everything. Maybe I don't want the surgery, ever thought of that?" he bit back at me harshly. "Just back off."

My heart thundered in my chest. I stood and grabbed my empty mug, or more like a soup bowl-sized cup. "You don't want the surgery? Well, if that's what you want, then fine. Go, say goodbye to your daughter because I will not stick around and watch you die or get sick." I stormed past him, not as dramatically as I would have liked, because it was still only 7 a.m.

I ended up walking outside and letting the warm air hit my skin. For the morning, it was warm. Summer was definitely here. Chris had followed, and I closed my eyes as his arms wrapped around my waist, pulling me back to him. I couldn't be angry; it wasn't my right to be. "I'm sorry. I didn't mean to snap at you. I just don't want to tell anyone, but I need you to respect my decision on this. I would do the same for you, Charlotte. I will tell my family, but in my own time, okay?"

I didn't want to fight, but he was wrong. I turned around in his arms and shook my head. "You tell them, or I will."

He looked at me and smirked. "You're threatening me?"

I nodded. "Indeed, hot shot. You need to tell them."

"Fuck sake," he muttered. "You're not going to drop this, are you?"

"Don't swear at me, and no, I'm not going to drop it. You kept this from me and that still hurts. They're your family, and they have the right to know. You will need support with this, Chris."

After finally getting him to agree to tell his parents, we headed back inside and lounged on the couch where we had spent most of the day, watching movies and playing with Lucy who was now on the floor and trying to roll over. She was getting so much bigger, and I knew we had other decisions to make about our future. Our future children if we could even have any more.

"You know Mum will want to move in here," he said with a slight grumble.

I hadn't thought of that. "I know." I paused a moment. "How about we have them over for dinner tonight and break the news that way?"

"I would like to see the doctors about the surgery before I tell them," he said.

Probably wise to do so. I reached up, pulling my hair into a high ponytail. "Okay, that may be wise. You'll be able to give them more answers after we find out all there is to know about this surgery. I hope Adam knows what he's doing—" I stopped talking, then groaned as I realised my parents wouldn't agree to this.

Chris laughed, knowing where this was heading. "Your parents will say 'Let that bastard rot to death'."

I sat up and frowned, throwing daggers at him. "Don't even joke about that, Chris. It's not funny," I warned. Nothing about him dying was funny.

"I'm sorry, it was a joke. But you will also have to tell your parents. I would like you to tell them that though. I don't think I

185

could deal with them here. Sorry," he said. I knew he wasn't really sorry though. It didn't bother me too much. I loved my parents, but they were too opinionated and made it clear how they felt when they left without a goodbye. I needed love, support, and someone to lean on. I was going to have two recovering men around, plus a child. I knew I would need help, but I was unsure who would actually help and who would try and take over.

"When your surgery is done, and you're all better, let's go back to the beach?" I suggested, lying back down and smiling. "We can rest there."

"Will you be mad if I can't get you pregnant again?" He put his hand on my shoulder, massaging it gently.

Closing my eyes, I shook my head. "I'd love more children with you, but I won't be disappointed. We have a beautiful daughter together."

I felt his lips pressing against my head as his fingertips ran up and down my arm. "The beach sounds like a good idea. You know, we can go anywhere you want to go. I don't want you worrying about work either."

"Chris," I warned, rolling my eyes. I knew exactly what he would say.

"We have enough money in our account to survive with me off. Trust me, more than enough. I will take a couple of months leave. If I get go signal for the surgery, I'd like it done as soon as possible."

I bit my lip, worrying. "Are you okay?"

"I will be fine as long as you're going to be by my side," he said quietly. I could tell he still felt guilty about everything.

I moved, so I was lying on my side, my hand running up his stomach and resting on his chest. "I'm not going anywhere." And I wouldn't be. What kind of woman leaves her husband when he's sick? I wouldn't do that to him. He may think it was easier, but I, for one, didn't.

We both bolted off the couch when we heard a loud scream filling the room. Neither one of us rushed to grab Lucy. Instead, we both clapped, and I grabbed my camera. Our baby girl just rolled over for the first time. It was more of a faceplant, but it was still exciting for us.

"Oh, come here, baby. Did that scare you?" Chris asked, crawling his hands and knees to reach her.

I smiled, putting the camera away and came over to them. Lucy was growing up so fast, too quickly.

Adam just appeared in the doorway with his briefcase and a bag full of takeaway for dinner whist we stood up. He winked and held the bag up. "Chinese food. Okay with you?" he asked.

Umm, of course it was. I rubbed my stomach, eagerly hungry.

Dinner went by quickly; I think we were all starving. Lucy went down after a bath and a play with Uncle Adam. We all sat out on the back patio desk, enjoying the warm evening. Each man held a beer in their hands as we played a round of cards.

I thought I heard a noise and looked at the men who both looked at me oddly. "Did you hear that?" I asked. Then I stood eagerly. I knew that sound all too well, or more precisely, I knew those heels very well.

A smile widened across my face, looking at Chris as he smiled back at me. "Thought you may need some company." He took my hand and kissed it gently.

"Oh gosh, you two need to get a room—one far away from the one I'm staying in, I suggest."

"Trust me. You'll need to be in the car at the end of the drive when these two get going." Adam teased and punched Chris playfully in the arm as they both laughed.

I poked my tongue out at my brother, ignoring him and letting out a squeal of excitement. I couldn't believe Chris had brought Ness here for me. I gave him a look and mouthed *"Thank you"* as I held her back tightly as she hugged the life out of me.

187

"Thank you for coming," I said as I fought hard to hold the tears in.

Ness's hold tightened. "I'm not leaving until Chris is well again. He will get through this, sweetie," she whispered quietly, and I realised Chris did tell someone.

He told my best friend.

CHAPTER TWENTY

"What about these?" I looked over at Mum, half rolling my eyes as she held up a baby pink coloured dress.

I shook my head, wanting to gag. "No, I don't think so. Plus, it wouldn't go with what we've chosen."

She sighed. "Charlotte, I honestly don't know why you want a black theme for your wedding."

Chris and I were in full swing of wedding preparations. We both decided on a darker theme, not exactly black, but Mum thought our wedding was going to be some Goth event. I had given up on trying to explain it.

"Oh, I really love this," I said reaching, picking up the charcoal-coloured dress. A strapless floor-length dress that would look great on Ness; she was my maid of honour. Well, of course, she would be. She was currently in the changing room trying them on.

Ness walked out in a knee-length one-shoulder. "Well?" she asked, doing a twirl.

"Love that dress on you. You're so pretty, Ness," I said, moving closer for further inspection.

Mum, however, shrugged. This was going to be a long day. I was a little more excited when we then moved on to bigger, whiter, prettier dresses. I couldn't wait to marry Chris.

I slumped down on the bed and let out a strangled scream. "Fun day?" Chris' humorous voice spoke beside me.

I opened one eye and looked to my left. "Next time, you're coming with me. Mum fought every decision I was making."

Chris put his laptop beside him and took his specs off, rolling on his side and running his hand over my stomach. "Did you find yourself a dress?"

I smiled. "I may have done; you'll never know."

"Can I convince you?" He asked, his hand sliding lower.

I slapped his hand away. "Ah, I don't think so. Your girl is starving, and I would love for you to make me some dinner."

He chuckled, moving so he was now on top of me. "I think I could cook my girl something to eat. What would she like?"

I pretended to think. "Take me out to dinner, romance me, and show me some of that Chris Rivers charm that he uses on the ladies."

He buried his face in the crook of my neck and laughed hard, his whole body shaking with laughter. He lifted his head and smiled. "You want me to woo you?"

"Hell yeah, I do, baby!" I grinned back wide-eyed.

"Alright then, get dressed into something sexy. I'll throw a suit on and take you out to dinner, baby. But just so you know, those legs of yours will be open when I get back home and for as long as I want," he said huskier.

I hooked my ankles around the back of his thighs and bumped my hips up into him. "Quickie first."

*   *   *

Ness and I brought out hot drinks into the sitting room and sat down on the couch. I grabbed the blanket and pulled it up over my legs a little as she did the same. She had been here a little over a week, and I was so happy to have her here.

I really needed my best friend right now. For my own sanity.

"What did they say today?" Ness asked, getting right to the point.

I ran my hand through my hair and groaned. I had my own migraine from all the information that we had received today;

doctor's appointments after appointments. I think my head was going to explode if it received any more information.

"They took Adam's blood work, and they're going to do some more testing on Chris. He's not really saying much though," I said. Chris wasn't showing any emotion at all today. He was kind of spaced out. We were having a silent fight; neither of us not knowing what we were mad at each other about.

Ness nodded, pressing her lips together and sighing. "I really can't believe it. It's scary to think he's been so unwell for so long."

I felt my eyes swell with tears. "It's pretty bad, Ness, and Chris plays it off like it's not that, but I mean the complications that can go wrong. I just don't see how he's going to wake up from this and remember who I am, or even wake up at all." I was so worried about the risks involved with these procedures. I felt like the only one who was worried that this could all go wrong and neither of them would wake up.

"Do you forgive him for leaving you and Lucy?" she asked.

The question caught me off guard. I hadn't been expecting it at all.

"No," I said quietly. Maybe that's why I felt so bad. "He left our daughter and me. I may be here, but I can't forget him for what he did to us." It was the cold hard truth. "I feel awful for saying that."

I was here working things out. I was going to try and try my hardest, but at the end of the day, if Chris and I couldn't get past the previous issue, I would have a very tough decision to make. Love or not, I still feared one day he would leave again.

Ness smiled. "So, you and him are shagging again?"

I rolled my eyes. I wish. "Seriously, you want to talk about my sex life. I'm more interested in yours." I grinned. Oh, how I had missed our girl talk and changing the topic from my non-existent one seemed a perfect idea.

Ness waved her hand around, trying to brush me off, but I knew better. "I'm not seeing anyone. I've had a couple of dates here and there, but they've turned out to be men who had a major commitment phobia. I want a relationship; I want what you and Chris have."

A lump formed in my throat. I hated that we were held on some pedestal. "We're far from perfect, but I will admit: Chris charmed the absolute hell out of me, right up until everything happened. We were so happy and crazy about each other."

"You still are. He's trying, and so are you. I know you both will work through this. Give it time." Ness smiled, taking a sip of her hot tea.

Time was one thing I wasn't sure we had. It was something Chris and I really needed to discuss. What would happen if this operation took a turn for the worse? There were so many unanswered questions that I needed to get the answers to. I just wasn't sure if I was ready to know them yet.

The sliding doors opened, and Adam walked in. I noticed the little look he gave Ness. There might be a romance brewing up and I was going to keep a close eye on those two whilst Ness was here staying with us. I smiled, saying nothing.

"Food's done. You girls ready?" Adam asked, snapping a set of tongs together.

Both of us nodded and said, "Yes."

I really wasn't in the mood to eat. I felt sick staring at the amount of meat they had cooked plus the salads we made; the headache I had didn't help. I rarely got those.

"Chris, are you going to be working still?" Ness asked. "Or, will you be working cases from home?"

Chris looked up, closing his mouth from the piece of steak he was about to place into his mouth. "I'm going to work from home. I can do all my cases here, and if I'm needed in court then I can still make it there. Work won't be an issue."

"Will your clients be coming to the house?" I asked him. I wasn't sure how I felt about any of this.

Chris looked at me; I could tell he didn't appreciate my tone. "No, this is our home."

Adam smiled, looking up and breaking the gaze between Chris and me. "So, Mum and Dad are getting into town around 11 a.m. tomorrow. Do you want me to go pick them up?" Adam asked, looking over at me and smirking.

Shit, I had forgotten about them coming here. They called last night to let us know they were visiting their only granddaughter. I just hoped they behaved. I looked at Chris who was looking at me still, obviously waiting for me to answer. "No, I'll take Lucy and pick them up."

"I will come with you," Chris said quietly. I just nodded.

Dinner was so weird. It was just an uneasy tension, and with so much happening these past weeks, I was beginning to feel exhausted and over it. The steak was good; that was a plus.

Ness hesitated, then spoke again, directing her attention to my brother. "So, any women keeping you busy?"

My brother almost choked on his drink. "Ah, no. I don't think I have time for romance now."

I smirked, looking at him and then Ness. I wiggled my brows at her, and she glared at me.

Barely touching my food, I jumped at the chance to go inside and clean the dishes and tend to my daughter. She was face down, rolling about with a blanket over her head. I couldn't help but laugh. Her bright eyes looked at me as she smiled. She was utterly beautiful.

"I can't wait until she's running around," Chris's voice came in behind me.

I smiled, keeping my eyes on Lucy bouncing her legs up and down. "Me either. She's going to be so full on, but it'll be fun."

"You're mad at me," he said quietly, taking a seat in the rocker chair while I lay on the floor with Lucy. She lay on her belly, trying to grasp the toys in front of her. The rattle was mere inches from her fingertips. Finally, she wrapped her little fingers around it and started to suck on it.

I looked up at Chris, shaking my head. "I'm not mad. I'm just worried."

"Please don't worry. I don't want you to worry about any of this, baby." He sighed, slipping out of the chair and lying on his side in front of us. Chris reached over and rubbed his fingertips over mine. "I know this surgery has big risks. I have a lot to talk to you about, and we'll make this decision together, if you don't feel right about something, then I will hear your concerns."

That made me feel slightly better about everything. "You promise?" I asked, looking up at him, our gazes locked on each other.

"I promise, Charlotte. You're my wife, the mother of my daughter. I wouldn't go through with something without talking about it with you first." He smiled at me, but it disappeared quickly; a sad look came across his face. "Do you still love me?"

I just stared at him as I sat up and leaned over. "Do you think I love you?" I asked sadly.

He shook his head. "I think you're trying to love me, but I hurt you too badly. You're trying, but I can see you slipping away from me, Char. It's okay. If this is all too much for you, tell me, and I won't fight you on it."

Was I really coming across like that? "How can you think I don't love you?" I asked through tears.

"Sometimes, I wonder that."

I looked up when his hands ran up and down my back, his thumbs brushing my tears away. "I am madly in love with you, Chris. That won't ever change."

He looked relieved when I told him I still loved him. I did. I was crazy in love with the man. How could I not be after he gave me a beautiful daughter? "I know we have things to work through.

I promise we will get through them." He pressed his lips to my nose, kissing me softly.

"Make love to me, Chris. Just make me forget this week." I breathed out over him, kissing down his neck, my fingertips running through his hair as his lips were pressed against my own. I moaned as his tongue slid over mine. Reminding me just how much I had missed kissing him like this.

"Get to bed. I'll put Lucy down." He groaned, kissing down my neck.

I tilted my head back, breathing heavily as his hands gripped my hips. "Chris, I need you now," I looked at him, letting him know I needed him to not be so gentle with me.

We had such a strain on our sex life since Ness had been here. Adam down the hall complaining didn't help either, and with all these doctor's appointments and Chris's late nights, we barely even touched. Tonight, I needed to be touched.

I needed to forget. I wanted to fuck. Just pure fucking. There was nothing tender about it—just raw and primal.

I was on edge, and when the bedroom door opened. Soon, I grinned at Chris who smirked back at me, closing the door and flicking the lock. My eyes were stuck to his body as he pulled his shirt off over his head, his stomach flexing as he unbuttoned his jeans, the trail of hair going down to his grey boxer shorts.

"You like?" Chris grinned.

I nodded, smiling and biting down against my lower lip, holding in the deep moan. "Oh, I like. A lot."

Chris slid under the covers and grabbed me by the waist. "Get on your hands and knees, baby," he demanded, his fingers skimming over my naked stomach and between my thighs.

I sucked in a quick breath, doing as he said while he knelt up, moving behind me and then lowering his head. Using his tongue, he gave my core a long wet lick. I bucked forwards, moaning as his hands grabbed my ass, squeezing and gripping me. I was fisting the sheets as he licked, sucked, and fucked my core.

"Oh, god. Chris, I'm close," I breathed out hard, as I rocked myself into him.

His mouth moved, and I felt his cock against me. "You want it hard, baby?" he whispered as he kissed down my back, a hand reaching up and groping my breast as he started thrusting in and out slowly.

"Yes." I giggled a little as he playfully slapped my ass.

His hand pushed my body forward, holding me down as he slid in and out. One hand was on my back while the other was groping my ass, thrusting deeper, harder, and rougher as I pushed up into him, silently begging him with my loud moans to let me come. He listened, and with one hard thrust, I came undone around him. I was gripping the pillow, sliding it down in front of me, and screaming into it as I started to come again.

My body was flipped over, legs in the air as Chris laid on top of me, slamming into me hard while he drew out my orgasm. His eyes glued to mine as he let my legs go; they fell to the bed, and I slid them up his thighs, locking him in.

"I love you," I whispered, cupping his face as I panted hard.

A smile came over his face. "I love you more, beautiful." He leant down, kissing me passionately as he came hard and deep inside me.

His thrusts slowed to a stop as we both caught our breaths. I smiled up at him while he placed a kiss on my forehead. "Hard enough?" he asked through his own hard breaths.

I turned, looking at the alarm clock beside us on Chris' side. "It's still early." I smiled.

He chuckled. "Well then, you know what to do if you want it again, baby." He pulled out and rolled off me. I grinned, moving on top of him and kissing my way down his chest, following the hair trail down as I got him hard again.

An hour later, we both lay curled up together, Chris stroking my hair as I ran my fingertips up and down his chest, both

196

of us blissfully happy after the extreme passionate lovemaking. I was more so too sore to move, and cuddling naked seemed a rare, but perfect idea. Neither of us had spoken much; we were just content the way we were right now.

I propped myself up on my elbow and looked at him. "Have the surgery. If you think there is a good chance, then I want you to have it."

Saying that, I could see the relief in his eyes. I knew this was his only option for a chance of survival. I knew there were greater risks of something wrong happening, but this also took away a lot of waiting with false hope if the other options didn't work.

"We don't have to decide now. Let's take some time," he spoke quietly, taking my hand and kissing it gently.

I shook my head. "Time is something you don't have, and I think this is our only choice. I know the tablets may be great for some, but your swelling is getting worse. I heard what the doctors said, Chris. I want you to have this surgery."

He let out a sigh. "You're sure you're okay with this? It's going to be an extreme and intense surgery for us both."

I didn't want to think about that. I lay my head back to his chest and held him tighter. "You're going to wake up. I know it," I whispered as tears leaked from the corner of my eyes. Chris not waking up was a chance I didn't want to take, but for him, I'd put aside my fears and agree to this just to make him happy. I was still his wife, and I would support him no matter what.

The next morning, the sun was hitting our skin as I opened my eyes and looked over at Chris. He was awake and already looking at me. "Morning, beautiful." He smiled, pressing his lips to my naked shoulder.

I smiled back, "Good morning, sleep well?"

His smile turned into a grin. "I slept extremely well, and last night was long overdue."

I held in my giggle. "Promise me something," I spoke sleepily. "Promise me that we'll make more time for each other each day. No more fights or silent treatment."

"I promise," he said as he moved closer, running his hand down my back and over the curve of my ass. "When do we need to pick your parents up? They still hate me, don't they?"

I had no idea how my parents felt about Chris at the moment. I hadn't spoken to them much since they left without a goodbye. "I don't know, but we've got dinner tonight, and I can only imagine what everyone is going to say." I groaned at the thought of the drama that would erupt once they heard the news of Chris's illness.

Chris looked at me and moved over, lying on top of my body. "As long as you're by my side, then that's all that matters. You and our daughter."

"Right by your side," I whispered as I lifted my head for a kiss.

He broke away from the kiss, our naked bodies heating up from the uncontrollable desire we had for each other still. "You think we could start the morning off right before terror wakes up?"

I giggled at the name he gave Lucy. I parted my legs more for him. "I think we could do." I smiled.

If only the rest of the day could have been as amazing as our morning . . . instead of the painful drama.

CHAPTER TWENTY-ONE

"Keep your eyes closed!!" I shouted, feeling panicked.

"They are! I'm not even facing you!" Chris called out back. "Wait, let me see you. Please, I just want to see how beautiful you look right now, baby, please," he asked. I could tell he was eager.

"Chris, I mean it. I will get so mad if they're open!" I warned. I was so mad with him right now. I had been trying on my wedding dresses at home. A friend of Chris' heard we were engaged, and she sent a gift over: a rack of dresses for me to look at. I was in awe of the one I had put on, but who do you think decided to come home early and surprise me? Yes, my bad timing fiancé who was now covering his eyes and facing the door.

"I promise, Charlotte. I didn't see, but you look beautiful," he called out.

I was hurriedly slipping out of the stunning gown and trying to get it back in the white dress bag. I zipped up the zipper and let out a sigh. "Okay, you can turn around now."

Chris put his briefcase down, and his arm dropped. He turned around and smiled. "Is it one of those?" he asked, walking closer as I pulled my shirt over my head.

I shrugged. "You, my dear, are going to have to wait until I walk down the aisle. The grassy one, since we're marrying at the vineyard."

He chuckled. "Baby, come on now. You're going to walk all over a ton of white rose petals."

"White, cream, or light pink, I'm undecided." I smiled walking over towards him. "I missed you today. How was work?" I asked wrapping my arms around his waist.

"I had court all day, and guess what?" His arms slid around my waist, lifting me up slightly.

I eyed him, even though his face wasn't giving any emotions anyway. I knew what he was going to tell me. "That's fantastic; you're so wonderful. You make me really proud baby." I kissed him on the mouth.

He shook his head, "One day, I will lose a court case, then you won't be able to keep guessing like this, beautiful."

"Not possible, and do you know why?" I asked him seriously.

"Why's that baby?" he asked, placing small kisses over my face.

I cupped his cheeks, pulling back. "Because my soon-to-be husband is amazing at what he does. You're charming, and I should know. You made me fall for you instantly."

"No need to lie." He smirked, playing around with me.

I laughed. "Come on, I'm taking my man out to celebrate, or did you have plans with the guys?" I asked, normally they went out after a big win and celebrated.

"Actually," he said as he scooped me up bridal style. "I've made plans for us."

"Oh, yes? What are those?" I asked, very curious.

Chris walked with me in his arms still towards the balcony, sliding the door open and walking outside, "Do you remember that place you always want to go and stay at? Not too far from here?"

I thought for a moment. I looked up at him as he sat down on the patio lounge and pulled me closer to his body, his hands playing with my hair as I ran my fingers through his. It then clicked, "Chris, you have work!"

He shook his head, "I took a few days off, and we're leaving tonight. Go pack; I want to spoil my girl this week."

*   *   *

200

I was hiding in the pantry, well, more like searching for some booze. I could only find a bottle of scotch, and I didn't think my mum or Chris's mother would enjoy being served that with dinner.

"Charlotte?" Adam spoke, entering the kitchen.

"In here," I called out, about to give up.

My brother chuckled as he walked into the pantry. "What are you doing?"

"Hiding." I sighed, slumping against the shelves.

He pulled out two bottles of Moscato and smiled. "Thought you might need these?"

"Thank you. I can't believe I about forgot them." I shook my head, "I don't drink, so I didn't think we'd need alcohol with dinner. I guess I've been distracted."

"Charlotte, stop and calm down. What's the matter?" Adam asked, entering the pantry and closing the sliding door. "Are you okay?"

I shook my head. "I feel so sick. I'm so worried, Adam. I told Chris to do the surgery. What kind of person am I?"

Adam sighed, loosening his tie that was around his neck and then opening the top two buttons. "Listen to me. Chris is going to be fine. You need to hear this though. If Chris doesn't get that surgery, he could die; we both know the outcome. You made the right choice. It's tough, and it's only going to get harder, but I'm going to go in and give my brother whatever he needs. I want him around because even the shit that happened when Lucy was born, he's a good guy."

I was on the verge of tears as I listened to Adam say all those things about Chris. "You're right; he's going to be fine. I just need to stop thinking the worst."

"And don't worry about Mum and Dad. They're being stubborn," he said more quietly.

I shrugged, scoffing. "They refused a lift here once they found out Chris was coming with me. That's just being plain rude."

I was really hurt when I called to confirm their arrival time. I suggested we go get a coffee before we come home, Mum said that sounded great. But I mentioned Chris joining us, suddenly it wasn't such a good idea; they had things to do apparently. I played it off as if it didn't bother me, and I didn't dare tell Chris. I couldn't bring myself to mention it to him.

"I know, please just don't worry about them. I'll talk to them both when they arrive here," Adam said, giving me a half smile.

"Okay, fine." I gave in, it was hard not to be around him.

"Good. Just remember: nothing is going to be more fun than a fucked up dinner with everyone fighting. It's going to a battle zone once they hear what's happening." He grinned and handed over the wine.

I looked at him with a mischievous smile. "You need to ask Vanessa out."

He laughed. "Excuse me?"

"You heard me. I have been watching you two, and through all the teasing, I can see you like each other." It was true. They fought like crazy, but I noticed the little eye smiles they gave each other.

Adam just smiled. "She's your best friend. Isn't there some sort of code?"

"I'm married to your boss; the codes are broken. Just go out on a date with her and see how it goes. Or Chris and I could get you both to watch Lucy while the two of us go out." I winked. That idea actually sounded quite nice.

He glared and walked out, muttering something under his breath.

I went back to stuffing the roast chicken I was making. I didn't cook things like this often. Chris and I didn't do the whole baked roast with the trimmings; we liked simple but new foods. Sushi was a favourite of ours to make together. I was a bad cook but learning. Chris, however, was a great cook.

202

I put the chicken in the oven and turned it up. I didn't have long until everyone arrived. I was running late. "Chris," I called out, throwing the tea towel on the bench and checking the potatoes.

"Yeah?" his sweet voice came up behind me. "What's baby mama doing? Cooking veggies for the first time could be dangerous."

I rolled my eyes, smiling as I put the lid back down. "Funny, aren't you? I've made vegetables before," I corrected.

He frowned, and then his smile grew. "But we didn't get around to eating them, did we? I think we skipped dinner."

I smiled at the memory of that. "Yes, we did, but anyhow, I need you to feed Lucy a bottle of milk, and if you're able to, could you please change her diaper as well?"

Chris lifted Lucy up, her bum near his nose and she let out a squeal of laughter, kicking her legs up. Chris lowered her and looked at me. "Help me? It's kind of gross." He scrunched up his nose.

I laughed, shaking my head. "Umm, I change her all the time. You've done it before, baby." I smiled.

He groaned. "Fine, I'll change her. Do you want me to wait until after she eats before bath time?"

"Yeah, she's going to eat her first baby food tonight." I smiled. I was so excited to see how she took to the gels and pure foods.

Chris came over and cupped my cheek with one hand, leaning down a little to my height. "It smells wonderful. Don't stress."

"I love you for saying that, it means a lot." I met him halfway for a sweet kiss before he went to change her.

I think the most amusing part of this whole dinner was that Lucy was making a huge mess. Her food was all over the place, her bib was covered, and the chair was filthy. I didn't care though. In the end, Chris gave her the bowl of apples and she finger-painted, eating a little along the way.

The worst part so far? Well, easy. When Chris' mum walked in with a cooked chicken, salads, and dessert. Didn't help when Mum told me she had brought salads and sliced ham too. I felt like utter shit as I had cooked the entire day only to be upstaged in my own home—at my first home-cooked family dinner.

The little things were getting to me. I kept trying to focus on the main things: Chris and Lucy. Those two made me smile.

"She's growing so much." Mum smiled. "I keep forgetting that she's almost four months old."

"Don't remind me; it's going too fast," I replied, taking a bite of my chicken. It was pretty good. Well, I thought so.

"Well, don't rush for anymore," Dad grumbled. "But you'll do whatever you want anyway."

I looked over at Adam, urging him to help me. He let out a slight cough. "So, Char, great chicken. It smells and tastes so good."

My mother-in-law then felt the need to reply. "It looks a little dry."

I looked over when Chris slid his hand over mine, giving me a reassuring squeeze. "Don't listen to them. I promise you it's good. Thought we were having vegetables though?" he asked quietly.

I let out a laugh. "You do realise no one, apart from me, is eating my chicken? You all took your mum's chicken, and the vegetables are in the kitchen because no one thought they'd taste good." The laugh that I had turned into a slightly dry throat. I gave up trying to win them over.

Chris stood. "Well, this is just perfect." He walked out of the dining room, scraping and clinging were heard, and then he entered the room again with a plate of vegetables and a gravy bowl. Sitting down, he then reached over and grabbed my plate with the chicken I cooked on it. "If no one else wants this, then I'm going to eat the whole thing." He placed it beside his plate of vegetables and smirked, dipping a piece of chicken in the gravy. "Oh, yeah, I'm going to have this also."

I could have jumped his bones right then and there. That was the sweetest thing ever, taking a whole roast just to make me smile. I had no words for what I felt right now. I was really smiling on the inside at him.

"You don't need to eat that, Chris. It's okay," I assured him.

"Don't be silly. My wife cooked dinner for everyone. No one is eating this, so I will. Why? Because you cooked dinner for everyone all fucking day and no one has done anything, but fucking complain about the food they aren't even touching!" He slammed his fist to the table, making the plates and glasses rattle.

My heart was pounding at how angry he was . . . over a chicken?

Luckily, Lucy was too content with her finger food to be startled by the loud bang.

"Chris, we were trying to help her," his sister Samantha said quietly.

"Too late for that." Chris scoffed. "You should have left the food at home and enjoyed what my wife served up."

"Son," his father warned.

Chris glared back at him, "What Dad? Going to tell me to shut up and do as I'm told? This is my home. You were all told to come here for dinner, Charlotte was so —" He paused, rubbing his temples lightly then looked at them all. "Char was so excited today, then you get here and bring your own food. That's what I call rude."

Everyone was silent; it was now even more uncomfortable than before. I sighed and looked up at Chris. He just shook his head and took a mouthful of potatoes. "This is the best dinner I have ever eaten in my life." He grinned wiping his mouth.

I couldn't believe him right now. He was amazing.

Dinner resumed to slow weird conversation about the weather and the holiday season coming up. I slid my hand over on Chris' lap, moving towards the middle of his parted thigh. I gave him a slight grab to let him know, later tonight was going to be all about him.

"Chris, how's work?" Samantha asked him.

"Uh, it's good. I'm taking some time off soon though, working from home," he answered, pushing the half-eaten chicken away. I begged him to stop. I couldn't watch him eat all that. He'd make himself sick.

"Why?" his dad asked him. "You've got a business to run. You can't do that from your lounge room."

I knew what was coming up. He was going to have to break the news to them. Chris went silent. I took his hand in both of mine.

I was right beside him. I was here for him and with him.

"Funny story. I actually got some news the other day. Well, around a month ago we found out," Chris started, looking a bit afraid to continue.

"Oh no you're pregnant," Mum gasped.

"No!" I shot back. Well, I don't think I was, but then again, I hadn't taken the pill since having Lucy. Oh shit, maybe I was pregnant. No, I couldn't be. I wasn't. Oh God. "Nice to know you're eager for more grandchildren," I instead said.

"Good. I think you both need to wait for kids," Chris's mum spoke up, smiling at us like she was helping us out with a decision.

"I have an acute kidney injury, adrenal failure," Chris just announced quietly.

The whole room went silent. I squeezed his hand, letting him know it was okay.

"How bad?" his dad asked quietly.

Chris sighed. "It's bad. I'm having surgery tomorrow morning."

"And you just tell us this now?" my dad said next. "How bloody considerate of you both!"

"I didn't know they'd do the surgery tomorrow. We were just told this a few hours ago," Chris shot back, glaring at him.

I knew the other part was coming up, and when Adam stood, I think I clung to Chris's hand tighter. "I'm giving him a kidney. I'm a match."

"Like hell you are! I won't allow you to risk your life for this guy." Dad stood up, pointing to Chris.

"He's my brother. I'm saving his life, and he will die if he doesn't get this soon!" Adam retorted, shaking his head. "I'm helping him regardless."

Mum looked at me, disappointment washed over her face. "I can't believe you're letting your brother go through with this, and for him!"

"I'm saving his life. She doesn't get a say in it anyway. This is my choice! Chris said no, and guess what? I am still doing it!" Adam bellowed, making me jump.

It was no wonder these two won cases constantly. Their thundering voices scared the shit out of me.

I didn't want to listen to any of the yelling. Ness and I looked at each other and seemed to have the same idea: take Lucy and hide with the wine.

She and I were in Lucy's bedroom. Samantha ended up joining us as Chris and Adam had a face-off with our parents. It wasn't a pretty thing we heard either. Dad had called Chris a deadbeat father, and Chris brought up my past eating disorder. That only made Dad wilder.

Chris's mum was yelling, refusing to let her son go through with some wild surgery that had such a low survival rate. He responded by saying he was a grown man and could make his own choices.

The fight ended when a loud smash was heard. I looked over at the other two who were beside me lying on the floor in Lucy's room, and I said, "I bet that was my plate of chicken."

The three of us then burst out into laughter, not because it was funny but because it was mostly true.

All I knew I had to do was remain strong and stay at my husband's side through all of this. Tomorrow was going to be hard on us all. I just needed to show Chris how much he was needed.

CHAPTER TWENTY-TWO

I smiled as I walked over to Chris. This was perfect here. "I love it!"

Chris looked at me, his smile spreading further over his face. "Yeah? You do?" he asked.

I nodded. "Yes, this is the perfect spot for our wedding. It's simple but elegant. The flowers and the view are just stunning, Chris. I love wine, and I love you. It makes sense to marry in a vineyard."

He laughed, taking my hand. "Yes. I think so too."

"I think about our future, and I see a life of happiness with you. A big family of kids: two girls, and two boys.

"Four babies? You want four kids?" he asked, his eyes widened.

I nodded. "Yes, I would like two of each. That way, they can have a little playmate." I walked over to where he was sitting and took a seat beside him. "Do you not see four kids in our future? What happened to a lot of babies you were dying to have?"

"I want you to be happy. I see two girls who look just like their mummy and two boys who——"

"Who looks just like their daddy," I added before he could say anything else.

"Well, yes, I hope so. I was going to say, who had a great head of hair." He winked, squeezing my ass.

"I want to get married here. It's perfect," I leant into his side more, looking around the vineyard that overlooked the large Rocky Mountains.

Chris looked down at me and smiled. "It is. I can't wait until you're my wife, Charlotte."

I agreed there. "Want to go back to our room?"

He chuckled. "You're insatiable. I can't keep up with you."

"Yes, you can, and all this wedding planning is making me want you." I was extremely turned on with all this wedding talk and the thought of Chris standing there in a tux. I knew one thing that would get him to our room quickly. I gave him a flirty grin. "We could go practise making babies?"

"Well." He groaned out. "When you put it that way, let's go."

Chris and I were staying up here for the night, doing the whole wine and cheese tasting. We figured it would be something different for us to experience, and it was. I loved seeing how the wine was made and trying new flavours. Then we set off through the forest bush walk track, having a picnic on the large rocks overlooking the waterfalls.

We got back into our room, and Chris took my hand. "Let's get in the spa. We've been walking around all day."

"That sounds nice. You feel like giving me one of your amazing back rubs?" I asked, giving him a cheeky grin as I pulled my top off.

He wiggled his brows. "Yes, as long as you give me one of your special rubs after the bath?"

I shook my head, smiling at how dirty he could be but made it sound normal. "Okay, and if you're a good boy, I may just even use my mouth as well as hands."

He laughed, pulling me into his body. "This is why I'm marrying you. Perfect wife ever."

"Only wife ever," I corrected him.

There was no way this man was ever going to leave, without me going with him.

*   *   *

I had felt sick all morning; my nerves were shot. Chris and Adam went in for surgeries today. In exactly two hours we needed to be at the hospital.

"Are you okay?" Chris asked, rubbing my back lightly as I was bent over the toilet bowl throwing up.

I nodded. "Yes. I'm good. Just worried for you," I said, rubbing my temples before I threw up again.

Once I had finally finished puking, I stood up, walked to the wash sink, and rinsing my mouth out as Chris stood and watched me. He seemed relatively calm for something that was something so huge.

"Don't worry about me. I'm good, baby. I promise. I just want to get this finished and then get home. Get back to getting us on track and watching Lucy grow up," Chris said as I turned around. I couldn't help but burst into tears.

He was so positive, and I felt bad for worrying so much. I gripped him tighter, afraid to let go. "Chris, I don't want anything to happen to you. I'm so scared. What if you don't wake up or what if you do but you can't talk or move? What if you forget me?"

Google was never good for any medical advice.

"Don't, baby. Don't do this," Chris said, I could hear his voice breaking. "Look, the odds aren't in my favour, but I'm going to damn well wake up for you. For our family. I love you so much."

I pulled back slightly, looking up at him and cupping his cheeks. "You wake up, and when you do, I will be right there waiting. Just don't forget about me. I love you so much, Chris."

"I love you too, baby, more than anything," he whispered, kissing me hard.

Everything felt like a blur downstairs. Chris was sitting quietly and talking with Adam now, and then Ness looked a bundle of nerves also. My parents weren't talking much. They were still mad about Adam doing this, and that I wasn't forbidding him to do it. Even Chris's parents were now staying here; they were acting as if everything was normal.

Lucy was rolling around the floor and drooling over her pyjamas.

I smiled and walked over, picking her up and sitting her in the high chair. "Hungry?" I asked her, showing her the jar of apples.

Her tiny fists banging down as she squealed excitedly, her mouth opening and closing fast. Chris stood up, walked over, and sat beside me. "Here. Go get dressed, and I'll feed her then bring her up."

I went back upstairs and ended up throwing up again. I hated this. The unknown of what was going to happen. I dressed up and went to Lucy's room when I heard her giggling loudly. Chris was changing her and trying to hold her down as she squirmed. She was going to be crawling without a doubt soon.

"Want some help?" I asked, walking in and going to her wardrobe.

"Thanks. This little Rugrat won't stop moving." He grinned, tickling her which caused her to laugh louder again.

Lucy was coming with us to the hospital. I didn't care what any of our parents said, his daughter was going to be there to see her Dad before he went into surgery. The drive there was eerily silent. There was nothing really to talk about. I wanted to cry, and I did at times.

"Well, this is me," Adam said, starting to look nervous. "Shit, this is really happening."

I wrapped my arms around him tightly. "I'll see you when you wake up," I said and kissed his cheek.

Adam and Chris exchanged hugs, both getting a little teary, and I had to look away before I started sobbing again. Adam then turned to Ness, and I fought my excitement when he kissed her. About time.

It was just us left. My parents and Ness stayed with Adam while he was being prepped, and I went with Chris, squeezing his hand, a little harder than normal. Lucy was fast asleep in the pram which Chris's mother pushed along for me.

I went into the room with him; he changed and was lying in bed. His parents came in, trying to lighten the mood with a joke, and then they said their goodbyes, wishing him good luck. Then when they left, I felt myself tear up again, getting up on the bed and lying beside him.

"You know, I don't want you to go into this surgery with any doubts or bad thoughts," I said as he played with my fingertips. "It needs to be positive."

"I know. I feel good about this, Char," he said quietly.

I looked up, and that's when I saw it: the fear in his eyes. Being strong was only going to work for some time until it wouldn't last anymore. I reached up, stroking his cheek lightly. "Chris, you mean everything to me."

"Same," was all he said.

I pressed my lips against his, pulling away for a mere moment. "I forgive you, Chris, for what happened with Lucy and the divorce. I forgive you for that."

"Are you saying this because I could die?" he asked.

I was horrified he would even think this. "No. I'm saying it because I realised I'm not angry anymore. Ness asked me the other day, and I said I hadn't forgiven you, but I have. We have our family back. I can't hold something over you when every day you keep proving to me that you're changing, and our relationship is rock solid. I love you. I forgive you."

That's when he broke down and began to cry, holding me ever so tightly as his body shook underneath mine. I held him back, crying as he pushed his mouth over mine, kissing me with a deep passion—giving me a kiss that rocked me to the core.

When we broke away, he used his thumb to brush away my tears. "I love you. I am going to get better, and then the three of us are going to go away. Anywhere you want, baby. I don't care about anything else. Just us. Even Bali, let's go there."

I smiled. "I'd love that. We can go to Bali and stay at the beach. Lucy will be able to play in the sand and water. We can just focus on us. I love you, Chris."

The door opened, and my heart dropped. No, not yet. It was too soon. He couldn't go in now. Not when we were making plans. He looked up at me and smiled sadly. "I will see you when I wake up. Make sure Lucy's in here too. I want to see my girls before anyone else."

No. It was too soon. I wasn't ready.

"I promise. I love you, Chris." I stood up as a team of doctors walked in. I sat down as they went over all the pre-op checks, and Chris signed a DNR form. I knew he didn't want to take any chances of being a vegetable.

As much as that hurt, I felt the same.

"Alright, Chris. Let's let you in the OR and back out here to your family," Dr. Patton said. I looked over at Chris and smiled at him.

I leaned over and kissed him. He pulled me back when I went to move away, kissing me hungrily. If we were at home, we both would have jumped each other. I smiled over his mouth. "I love you, Christopher. I will see you soon."

"Love you too, baby. Give Lucy a big hug and kiss for me," he said and kissed me one last time.

The nurse with the paperwork was about to leave, but I grabbed her arm gently. I couldn't not do this. I would never forgive myself if I let it happen. "The DNR, if something happens before the transplant. You tell them to save him. He's not thinking. I need you to save my husband, please. He needs to come home with us. Save him."

She glanced down at Lucy and nodded. "Your husband will be fine."

As soon as I was alone, I burst into tears.

I sat in his room with Lucy and just sobbed my heart out. I had the overwhelming urge that something was going to go wrong.

Composing myself, I finally walked out, and instantly I was met with both of our parents, Chris's sister, and Ness. I put on a brave smile, but it was hard to do.

"How are you?" Samantha asked. "How's he?"

I nodded, "Staying positive. He will be fine." That's what I had to do.

In all honesty, I didn't want to think about what Chris was going through right now. Because if I did, the severe disadvantage we were at would really sink through. I needed to figure something else out. I needed to just try and think about anything other than what was happening.

"How's Adam?" I asked, changing the subject.

"Good, he will be out in a couple of hours." Ness smiled.

I grinned at her. "So, I think you and him are good together. About time."

"I know." she laughed. "Trust me, I know."

We all went into the café at the hospital, sitting at a table with some light lunch. Lucy was wide awake, and I needed to feed her. She was being such a good girl especially for someone who's been in the pram most the morning.

"Are you going to stay here the entire day?" Dad asked.

I nodded. "Yes. I want to be here for Chris when he wakes up."

I saw the looks everyone was giving me. They weren't as optimistic as I had been. In my mind, Chris was going to be okay. They never said anything; I could see they wanted to, but I was a hormonal mess right now and just didn't want to think about anything else.

"I might go back to the room while Lucy sleeps," I said, sitting around with everyone talking about the side effects doing my head in.

Ness stood up. "I'll come with you, and Adam will be out soon. I want to see him."

I smiled. "Yes, he will. That went fast."

215

Ness and I walked back to the room. People rushing around us just seemed like a blur. I couldn't feel anything; I just felt numb. I wanted to cry again, but all my tears were dried out. It had been one hell of a year for crying.

"Are you hungry?" Ness asked me as we sat down.

"I am, but I can't eat. I feel too sick at the thought of eating. Lucy doesn't even know what's going on. She's just happy and content being here and playing with her rattles." I laughed, picking her up and sitting her on my lap.

Ness laughed. "That's true. I will go to the vending machine. You need to eat, Charlotte. I'll get you some sandwiches. I won't be long." She stood up and left the room, leaving me alone to overthink and worry.

When the door closed, I looked down at Lucy, holding her close and rocking her gently. "You know, your Daddy loves you so much. He's a little sick at the moment, but he's going to be better, I know it."

The door opened again. Mum walked in smiling big. "Adam is awake. He's doing well, and the surgery went smoothly. Are you coming to see him?" She asked.

I smiled, relieved my brother was okay. "You go. I will be down to see him a little later. I just want to wait here first," I said as Lucy played with my necklace that Chris brought me. A locket pendant with a photo of him and Lucy inside.

Mum gave me a look of disappointment. "He may have just saved your husband's life. I think you need to get down there now."

And before I could stop the words from muttering out of my mouth, I spoke, "Fuck off."

The loud gasp that escaped her throat was loud. "Charlotte!" Mum snapped.

"No, don't you Charlotte me. My husband is in surgery, and all you're worried about is Adam. I am worried about my brother too, but Adam is awake and doing well. Chris is still in

216

there, with a 40% survival rate, so don't you dare come and lecture me on where to be. I am where I needed to be, with my daughter whose father may or may not live. You and Dad disappointed me by not wishing him all the best," I snapped. I was so furious at them right now. "You could have said good luck."

"Charlotte, he left you when you gave birth." She shook her head.

"Get over it. I sure have. There are more things to worry about, and Chris feels shit enough as it is, and all you keep on doing is making him feel worse with your little digs about whether or not he will do it again. Chris is my husband, and I love him. He's Lucy's dad, and that won't change. You don't even know the full story, so back off and get out of the room now!" I couldn't believe she was bringing that up again at a time like this. It's all they talked about, and I just wanted to move forward.

I don't know how long it was, but I dozed off. I was exhausted, only waking up when a light tap on my shoulder woke me. The room was dark but warm, and I noticed Lucy fast asleep holding the little bunny Chris had brought her. Mum was in the room, stirring as I stood up, trying to hide my yawn. "Sorry." I blushed and jumped up when I noticed it was a doctor.

The Doctor smiled. "It's okay. I just came to let you know about your husband."

My heart rate picked up. "How is he?" I asked, feeling relieved he was out of surgery.

"Mrs. Rivers, Chris is now in recovery. We encountered a slight complication, but the transplant itself had been a s smooth and successful procedure."

I cut her off, my stomach in knots. "What? But he's okay. He's in recovery, right?"

"Chris became hyperkalaemic and went into cardiac arrest. The doctors were able to save him and do the transplant. He's very lucky to be alive. Without the transplant all ready to go, things may have taken a turn for the worse," she said sadly.

I felt relieved that the transplant went well. I was scared as hell about everything else. "Is he awake? When can I see him?" I asked, wanting to go and kiss him and just be there for him.

"Charlotte, that's what I came to talk about. Unfortunately, when we took Chris out of anaesthesia, he didn't respond as well as we had hoped. He's unable to breathe well enough on his own for the moment. He is on a ventilator."

My stomach was in my mouth. "What does that mean?" I asked. "How long will he be on that for? I mean, when will his breathing respond normally?"

"Mrs. Rivers, you need to understand. Chris went through a very invasive and risky procedure; the success rate isn't high at all. Unfortunately, Chris may never be able to breathe on his own again without the help of the ventilator, I'm sorry. You may need to prepare for the worst. I will take you to him now if you like."

Mum sucked in a sharp breath. I felt her hand taking mine as I seemed to fall backward into the chair. "Go and see him, I will stay with Lucy," she spoke, and I clutched her hand with both mine. I was trying so hard not to break down.

I nodded. "Yes. Please stay with her. I need to see him," I said softly, the tears in my eyes leaking down, raining over my cheeks.

As I made my way into the ICU, the only thing going through my mind was that he had to wake up.

I needed him, more than he would ever realise.

CHAPTER TWENTY-THREE

"*Shave it, please.*" *I laughed, running my fingers over his five-week-trimmed beard.*

Chris shook his head. "Not a chance in hell, baby."

I pouted, groaning. "Please, Chris, I don't want our wedding photos to have you with a beard in them."

"You don't complain about it when my face is between your thighs," he said lower, leaning over and kissing my cheek.

I felt my cheeks heating up. "That's completely different, and you can't talk like that here."

Especially since we were at his parent's place. Chris flashed me a grin, ignoring what I was saying to him as he slid his hand under the dinner table and ran it over my lap, moving towards my parted thighs which I tried to close but was too slow. "I want you now," he said quietly, a huskiness in his voice.

I shook my head. "Chris, they'll see us. It's daylight."

I couldn't go and have a quickie while his parents were in the kitchen getting lunch ready.

Chris ignored me, standing and taking my hand. He led me down the hallway and opened the laundry door. The washing machine on was quite loud. I turned around to see him, and he closed the door, not hesitating to pull me close and clamp his mouth over mine. His tongue dominated my mouth as we kissed hungrily.

His fingers worked on getting my jeans undone. I shook my hips to help him get them down as I slid my hands up his arms, feeling the muscles in his biceps under his sleeves. Our mouths parted quickly as I slid his shirt up over his head, staring down at his toned chest. I groaned. He was definitely a sight to behold.

"God, you're hot," I growled, running my fingers up and down his chest and undoing his jeans.

I held in the giggle as Chris lifted me up by the ass and placed me on top of the washer. "I need you badly. I need you all the damn time. I can't focus."

His words were so arousing, the way he spoke and how he looked at me. I smiled. "Take me, Chris. Hurry before someone comes looking for us."

"Did you take it this morning?" he asked, referring to my pill.

I bit my lip, shaking my head as I reached in the front pocket of his tight boxers and pulled his hard cock out. "Nope."

He stepped forward, running his cock up and down my wetness. "Christ, baby, I want you pregnant so bad."

We were going to wait until our wedding night but fuck it. I didn't care anymore.

Chris slid deep inside me, stretching and filling me. I moaned loudly until he claimed my mouth with his again. I held him tightly as I wrapped my thighs around him, thrusting up to meet him. The vibrations add a new kind of pleasure for us both.

"Fuck!" he growled. Thrusting harder and faster as I dug my fingers into his ass.

I broke our kiss as I came, tightening around him as I milked his hard cock into his own orgasm of pure bliss. I was fucking him back as he moved harder, both our orgasms died down, and his thrusts slowly stopped. Chris half slumped against me as we both caught our breath.

"I love you," I whispered, beginning to kiss him again slowly.

He kissed back until the laundry door opened and I quickly hid into his chest.

"Eww! Oh my god, I didn't want to see my brother screwing his girlfriend!" Samantha squealed out.

Chris glanced over his shoulder. I was glad his boxers covered his ass and that his jeans were just underneath. "Fiancé, and get out now!" he growled.

The door closed and we both heard her. "Mum you need to buy a new washing machine! Or wash the clothes again!"

Both Chris and I laughed; he pulled out and fixed himself up then helped me do the same. "I can't wait to marry you next weekend."

"Me either, it's going to be perfect. You can have the beard if you want it," I said, playing with his chin.

He grinned, shaking his head. "Nope, beard's gone for the wedding. Hopefully, a baby's on the way soon after." He winked.

I hoped so too.

*   *   *

It had been three days, and Chris was still asleep.

I knew he signed a DNR, but I wasn't turning anything off. Saying it and doing it were two completely different things.

I was a mess. I didn't know what to do or think anymore. Sleep was something that was rarely happening to me. I was sick to my stomach each day. I couldn't keep anything down. I just threw it all up.

Adam wasn't allowing me to see him. He was in some self-pity slump, blaming himself for what happened and thinking it was his fault for pushing Chris into doing the surgery.

Our parents . . . well, they rarely came in and visited. I was in here with Lucy most of the time. Just me and her, playing on the floor with her toys. When she slept, I lay down and cuddled Chris, hoping he wakes up and tell me this was all just a bad dream.

I needed it to be a bad dream.

I sighed, leaning forward and rubbing my fingers over Chris's shadow of growth. His beard was definitely sexy on him. I'd never let him shave if I had it my way. I leaned forward and placed a kiss over his mouth. Part of me was hoping my kiss would awake him miraculously.

His breathing tube came out yesterday. He was getting stronger on his own. I was proud that he was fighting. I could see it, even if it was small things. I knew he was fighting to wake up.

"I love you, Chris. You need to wake up for me, baby. I need you to kiss me back," I whispered softly as I placed another kiss against his mouth. Carefully running my hand through his hair, trying not to lean on him too hard.

When the door opened, I pulled back. Looking over, I spotted Samantha walking in with two coffees. "Hey, thought you might like this. How's he doing this morning?" she asked, handing me my drink and then kissing her brother on the cheek.

I kept my hand on Chris's hand; I rarely let it go when I was in the room with him. "He's doing well. He went well through the night, and they said his blood was looking good. The swelling has reduced. It's basically just a waiting game now."

"Well, waiting sucks." She smiled, looking at Chris. "He's just getting some sleep in, preparing himself for when he wakes, and Lucy is all over him, as well as you." She winked at me cheekily.

I laughed. "I won't be all over him." *Much*, I thought to myself.

"Do you want to go and see Adam? He's up and awake. I don't mind watching Sleeping Beauty over there," she offered.

I peered in at Lucy and then looked at Chris. I hated leaving him, but I should go and see my brother. "Text me if anything changes with him," I asked, standing up.

"Of course." Samantha nodded.

I leant over and kissed Chris on the mouth. "I love you. I will be back soon," I whispered and then kissed Lucy.

I made my way down to Adam's room, pushing the door open. It was Ness who I first saw, looking tired as my brother read the paper. He looked up, peering over the top page. I could tell he was about to protest.

"Don't bother. I'm not in the mood to listen to you kick me out, and I won't be leaving anyway," I warned taking a seat.

Ness laughed. "She told you. Now, be a good boy and be nice, or I won't bring you back a treat."

"What am I? Five?" Adam snapped back, obviously in a grumpy mood.

She stood up, walking out, and closing the white door behind her. "How are you feeling?" I asked.

He sighed, shrugging. "I'm fine. I feel okay."

"That's good. When do you get to leave?" I asked, trying to get him to talk more.

"In a day or so. But who gives a fuck about that when Chris is in there, still unconscious," he grumbled.

I pinched his forearm. "Don't. Chris is sleeping, he's breathing on his own, and not unconscious, so stop it. I need you to be positive. That's all I need from everyone else as well."

Positivity—that's what I had to have around me.

Adam nodded, blowing out a hard breath and yawning. "Mum's driving me insane. She won't listen when I tell her to stop fussing over me."

I laughed. "Yeah, I think you secretly love it."

He shook his head. "Don't be ridiculous."

"Did you hear what Mum did to Chris?" I asked, getting more comfortable in the chair.

Adam shook his head. I then began to dive in and fill him in on all the details about how they still blamed him and that's why they never wished him all the best for his surgeries. By the end of me speaking, Adam was livid and ready to get out of bed. I had to force him to sit back down in case his stitches split open.

My phone beeped, and I looked down at the message. "It's from Samantha," I said quietly as my eyes skimmed over the message. I stood up and kissed Adam on the cheek. "I need to go back to Chris. I'll be back later with Lucy."

I then took off down to my husband's room.

As another week passed, I was failing at staying positive. I was feeling more and exhausted. The nerves were playing up, and I couldn't stop feeling sick. I knew what was going on. I just didn't want to admit it to myself.

I picked Lucy up and lay her on the bed beside Chris. He was doing the same as six days ago. He was just sleeping, so I read *Sleeping Beauty* to Lucy each night before she went to bed and she kissed her daddy goodnight. I secretly hoped he wake up, but he didn't.

"You want to cuddle Daddy before you sleep, beautiful?" I asked her, Lucy rolled to her tummy and tried to push herself up. rocking back and forth she spoke a blubbering ramble of words that didn't make sense.

I smiled, and then my heart almost stopped.

"Da-Da!" Lucy's little voice spoke.

Clear as day, she said 'Dad.' I had tears as she kept repeating herself over and over. "Chris, do you hear this?" I said getting my phone from my bag and filming her for him to watch later.

"Da-Da! Da-Da!" she squealed excitedly. I smiled watching her.

When she went to reach for a tube coming from his arm, I stood up and lifted her off him. Her mouth then turned to my breasts and opened wide. I had to laugh. She loved her milk.

I changed her into a pink pyjama suit and then fed her until she passed out. Her little snores told me she was out like a light for the rest of the night. I laid her in the bassinet of the pram and covered her with a warm blanket. She was sleeping much better lately. Seldom waking until the morning.

"Good night, princess," I whispered quietly and kissed her cheek.

Lucy's long black lashes fanned down her cheeks. She was so like Chris when she slept. I couldn't wait until she was able to crawl around, and then walk. It was something I looked forward to.

I walked over to Chris and pulled his covers back. Carefully, I lay down beside him and draped my arm over his chest, feeling the outline of his hard torso. I kissed his cheek and slowly stopped fighting the sleep that I desperately needed.

I needed him to wake up, to kiss me, and to just tell me that he loved me. I loved hearing that; the way he looked at me when he said it always showed me just how much he loved me. I could feel it. Every time he told me, I felt it.

I loved him more than anything.

To me, the fights we had were in the past. I didn't care about him leaving me anymore. I knew what I wanted, and that was for him to wake up and be here with me. With us.

I needed Chris to wake up. I needed him to know I was more than committed to him. To our marriage and relationship. I wanted to make it all better again. I knew I wasn't the best wife I should have been. I was going to try harder, and do more for him. I didn't blame him anymore. He was forgiven. Although, it may not be completely forgotten, I was going to try and forget it.

I wanted new memories with him.

My dreams became vivid again. This was the only time I got to pretend Chris was awake. It seemed so real. His hands were running over my body, holding me closer as he kissed the top of my forehead. I could feel his warm lips against my skin. His long fingers ran through my hair, tugging the way he did when he woke up and wanted me to wake.

I smiled, enjoying the warmth of his body. My hand ran up his chest, and my leg was hitched over his groin. I never wanted to wake up from this dream. I wanted to feel this moment forever until he woke up.

But I soon did; my eyes wanted to stay closed, but they couldn't. I knew it was dark and that I hadn't slept for too long.

My eyes fluttered open, feeling a hand over my stomach as his husky sleep-laced voice spoke. "You're pregnant."

I shot my eyes back open. I couldn't believe it. "Chris?" I whispered.

He nodded, giving me a sleepy, tired smile. "I'm here, baby. You were crying."

"Chris, you're awake," I said, realising that I was indeed crying.

He ran his hand to the curve of my neck and pushed his mouth to mine, kissing me so hard, as if it was going to be our last kiss ever. The dryness of his mouth against mine didn't bother me. I didn't care about anything other than him being awake and here.

I pulled back when I realised what he had mentioned before. "I love you, Chris," I smiled, so happy.

He smiled back. "Not as much as I love you." His eyes widened. "Lucy? Is she okay? And Adam?"

"They're both fine. Both are doing okay. Adam left a few days ago, but Lucy and I have been staying here," I said, laying my head on the pillow and smiling. "I was so scared. I should call a nurse and let them come to look you over."

Chris shook his head. "No, don't. I just want to look into your eyes. Tell me you're pregnant again, Char," he said, rubbing my stomach again softly.

I wasn't sure if they were mine or his, the salty tears hit my lips as I kissed him nodding. "I am. I had a blood test taken yesterday here. I'm six weeks, so it's still early."

He held me closer. "Christ, baby. Oh, fuck, I am so happy."

I started crying. It wasn't from a fear of being pregnant. It was relief. It was a nervous excitement that I could finally let it out. I had tried to just block it out and not think about the baby growing inside my stomach. I didn't want to have another baby if Chris couldn't be here with me.

"Baby, I'm sorry. I know it's not what we planned, and Lucy's still young," Chris started.

I shook my head. "No, it's not that. I'm just happy you're awake, Chris. I'm happy we're pregnant again."

"I promise I'm going to be here for you, baby." It then came through his eyes as he realised what he hadn't asked. "The surgery?"

I smiled again, stroking his cheek as I leaned closer and said, "It was a success."

CHAPTER TWENTY-FOUR

I was so nervous.

Nervous didn't even describe what I felt right now. I was sick to my stomach with giddy excitement. I married the love of my life today.

He was dashing as he stood in front of me, his arms wrapped around me possessively as we danced our first dance together.

I smiled up at him, unable to hide it. "I love you," I said happily.

He grinned back. "I love you too Mrs. Rivers. Damn, you look so beautiful right now. You took my breath away when I first saw you walking down the aisle."

"I am so in love with you. I want it to be like this forever, this perfect moment where it's just us,"

"And a room full of people watching us?" he added.

I laughed, gripping his tux jacket firmly. "Can we skip to our honeymoon?"

"If you want to." He winked. "I am going to fuck you crazy on the plane."

I giggled. We were taking his dad's private plane to wherever Chris was taking me. I had no idea. This was Chris's surprise for me. Somewhere where I wouldn't have a clue. But apparently, I would love it.

Chris spun me around, the music coming to an end. My feet were killing me, and my dress was a little too tight after eating so much. I loved it though.

I pulled Chris over to me off the dance floor and back to our table. "You should give me a clue as to where we're going. I haven't even packed anything."

"You won't need to wear much." He winked.

I laughed. I married a dirty man with sexy wicked and naughty thoughts.

Chris picked up his scotch and took a mouthful. He licked his lips and leant back in the chair. "We can leave in around an hour unless you want to stay the night here and leave in the morning. It's up to you."

"How long does it take to get where we're going?" I asked, curious as I tried to think where he was taking me.

"Twelve hours or so. You do know you're not sleeping tonight, Charlotte," he said, reaching over and stroking my cheek.

I looked at him, cocking my brow as I scoffed. "Yeah, because you can have sex for that long."

"Don't laugh, baby. You're ovulating, and I plan on taking full advantage of you tonight and tomorrow." His hand cupped my chin, thumb caressing me as he leaned closer and kissed me.

I was definitely at the peak of ovulation, and Chris and I were excited to be trying to make a baby, not that we hadn't been trying every other day. I smiled at him. I loved that he was so excited to try and have us pregnant.

Tonight was going to be a night I wouldn't forget. And I might not be able to walk much tomorrow.

I kissed him back, biting his lower lip. "I can't wait, Mr. Rivers. Today has been perfect. I am so happy right now, so happy that I got to find the man of my dreams and marry him in a beautiful place. I love that we're starting a family together and it just feels like a dream. I feel so lucky to have met you, Chris."

"I feel exactly the same, Char. You're everything I could have dreamt of and more."

*　　　*　　　*

I held Chris's hands as I helped him into our bed. After he woke, he stayed in the hospital for three more days before finally being able to come home today. I was so excited to have him here and happy that he is recovering. When he was told what had happened and how they had ignored the DNR due to my requests, he hadn't been as angry as I worried he would be.

He was grateful because it showed him just how fragile life is, and if they hadn't listened to me, then he wouldn't be here now.

He was under strict orders to take it easy.

That was something I was not going to risk. I was going to make sure Chris was relaxed, calm, and taken care of. Even if it meant me sleeping in another room with Lucy, so he didn't get interrupted through the night.

"Can I get you anything?" I asked him, pulling his sweats down, so he was just wearing a pair of boxers. I moved up and began to unbutton his shirt. My eyes went to his stomach with the bandage padding. I had to change that each morning and night to keep the incision clean and germ-free.

Chris yawned. "I'm good. Thanks, baby."

I felt bad for him. I knew me doing everything for him bothered him a little. He didn't like feeling helpless.

"Are you hungry? Thirsty?" I wanted to make sure he had everything he needed.

"Come here," he said, holding his hand out. "I just want you to kiss me. That's all I need."

I smiled, feeling my heart melt. "I can kiss you."

My lips pressed against his, slowly parting as he swept his tongue in my mouth and kissed me. This, I let him take charge of. I didn't want to lean into him in case I hurt him. Chris had other ideas though, pulling me close and holding my cheeks with his firm grip.

He pulled me up, my thighs on either side of his lap as I straddled him. I could feel him hard and push against me. I let out a low moan as he flexed his hips upright and that's when I pulled away, breaking our kiss.

"We can't," I said sitting back. He gave me a sad pout. I felt myself caving, but I had to remain strong because I knew if he would, he'd have me naked and fucking him slowly. "Chris, no."

"Why not?" He put on a charming grin.

"You just had surgery and need to keep your heart rate down. Please don't make me feel bad. I just want you to get better and then we can have lots of sex."

He chuckled, his hands then went down my hips, lifting my top up just above my belly button and placing his hands on my flat stomach. "I can't believe we're having another baby. Don't overdo it, Char. You need to rest as well and take care of our baby while he or she grows."

"I know. Don't worry about me though. I will take it easy and slow down," I assured him. "I should go find Lucy and get her fed." I then looked at him, my head tilted to the side. "You said I was pregnant in the hospital as soon as you woke up. How did you know that?" I asked curiously.

He pulled my top down and held my hands. "You kept throwing up before my surgery and crying as well. It was just like when you were pregnant with Lucy. I didn't think anything of it until I looked at you before they took me in. I knew then. You had that look about you, and your boobs looked bigger."

"Oh, so my boobs gave it away?" I laughed kissing him.

He nodded. "I love you, so when do I get to hear my girl say, Dad?"

Chris hadn't heard her say dad yet, due to she wouldn't say it again. I showed him the clip, but it wasn't the same. I wanted him to hear the words come from her mouth.

"Soon, I hope. You need to take your pills and have a rest, baby." I started getting off him until he stopped me.

He just stared at me, a blank look on his face before he spoke, "I can't thank you enough for what you've done for me,

231

Char. Sticking around and taking care of me like this. This year's been tough, but I'm going to make it up to you. You deserve everything."

"All I need is for you to get better. When you didn't wake up, all I thought about was what if you never woke again? What if I never got to talk to you ever again? Or what if I never feel your kiss again? I know this year was tough on us, but we learned a lot too. We got through it, Chris. I know we can get through anything that comes our way from now on." I leaned forward and rested my forehead on his.

We stayed like that for a moment, until we could hear everyone downstairs getting rowdy. I sighed. "I am not looking forward to this, and apparently, I'm not capable of taking care of you and our daughter at the same time."

"Don't tell them about the baby, not yet. It's still early," Chis said softly. "I just want it to be our secret for now. Something we can talk about when we're alone."

I agreed with him there. "I like that."

Thinking it would be easy with everyone around just proved how insane I was. Days later, it was chaos and doing my head in. Chris was snappy and becoming angrier when he wanted to do something, but his body just let him down.

I looked at Lucy and kissed her forehead. "Love you, bunny," I whispered and put her on the floor. She was crawling around, dragging her little legs over the ground more and more. Chris did love to sit and watch her.

He loved it even more so when she said 'Dad.' That happened every day. Still no sign of the word mum.

"Charlotte, go we will be fine. I promise," Mum said softly. I was tempted to take Lucy with me to my doctor's appointment, but our parents insisted she was okay here with them.

I walked over to my husband laying on the couch and bent down. "I'm leaving now, okay? I won't be long."

"Don't be." He sleepily smiled back. "We'll tell them after this. Okay, baby. Hurry back."

My appointment went well. I was now just under eight weeks pregnant, and our baby was growing well. I made sure to get a photo for Chris so he could see as well.

As I walked into the house, I heard loud yelling. "What the hell?" I muttered to myself. This couldn't be happening.

I came in to see my parents, Chris' parents, Samantha, Ness, and Adam all going at it. Chris must have gone back to bed.

"You don't know what he did!"

"Oh, to hell with it. I damn well do know. He's made up for all of that!"

"Fuck, stop bringing the past up. He's a good guy and treats Charlotte right. You need to get over it."

"He should be at home with his family."

"She's struggling to look after him and their daughter. She needs us here."

My heart rate picked up as my eyes scanned the room to try and find my daughter. I dropped my bags on the floor when I saw her. My heart was now in my throat as I raced over.

"Oh, my god! Lucy, no!!" I screamed out loudly, trying to catch her before it was too late.

What followed was a sound that broke my heart; her screams or should I say high-pitched screaming squeals filled the room as she fell onto the fireplace. The heat of the glass burned her small body.

Everyone rushed over, trying to take her from me and telling me what needed to be done as I picked her up and raced into the bathroom. I was hysterically sobbing as I quickly stripped her off while the tub filled with cold water.

"What the fucking hell is going on down here!!" Chris's voice thundered, making Lucy scream more and me jump slightly.

No one answered.

"Charlotte." Chris walked in and looked at his daughter. "Christ, what the fuck happened!"

"She fell, Chris." I sobbed, "No one was watching her, and she . . ." I stopped, holding Lucy as she clung to me sobbing her dear little heart out. "Someone didn't put the safety stand over the fireplace, and it was on. She was standing up and slipped, falling on her arms." I cried.

Chris was down beside me in an instant, taking Lucy from me and putting her in the water. She screamed as her hands hit the coldness. "Shh, baby, it's okay."

"Should I call the hospital? I don't know what to do," I said through tears still.

"No, her hands aren't blistering. We will wrap them up and keep an eye on it. It doesn't look that bad. You got her before any real damage was done," he said, leaning over and kissing me as my husband took care of us.

When Lucy finally settled and was fast asleep after having a dose of Panadol, I found it extremely hard to take my eyes off her. Chris had to pull me from her room.

"How was your appointment?" he asked.

I forced a smile, "The baby is good. Just one and growing good. I'm so sick to think about what happened, Chris. They were all yelling and fighting. It was like a pack of animals having at it with each other.

He nodded, agreeing. "I could hear them. I'm going to end up back in that hospital if they don't leave. It's too much stress that neither of us needs."

Chris led me down to the kitchen where everyone was waiting.

His mum was the first to speak up. "How is she? God, we just feel awful for what happened."

"Good, so you should," I snapped. "I can't trust you around my daughter, neither of you was paying attention to her!"

"Charlotte," Mum started, and Chris put her in her place once and for all.

He held his hand up, silencing her. "Get out. I mean it. I can't listen to you for another damn second. I swear to God, I am on the verge of throwing you all out on your damn pathetic arses! Never in my life have I heard a woman bitch and moan so much. You can't come in here and expect to run this place as if it's your own goddamn house."

"Chris," my father warned. "Enough."

"No, it's not fucking enough. For months, I have listened to you and her go on and on about what happened. Yes, it happened. I admitted that I screwed up, but Charlotte forgave me. She took me back, and now we've moved on. The last thing she needs is stress. She's bloody pregnant again, and I swear if anything happens to this child, I will be out for blood. I am done and over the drama," he roared; his voice was so loud. I had never seen Chris this angry in my life. His hands were white from clenching his fists together.

"Pregnant?" Samantha and Ness gasped.

"Chris, you need to sit down and take it easy brother," Adam said, breaking everyone's silence.

Chris shook his head, finally speaking calmly. "I need everyone out of our house. You've proven you're all too childish to take care of our daughter. She could have been seriously hurt."

"And we've apologised," my mum said.

"So have I," he sarcastically retorted back. "Still not good enough, is it?!"

Judging by the look across her face, she knew he was right.

EPILOGUE

After a struggling five years, we could gladly say Chris' health was back on track. So much had happened, much more than we ever anticipated. Neither of us was prepared for a lot of the things to come. Somehow, we got through them with each other's help.

Adam and Ness finally got married. They ended up having a three-year-old son, Harvey, who was just like Adam—quiet but knew how to throw a tantrum. It was exciting that my brother got to experience what Chris and I had. Although they both say one is far too much for them, I think they'll have more.

My parents decided Chris wasn't so bad after all and let him off the hook. They didn't come around a lot, preferring to travel and live the senior's life of touring and exploring with their campervan. I did miss them, but it was what they needed. They were too in my head, suffocating me when they stayed for more than a week. After Chris told them all to grow up and move on from the past, it was never mentioned again.

Chris' father had passed away, three months after his surgery. That devastated him; all of us were shattered. He dropped dead from a heart attack just after a family dinner at Chris' parents' house. That showed us all, just how precious life is. Nothing could have prepared us for that shock. Chris still struggles with it daily, and his kept herself busy with helping us out when she could. Samantha was great too; she loved babysitting.

Lucy was already walking and talking; a high-energy ball of fun. There was not a day where she would just sit still and play quietly. I was on my toes, running after her and trying to keep the little miss occupied. Chris was great with her; he was a fantastic father. I couldn't be prouder of him.

He and Adam both quit the firm and bought a business closer to home. They're now both working together with their own firm, and business has been better than ever. Funny how many clients came to them after they quit the big company.

It was a quiet summer. Chris and I had renovated the little cabin we bought when we split up for that short time. It felt like a lifetime ago. Speaking of which, the day I finally came face to face with Katie was a memory I will happily remember.

Chris and I came out of the movie theatre from one of our date nights that we went on each week. Katie was standing on the side of the footpath, looking absolutely stunned to see us both. I didn't speak to her. I let my hand do the talking and smacked her good and hard. The bitch didn't know what hit her.

I walked out of the kitchen and onto the deck, looking over at my husband who lazily lay in the hammock with our five-week-old son, Arlo, fast asleep against his chest. I leaned forward and kissed his small head and then kissed my husband on the lips.

Chris's eyes fluttered open and he smiled, reaching up and stroking my cheek. "I fell asleep?"

"You did. Are you sleepy?" I asked, keeping my voice soft.

Chris looked down at Arlo, then back towards me. "He's a night owl. The others slept all night but not him. I feel so old."

I laughed softly. "You're not old, and he knows it's Mum and Dad time when the kids go to bed. He's making sure you don't get to touch his mummy."

"I'll touch his mother however I want. She is mine." He winked. There was a dominance coming through his voice that sent a shiver throughout my body.

After all this time, he still drove me insane. I ran my hand over his board shorts and cupped his cock, pushing down and feeling him harden with a groan. He flexed upright, and I bit my lip. "Tonight, you're mine. As soon as Arlo's down, so am I."

"Devil woman," he muttered as I walked away and back inside to check on the others.

Our daughter, Lucy, was sitting up on the couch with her little brother Finn, and sister Billie. The twins who are now three were a massive surprise to us. The entire time we had been told we were only expecting one baby—another girl. But during the final scan, baby number two made an appearance and sent us into a panic. Chris was more than excited. He couldn't wait to go out and buy things for a boy. His first son.

We had four children—two boys and two girls. Just like we always planned on having. We had our perfect little family. We were so convinced we'd never fall pregnant again after the twins, but Chis wanted to give it a shot. I didn't hesitate to agree with him. Three months later, I was knocked up and cooking a baby. Chris' sperm was well and truly just as powerful as before the surgery.

He didn't need to worry about being infertile. I was eager for another child, just as much as he was.

"Mum, I'm hungry," Lucy stated. She was exactly like Chris.

I smiled. "Good thing it's time for dinner. Let's get up at the table, and I'll bring your food over."

Three of my children sat up and waited for dinner to be brought over. I admit, as stressful as they can be, they're the love of my lives.

"Hun?" Chris called out. "Can you take him while I get up?"

I walked out and lifted up Arlo; he was wide awake, just looking around and being placid which was rare. "Come eat, handsome." I smiled.

"I plan to," he said with a wink. "All night long I will eat well."

"Chris, god, you're insatiable." I sighed.

A throaty chuckle followed me inside, his hand giving my ass a slap. "Only for you, baby. Indeed I am."

The kids sat at the table, all eating their chicken and chattering loudly about who was swimming in the pool first and who got to be on Dad's shoulders. I sat there quietly, watching them all until Finn began to cry and cover his face with his tiny hands.

"Don't worry, Finn. You'll get to come in. Boys need to check the water first." Chris reached over and rubbed his mop of black hair. All our children had Chris's dark hair and big blue eyes. Poor me didn't get much of a look in.

Finn grinned and sat up straighter. Lucy laughed at him. "Baby," she teased.

"Am not. I am big and strong like Daddy!" he said back, looking at her and frowning.

Billie decided to get in on the fight and giggled. "I'm stronger."

"No, me!" Lucy laughed.

"I think you three need to finish eating, then its bath and bed," Chris warned, his voice coming out sterner.

Of course, all kids listened to their daddy and ate the rest of their dinner. When Arlo decided to cry, that was my cue to go and get him ready for his bed. Just once, I wished he would sleep more than two hours at a time before waking up for his next feed.

I tucked him up in his cot and kissed his plump lips. Turning his monitor on, I walked out of the room and headed to the other room where Lucy, Finn, and Billie slept. All three of them seemed to sleep better in the same room here. At least we knew they wouldn't wake up fighting like at home.

Chris was reading them a story, one each they chose, and he would sit down every night and read to them. No matter how long the book was, he'd read the whole thing.

"Good night," I whispered, tucking Lucy in who had passed out with her little bunny rabbit. I then went to the next two and kissed them both.

I felt Chris's hand slide around my waist, and I melted into him. "I could sit and stare at them for hours. All night, if possible," he whispered softly.

"Me too. They're perfect," I said quietly.

Chris ran his hands up and down my arms, his lips kissing the back of my head. "Would you like a bath? Since we have around an hour and forty minutes before Arlo wakes up."

I smiled and turned my head back, looking up at him and smiling. "I'd love a bath with you, baby."

Chris had spun me around, lifted me up, and carried me bridal style down to our bedroom and into the ensuite. Sitting me on the bench, he kissed my cheek and began to run us a bath, filling it with bubbles and bath salts.

"How are you feeling today?" he asked, massaging my shoulders softly.

I let out an involuntary moan and sunk further down into the water. "I'm good. Tired but happy. What about you?"

"I'm more than happy. I have everything I ever wanted. You, healthy children, and my health."

I thought about him being sick and when I worried he wasn't going to make it. I ran my fingers up to where he lay and held onto his hands. "You're not going anywhere, Chris. No one will take you from me. You're healthier than ever, and you've got four little children who adore you."

"No one will take me anywhere, baby. I'm here to stay with you and our children. Life's pretty damn good at the moment. I feel happy and complete," he said and resumed rubbing my shoulders.

His lips slowly began to kiss back up my stomach, stopping and starting again as he teased me. A hot tongue burned its trail path as he licked each breast. Sinking deep inside me, I couldn't stop the loud moan. I felt the hottest desire for him right now.

Our bodies moved together, grinding into one another's as our lips barely stopped kissing. Both moaning, grunting, and gasping as each stroke took them to new heights. My hands clawed at his back, gripping his ass hard as I reached my climax, shuddering underneath his sweaty body. I let the pleasure overtake me and melted into it.

Chris groaned and thrust, pumping deeper and faster as he neared his own orgasm. "Char, fuck. You feel so good. I'm not going to last much longer, baby."

I moaned. "Get off me then. I want to ride you."

He pulled my body as he rolled. I cried out loudly as I began to move up and down, feeling him deeper as I rocked up and down, back and forth. Chris latched onto my breast, licking and sucking. He wasn't worried about my breast milk. He moved his hands and gripped my ass tightly, pushing a finger into my ass, thrusting it in and out, causing me to explode again.

This man was insane, absolutely sex-crazed, and mine.

"Oh, god. I'm cumming so good." I could barely see straight as he rolled us again, plunging into me from behind.

His fingers were digging in as I felt him get harder. *The sex drive of this man!* I couldn't keep up. In no way did I think we would still be having sex like this after having our fourth child. I wasn't complaining though. I loved every second of it.

Chris pulled out. "On your back, sweetheart. I want to finish making love to you."

How could I refuse that?

I rolled over, completely naked and sweating, staring up at Chris. Smiling as he knelt in front of me and slowly lowered down. I ran my hands up his chest and wrapped them around his neck, pulling him closer.

"Marry me?" I whispered. "Marry me again, with our children and family. I want to marry you again, Chris. You make me so happy. I want to renew our vows after all that we've been through. I've forgiven and forgotten all the bad times we had. Us—now, this is what it's all about. Our love is stronger than ever. So Chris, will you marry me?"

He looked at me, a smile forming further over his handsome face, and saying the word that I said six years ago: "Yes."

The End

ACKNOWLEDGEMENTS

My loyal readers – Thank you so much. Without you and all of your support, this wouldn't be possible still. I am so grateful for the love and support you constantly give me that pushes me to be the best writer and storyteller that I can be.

To Winnie, and the wonderful editing team I have. You are amazing, and I am so grateful that you gave me patience and understanding, and let me tell my stories the way I dream them to be. From the cover, to the end of the book . . . I am extremely lucky to have you on my team.

My family and close friends. You know who you are. Thank you for always being there and cheering me on. Thank you for supporting me when I'm not sure of myself. Thanks for pushing me to be the best that I can be.

Dad – You mean the world to me. I love you.

Sweetly, Mel xx

Do you like romance stories?
Here are samples of other stories
you might enjoy!

WOLF
IN THE NIGHT
BOOK ONE OF WOLF IN THE NIGHT SERIES

MELISSA BENDER

PROLOGUE

ELLE

"I can't do this anymore. I'm sick of the damn secrets, Justin!" I yelled as a strangled sob escaped my throat.

My knees buckled underneath me, and I bent forward, gripping the counter to steady myself while the man in front of me just stood there and said nothing. He didn't try to catch me; he didn't do a single thing except damn well lie to me, probably for the last five years.

"Elle," he started, but he sighed and bowed his head. "I'm sorry. I don't know what you think you saw, but you're wrong."

I wiped my cheeks with the palms of my hands and glared at him. "Wrong my ass!" I hissed and stood on my feet, marching straight past him and into his office where his laptop was. I was sure of what I saw, and I knew I wasn't wrong at all. My own damn eyes have seen it.

"What the hell do you think you're doing in here? This is my office, Elle. Get the fuck out!" he shouted as he came running behind me, but I ignored him.

I clicked through the files and went through all of them, but there was nothing. He had deleted them.

I spun around and narrowed my green eyes at his dark brown ones, his hand running up and scratching his chin that was covered with a black week-long stubble. I couldn't believe he did this to me—to us.

"Tell me the truth. Who is she? Who is that child?" I asked, my voice trembling as much as I tried to fight it off.

I didn't want to cry. I was so sick of crying this week. I was sick of feeling like this. I hated feeling so betrayed by him.

He shook his head and slammed the laptop screen down hard. "I don't know where your accusations are coming from, and I don't know about any woman or child. Maybe you have seen something from the internet and thought it was saved on here. You just proved your point that there was nothing; it's clean."

My fists curled into hard balls, and all I wanted to do was punch him hard where it would really hurt. "It's clean because you deleted it. You fucking erased it all. I know what I have seen. There were at least twenty photos of them! Why are you denying this?" I shouted so loud that my throat hurt, swallowing hard as I blinked more tears back.

I tried to move away but he grabbed my shoulders. I ignored the burn from his grip as he kept me in place and stared down at me. His breathing hardened and his nostrils flared as he shut his eyes for a moment before opening them slowly, trying to calm himself down. "Elle, you need to calm down. You're getting worked up over nothing."

I was bewildered. *How could he say something like that to me?* "What did you just say to me?" I asked quietly, keeping my voice surprisingly steady.

He was holding me in place forcefully. "Settle down, or I'll kick you out of my house."

My eyes widened in shock. *How dare he threaten me with that?* I'd only just moved in with him not even a month ago. If that's how he wanted to play, then fine. Fucking fine!

"I'm done, Justin. I can't do this shit anymore. I'll leave tomorrow if you want me out." I pushed him off me with all my strength as he tried to block my way and headed for the spare room. He could have our room for all I care. I just didn't want to be anywhere near him tonight, not until I figured things out.

I couldn't hear any noise from him, but I knew he was still in the house, probably drinking some scotch, watching a game, or talking to his other woman. Sleep slowly started to come over me after hours of crying and thinking about the woman and the child in the photos. Soon, I was in a deep slumber, dreaming of that little boy who looked no more than five years old.

When I woke up, I felt arms around my waist, a hard and warm body pressed to my back, and light kisses being placed against the nape of my neck. I had no idea when Justin had even come in here, but I didn't care. I was still leaving him.

"Elle, let me take you out for lunch, and I promise I'll explain everything. Please, baby, don't go." His quiet voice was laced with sleepiness and desperation.

I let out a yawn and slowly turned around in the bed, looking into the eyes of the man I once trusted with everything. He knew my entire past as well as my deepest and darkest secrets. The things we had done together were a hidden part of us, and now this. *How could he not want to open up to me like I did to him?*

I had told him about my childhood. He had been there for me when my mother passed away few months ago. He helped me when my father demanded that I move in with him and his new wife. My dad was an abusive drunk who left my mum when I was four to be with other women. My three older brothers protected me with their life. Every boy that came near me was warned several times that if they hurt me in any way, my brothers would come after them. Justin was the only guy who wasn't worried. Sure, he was older than me; he was thirty-six, and I was twenty-two, but the age didn't seem important. We had only officially started dating three months ago. He didn't want to tell everyone because of our age difference, even though we've known and been together for years—three years.

"Elle?" he spoke again. I had been too upset to respond.

I nodded, reluctantly agreeing to his offer, mostly to get him off my case. But I was willing to give him the chance to explain things. "Fine."

Five hours later, I wanted to kick my heels off and soak in the tub, but I wasn't even halfway through my day. I had stacks of paperwork to arrange and appointments scheduled for people to come and go through rental properties. I spun around in my leather swivel chair and looked out the large floor to the ceiling window, enjoying the view of the mountains half covered in snow. It was so beautiful to look at—so peaceful and relaxing after a stressful evening.

I snapped a picture and sent it to my best friend who I'd never actually met, but she was already like sister to me. She was my rock through this. I loved that she never judged me for any of the things I had done. She was just as wild and crazy as I was at times.

She replied to me: *'OMG so pretty!'* and we texted each other for a few minutes until I told her I had to go. I told her about my fight with Justin, and she threatened to fly over and slap him for me if he hurts me. I knew she would too.

My heart was hammering, and sickness filled me as I looked up when I walked out onto the sunny and busy street. I immediately spotted Justin standing outside, looking handsome in his business suit. I always loved seeing him dressed like that with his hair perfectly tossed up and done. He looked really sexy.

A smile was plastered on his face, but something felt off. He seemed nervous, and that scared me a little. Justin never got nervous over anything. He was mister cool, calm, and collected most of the time.

"Hi," I said quietly. "Where do you want to grab lunch?" I asked him. He usually decided where we went to eat, and I liked it that way. I was too precise at times, and food wasn't an easy choice for me. I normally changed my mind a lot with ordering.

"Let's go to that place you like, baby." He reached out casually and held my hand, leading me down through the crowd of people and towards the small café I loved. Justin ordered lunch for both of us—a tossed salad with an iced tea—and grabbed us a table outside the café to watch the lunch hour rush pass us by.

"Elle, I have something for you," he spoke and pulled something from his bag beside him. I hadn't even noticed he was carrying it with him. "Open it." He urged with a nervous smile.

I frowned when he passed over a yellow envelope and set it down in front of me. "What's this?" I asked, confused, as I slowly pulled out the thick paperwork.

"It's for you. The house I bought years ago is now yours. I want to have it in your name, and I want to prove I'm serious about us, Elle," he spoke, now looking confident.

I shook my head. I wasn't expecting this at all. "I don't get it. Why?"

He shrugged. "You're not walking out on me...You're the other woman."

His words hit me like a ton of bricks. I raised a brow and blinked before finding my next words. "Excuse me?!" I spoke a little louder, gaining some looks from an elder couple beside us. "What do you mean I'm the other woman?"

He shrugged again. "You know exactly what it means. You're the other woman, and that is all I'm going to tell you."

"What do you mean? You owe me an explanation, Justin. Who is that woman and the child? Is he yours?" I felt like a broken record on repeat. *Why couldn't he just answer my questions?*

"I don't owe you anything. You're getting the house, so smile and say thank you." I could tell I was starting to piss him off. The way his eyes darkened told me he wasn't in the mood to be pushed. I should have listened, but I didn't.

"How are you telling me that you're committed to me when you just dropped that on me? All you said was that I'm the other woman. I don't understand. I need answers. I needed them yesterday and today." I closed my eyes, breathing in and out slowly to calm myself down before I continued speaking, "It's too late. I can't break anymore. I'm so broken that I feel nothing. I don't feel anything and can't comprehend any more of your pathetic bullshit."

Justin slammed his fist on the table which made me jump slightly. The cutlery rattled as he leaned closer over the table. His voice was low, and I knew he was being serious. "I tried to make you happy. I fucking tried everything, and it still wasn't good enough. You're not leaving me. I will be the one to walk out of this so-called relationship. I'm done trying to fix you. I'm done trying to save your fucked up miserable self."

My eyes were slowly filled with tears. I couldn't eat, and Justin didn't look in the mood for his meal either, but I was not going to sit here and let his words stew over and over in my mind. I grabbed my handbag and the envelope before standing up. Justin's eyes widened as I slap him hard across the face, the noise causing more people to look at us. I couldn't care that we were in a public place; he just humiliated me. I had been fooled by his charming ways and seductive words. And for what?

Lies and broken promises.

"Go screw yourself in hell!" I spoke each word bitterly, letting him know how pissed I was. I turned and made my way back to the office as tears slid down my cheeks like a raging river.

I couldn't believe he had done this to me. I was numb. I was embarrassed. I was hurt.

I was shattered and heartbroken.

The rest of my work day was a daze; I couldn't focus. I knew I would break down if I keep thinking about what Justin had said to me. I could do something crazy, and I knew my best friend would fly over and kick my ass if I did. She told me she would do so. I believed her without doubt. I knew she would drop everything and come to me.

But my shock only got worse when I came home. The house was quiet. A strange feeling swept through my body as I walked into the kitchen and set my bag on the black marble counter top. Slipping my heels off and walking towards the bedroom we shared, I pushed the door open and held a hand to my mouth as the room was empty. The next place I checked was his office, and it was empty as well. Everything was gone.

He left me. He really left me.

I was now alone and had no idea what to do. *How could I face my family and tell my brothers that I was now single? That the man they accepted was a fake, a fraud, and a liar?*

How could have I been so stupid? How could have I ignored the signs of this heartbreaking and sickening betrayal? The late-night works and the change in his behavior... I thought everything was just fine. Our sex life was more than amazing. Gosh, we were far from lacking there. So how could have I been so blind as to see that he had a family?!

I sat on the couch and laid down, letting more tears fall. I couldn't even cry loudly. I fell asleep, crying silently. When I woke up, I was hoping it was all a dream, but the memories of yesterday came back.

I was a mess; I wanted to feel something, to believe that this was all a sick joke, but deep down, I knew it wasn't. I knew he was serious, and now, this house he had bought was mine. I didn't even know if I was going to stay here. I needed to leave, escape, and get away. Antarctica seemed all right. I loved the cold, and penguins looked friendly enough, but that wouldn't help. They'd all probably leave me too.

How did my life get like this when Justin had only asked me to marry him two weeks ago? How did this happen? He wanted to have babies soon. He wanted me to be his wife; he asked me that during sex. Well, no. He told me that he was going to marry me within the week as he screwed me from behind, his hand roughly grasping my breasts. It was his favourite position, not mine.

But then other things happened, and he made stupid decisions, not thinking about it thoroughly. That all led to me putting our marriage on hold. I couldn't marry him when he was being so thoughtless at times, making me cry far too often.

My stomach was churning at the thought of what would have happened if I had ended up marrying him last week and found the photos then. *Would he have divorced me?*

This was all too much. I needed to get out of here and start over. I couldn't face anyone, especially him again.

I stood up, went into my bedroom, and grabbed a suitcase, packing everything up that I needed to start a new life—mainly shoes and clothes. It wasn't much, but it would do me good until I got settled elsewhere. I couldn't stay in a house that had too many memories, especially bad ones.

I made my way outside the house and threw the suitcase into the back of my BMW before sitting in the driver's seat. I put my shades on, cranked the tune up, and started driving. I wasn't going to cry anymore. I drove past a couple sitting at the bus station, and my heart was aching at how happy they looked. If only they knew how crushed one of them would be years later. Love is a waste of time, and I wasn't giving anyone the chance to get close to my heart again.

I had no idea where I was heading, but I kept on driving. When I run out of gas, I would go to the nearest inn and make that place my home for a while. Hopefully, it would be somewhere freezing cold. I hated the heat. I hated it greatly, just like how I hated Justin right now.

My eyes drifted out at the sunny sky. Slowly, my eyes brimmed with tears as much as I didn't want to cry for him anymore.

I had been driving for most of the day, getting tired and ignoring the calls on my phone as I pulled into a small town. Of all the places, it was just my luck that I ended up here. I was a little scared at how empty it looked after 5 pm. I parked my car in front of a hotel and went inside, booking myself a room. The male concierge looked at me intently but didn't say much as he slid the room key over.

I needed to find a decent home to live in—a cheap place to rent—as soon as I could, until I figured out what my next move would be. *How I was going to start over when I knew no one?* I didn't even have any references for the real estate. I'd never lived anywhere other than home and with Justin.

Just thinking about him made me grind my teeth together.

I also have to call my boss, Timothy, and inform him that I needed to take some time off. He and I got along like great friends, often going out for dinner together on a Thursday evening. He was a charming older man but he had never been married. Not a lady's man though. He would always tell me about finding the perfect life partner; how you would know if you're meant to be with someone just by looking into their eyes. He hadn't found that someone yet, but still hadn't given up hope.

I dialed his number, and he picked up. *"Hello? Emmanuelle, is that you?"* he asked, always so caring.

I smiled. "Yes, it's me. I'm sorry to do this, but I need to take a break."

"Don't worry your pretty head, sweetheart. Your brother has already called me. I'll tell you now, young woman. If I ever see that idiotic ex of yours, there will be words exchanged," he said in a stern voice. I could picture him pushing a pencil into a sharpener as we spoke. Although Tim wasn't much of a fighter, he knew how to cut someone deep with his words.

Ending the call after listening to him ramble on and on about what a waste of space Justin was, I started heading to the bar across the road. A strong cocktail would go down nicely with this horrid heat. My body began to react in a way I'd never felt before as I walked into the bar, noticing all the men looking at me.

Weirdly, I was drawn to the man at the end of the bar.

*   *   *

JUDD

Here I was, sitting at the bar and having a few drinks with the pack before I headed home when a woman walked in. I saw her from the corner of my eye and turned my head to get a better look.

Starting from her heels, I scanned up, taking in every inch of her beauty. She was wearing a pair of black heels with red soles. Her legs were tanned and seemed to go on forever as they went up to a pair of navy shorts. My eyes then went further up, looking at the white tank top that showed off her perfect perky breasts.

I wanted to smirk and tell the woman to head on home, back to the city where she belonged. This was no place for a woman like her. Human of all things. But my pants started getting tighter; the throbbing getting worse the closer she got to the bar. There was something about her—something different.

She walked up and sat on the stool beside me. My beta gave me a look, and I smirked, telling him to say nothing with just a look of my eye. The woman ordered a cosmos from him— whatever the hell that was—and Ty nearly passed out from confusion. The woman blushed a cute pink and mumbled something under her breath, changing the order to a corona and lime.

I was trying to ignore her, but I'm a gentleman at heart. And well, it's not every day you see a woman this beautiful walking into this run-down bar—a place where we had our pack meetings. No stranger dared to come in, and it was obvious she'd pissed a few of the boys off. Women weren't allowed in here. This was the place where we came after a hard day's work out before heading in for the night.

The woman finished her drink, and I decided to speak up. The bar was completely silent. The others were waiting to see if I'd kick her out, warn her off, or threaten to kill her, but I had no plans of doing that. "Another?" I asked, glancing at the men who resumed their talk to avoid their alpha's glare.

She just looked at me, unsure as to whether I spoke or not. She nodded, licking her plump red lips as she looked somewhat nervous. I ordered another one and she finally spoke, her voice hitting me right in the heart. "So, cowhand. What's your name?"

I was never a man for small talk, but she was obviously passing though, so it didn't bother me too much. The cowhand reference had me smiling. If only she knew what I really was, or that she walked into a bar full of wolves. I decided to answer her after she stared, waiting for me to speak. "Judd, and you?"

"Nice to meet you, Judd. I'm Emmanuelle, but that's a mouthful, so Elle would be fine." She blushed again, and I frowned, wondering why she would be nervous. My eyes scanned for a ring or some sign she was taken—she'd have to be. No way was a woman like her single. "So, Judd. What is it that you do around here besides drink alone in a bar full of men?"

I fought the urge to laugh, giving her a simpler answer. "I work on a ranch. I have horses, cattle—" She cut me off before I could continue.

"You ride horses?" She looked at me excitedly, her eyes sparkling in delight.

I chuckled lightly. "I do, indeed, daily."

"Well then, a stranger who rides a horse is something I didn't expect to meet in the middle of god knows where I am. I think I took a wrong turn somewhere." She giggled lightly and smiled back at me.

The way she laughed was different. I could see a sadness masked behind her eyes. She was covering something up. "Tell me, Elle. Why are you driving around by yourself? Don't you know how dangerous that is?"

Her smile dropped. "I'm not driving around. Well, I am, but I'm taking a road trip."

I was curiously amused by this. "A road trip? And where are you headed?" I asked, leaning closer to her as I motioned for Ty to grab me another jack and coke.

"I have no idea. I am sick of planning everything, so I'm living in the moment. All right by you?" she asked, cocking her brow up at me.

Ty let out a slight cough. He was warning me to quit while I was ahead. I didn't listen. "Hopefully you don't get lost then. Wouldn't want something to keep you from your safe travels, Elle," I said, looking at her as I blurted each word lower than the last. "Never know what's out there."

She was drawing me in, playing with a fire that she knew nothing about. "Why are there no women in this bar, Judd?" she asked, and I felt my cock leaking pre-cum just from the way she spoke my name.

"No idea, Elle." I smirked as I glanced around the room. "Never even noticed."

After a few more drinks and light conversation, she ran a hand through her long black hair, showing off a pair of diamond studs as she yawned. "I'm sorry, Judd. I think I'm going to head off. I've got an early start tomorrow morning before I head on my travels." She then opened her purse and started fumbling, as if she was looking for something. She placed her room key on the bar, and I could see the room number for the hotel across the road.

I touched her arm lightly as I realised she was looking for cash. My fingers felt like they're on fire just from that light skin contact. "It's on me. No need to pay." She looked down at my hand, quickly pulling away as she closed her bag up.

She picked up the key and smiled at me, which in turn caused me to notice her dark green eyes. "Well, ma'am, I hope you have a nice evening." I stood as she got up from the wooden stool.

"Thank you for the drinks, Judd." She smiled again before heading towards the door, and I stared at her ass that had me wanting to grip it firmly.

As she walked past everyone, the boys stopped talking again, staring at her. I let out a low growl that only the boys would hear, warning them to look away. Elle wasn't fresh meat for them to sink their claws into. I caught her turning and giving me a glance, as if she was trying to figure out what was going on.

"She's human," my beta said quietly, watching the door.

I gave him a dark look, frowning. "I don't give a fuck."

He shook his head. "You rarely give a fuck about anyone. Just leave her alone. She'll be gone tomorrow."

I let out another growl, clenching my jaw. "What the fuck do you think I'm going to do to her? Kill her for trespassing? She's a fucking human who has no idea she's in a town full of werewolves. Watch her tonight! That's an order, and nothing better happen to her!" I snapped, warning them all. My eyes darkened as I made it known to everyone in here. "No one touches the human!"

Ty looked at me, bowing his head in submission at my order. I knew what he was thinking though. The last thing I needed to do was get mixed up with an outsider, a pure human of all things. But what the fuck was I meant to do? Sit around and let her leave town? Never see her again? I had another drink, trying to distract myself, but my thoughts kept going back to Elle. The only thing I could think of was whether or not she meant for me to see her room number. I decided to take a chance and stood up, throwing down a twenty and heading out the door, not worrying about the change.

I went to the hotel across the bar and headed to the second floor. I walked down the hall, counting room numbers as I went. I got a few doors from her room and heard soft moans; the smell of her arousal was hard to miss. The closer I got to her room, the louder the moans became. As I walked up to her door, I noticed it was left ajar, and I could see what's inside. A low growl escaped my mouth, knowing that anyone could have walked in and seen what mine was this way.

When I peeked through the door, I saw her lying back on the double bed touching herself. One hand was on her breast while the other was in between her thighs. She moaned a little louder until I pushed the door open. It made her stop what she was doing and sit up, looking right at me with wide eyes. She bit down on her lip and stood up as she hurriedly reached for the silk robe lying over the chair, obviously embarrassed.

"Leave it," I spoke up, keeping my eyes on hers orbs.

She looked up; her eyes went down my body and stopped at my belt. I'm sure she could see the big bulge in my jeans. "Judd." She breathed out, her cheeks flushing as she looked away.

"Sit back on the bed and spread your legs," I replied, kicking the door shut with my foot before walking towards her.

She was the most beautiful woman I had ever seen with her fulsome breasts and curved hips. She was, in a word, pure perfection. She walked over to the bed and sat down on the edge, following my command.

The alcohol had gone to my head, and all rational thoughts left my mind. I shouldn't have done this, but I couldn't hold back. I needed to have her. I stripped my pants and underwear off, cock standing in attention as I dropped to my knees. I reached up and moved her hand out of the way as she tried to cover herself. She looked at me shyly with those come-fuck-me eyes, and I knew exactly what she wanted. It was what we both wanted.

I spread her thighs open and tasted what I had been craving all night—possibly all my life—for the first time, and it was like heaven. She flinched as my tongue licked down the inside of her thigh, teasing her until she grabbed the back of my head and pushed me into her smooth, bare pussy, silently begging for more.

I continued to worship her magnificent core and began tongue-fucking her. My hands roamed up her body until I found her breasts. I rubbed and pinched her nipples until they were at full attention. She was biting her lip to keep herself from being loud, so I took that as a challenge to make her scream. I found her clit and began circling it with light slow strokes.

She cried out loudly, and my cock jerked as she thrust upright and grinded into my face while she came, covering me with her glistening wetness. She tasted better than she looked, and I needed more.

Without giving her a chance to recover, I jumped up and scooted her further up on the bed. I flipped her on her stomach, grabbed her hips, and lifted her ass in the air. I guided the head of my cock up to her already soaking wet core and slowly eased in. I stopped just as the head of my cock was in and savoured her tightness, stretching and allowing me to enter.

The feeling around my cock was enough to almost make me cum. I had to stop and then start up again. Nice and slow, in and almost completely out before I slammed my cock back into her pussy, enjoying the way her tits bounced as I fucked her. Wanting to keep this going for a bit, I took up a nice steady pace of fucking that delicious pussy.

I reared back to get a good look at her ass as I pounded her, giving it a nice hard smack. She jumped and whimpered. A red hand print formed on her white skin and that just made me want to fuck her even harder. At this point, she was biting and moaning into the pillow. My balls smacked against her clit with every thrust in, sending shudders throughout her whole body each time.

After a few more minutes of me pounding her, I stopped and lay down on my back. She got up and straddled me, positioning herself on me and eased her pussy down onto my cock. Once buried inside her, she began to ride me. I played with her perfect breasts with my hands as she began to fuck me faster.

Her head was thrown back as her body was bouncing on top of me, and I began to thrust up to meet her. Wanting to taste her again, I sat up a little. I licked and kissed the underside of her left tit and worked my way up to her nipple, sucking it hard which caused her to cum again. With the feeling of her pussy tightening around my cock, I knew I was getting close to cumming myself.

I pulled her down to me, grabbed her hips hard, and began to thrust in and out of her with such force that made her bounce a little each time I did. She was moaning in my ear which made me fuck her harder and faster until I quickly pulled out. She then wrapped her hand around my cock and started jerking me. I grunted, as shots of fluid burst in between our bodies.

I ran my nose down to the side of her neck, and I fought control of letting my wolf take over, wanting to sink my teeth into her soft skin. Instead, I placed a soft, lingering kiss just below her ear and loosened my hold on her body.

She just looked at me and sat up, naked and covered in my cum. What a sight that was! She lay back on the white messed up sheets while I stood up and went into the small bathroom to grab us some towels. I cleaned myself and got dressed in silence. Elle just lay there on the bed with the blankets draped over her still bare body.

She looked up at me through those green orbs. It was obvious that she'd never done anything like this before. I never kissed her. If I did, she'd feel it too. Hell, she just had my cock inside her. Of course, she felt something.

"Elle," I said, not looking at her as I sat on the edge of the bed.

"Don't," was all she said. Her voice sounded as if she was seconds away from crying.

With that, I nodded, understanding that this was just a fuck. I stood up and walked to the door, not looking back as I knew I wouldn't be able leave if I did. I ignored the pain in my chest. I headed for my ute and hit the engine, putting all my focus on the events for tomorrow that was needed to be done. I just hoped the young wolves didn't go running and stir the bulls up again through the middle of the night.

I arrived home, and my boots hit the dusty gravel as I made my way towards my house. My mind kept going back to

Emmanuelle the entire drive. I tried to forget about her because at the end of the day, all I was to her was a stranger who rode a horse.

If only she knew, she was so much more to me than she could ever imagine.

She was my mate.

CHAPTER 1

ELLE

I barely slept a wink, and my mind was buzzing. *Did that really happen last night? Did I sleep with a stranger?*

The soreness in between my thighs told me yes, and it was completely amazing!

He was not the type of man I would ever go for. He was tall, so much taller than me. His arms were strong, and his chest was all muscle. His cock, oh my god. I don't think I had ever felt something so thick in my hand before. He took complete control of my body, and I followed.

I allowed him take me how he wanted, and for some reason, I had wanted him to cum deep inside me. But that would have been so careless though.

I needed to leave this town. I was slightly embarrassed that I had flashed him my room key number that way, giving him a hint to come around. The alcohol and the way Judd spoke and looked at me completely turned me on while I was sitting in that bar. Incredibly turned on and extremely wet, my god. Not even Justin had made me feel that way.

All I could think about was Judd's naked body and how muscled he was. I could still feel the slight burning tingles from his touch all over my soft flesh. I wanted that feeling again, especially when I orgasmed. My god, that was the most intense and most pleasurable experience of my life! Every other climax was put to shame.

Now, I was horny and slightly depressed. I'd never get to feel that again.

Wow, I needed to get a life. *It was a one-night stand, Elle. You're acting as if it was something more and meaningful.* I sounded clingy and desperate.

Being desperate is one thing I'm not.

I'm not falling for a man like Justin again. I wasn't going to give my heart to anyone after what he had done to me.

Slowly, I got up and made my way towards the shower. I needed to wash and get ready to leave. There was no way I could stay here anymore after what had happened. Deciding to skip this town was the right thing to do. I didn't belong here; it was strange and eerie. People weren't friendly. They looked at me like I'm some crazy criminal who had two heads.

I tied my black hair into a messy bun and pulled on the clothes I wore yesterday and a thin cardigan. I stared at the bed once last time, remembering what had happened in there hours ago—our bodies clinging to each other, grasping in need and want.

I did find it odd how Judd and I never kissed; not that it bothered me. It was just a one-night stand; nothing romantic about it. Denying that I didn't want to kiss him was a lie. I badly wanted to feel his mouth against mine.

The cool breeze hit my exposed legs as I walked outside, getting another eerie feeling that I was being watched. I hurried to my car, sat on the driver's seat, and locked the doors immediately. Judd's words scared me a little too much than I would admit, travelling alone. Yes, he was right. It definitely wasn't the best idea. Now, I could kick myself in the ass. This seemed like an episode of Law and Order or Criminal Minds. A strange quiet town where murders are bound to happen.

Like hell I was going to end up eaten alive or attacked by some wild animal. I got out of the place quickly.

I had no idea which way was out of town. I kept going straight and trying to follow the signs. My Navman was not even recognising the place I was in right now. I think I really was lost.

"I don't know where to go," I said quietly to myself, chewing on my lower lip, and I let out a sigh.

The night sky was beautifully lit up with a midnight blue and silvery shining stars glowing across. I peered out the dash, wanting to stop and take a photo, but I remembered what Judd had said. *Were there crazy people out here?*

Looking around, I couldn't see anything strange. As if! I don't believe in stupid things like that.

I pulled over on the side of the road. I grabbed my phone and I snapped a photo of the scenery. It was a gorgeous sight, something so rare and beautiful. I never got the chance to see places like this.

The smell of dust and grass filled my nostrils. My stomach was growling from the hunger, and I felt thirsty. Maybe I should have stayed in town or tried to look for a vending machine for food. I had eaten most of my snacks on the way here. Water was the only thing in my bottle, but I needed caffeine or vanilla coke.

Driving back on the road, I took another turn and found it to be a dead end.

Just my luck that the petrol light flicked on a glowing red.

"Fuck me." I groaned. "You're kidding right now!"

I slapped the steering wheel and managed to pull off onto the side of the road. My car came to a slow halt as it stalled to a stop. I couldn't see much of where I was: an old fence blocking off a large overgrown paddock.

Peering through the window, I wasn't game to go outside again. I swear I could hear howling noises, and that was frightening me. This countryside frightened me. There, I admitted it. I liked the city better. Bright lights and shops—lots of shops. This place had barely anything. It looked to be set back in the old days—the old-style country.

My thoughts drifted back to Justin; how he just left me like that. If he wasn't guilty, he should have fought for us. Then again, if I really loved him, I wouldn't have been bold and let another man fuck me into the mattress like that. Touching myself as he walked in... Oh lord, I was now flushing with embarrassment again.

I blame the heat.

Yes, that's what I blame. If it was cold, I would have been cuddled up in bed and crying my eyes out. Instead, I was horny and naked, fucking someone who I just met.

Pushing him out that door was all I could do. I couldn't bring myself to listen to him tell me what had happened was just some fun, some steam for him to blow off after a hard day's work. I knew, as soon as he walked out, he was going to try to find a way to take off without saying what that really was.

Just a fuck.

I closed my eyes for a moment. Oh god, my brothers. They were going to freak out, and possibly ground me. They're way too protective of me. If I were up to them, I'd be living in a locked room and attending church every Sunday. Sex before marriage was a big no for them. Many times they had tried to get me to see the right way, but being me, I was free-spirited, believing in the moment. I had no idea what happens when you die, but I think you just go to a place with all your loved ones and celebrate the life you had.

My phone flashed, and I sighed. Typical. Of course, Justin writes to me now. I deleted the message without looking at it, tossing the phone in the glove box compartment.

Squinting my eyes, I tried to get a better look of where I was.

Soon, sleep began to overtake me again, and I was out like a light, curled up in the front seat in the most uncomfortable position I had ever been. Why did I leave the hotel? Oh, that's right. I couldn't stand being in that bed any longer.

I was woken up by a rumbling. At first, I wasn't sure what it was. Then I began to fully wake up in panic. The car was shaking slightly, and my first instinct was that it was an earthquake. The ground was going to cave in, and I'd die in my car.

As I looked around, I got distracted by the grass moving. I was thinking that velociraptors from Jurassic Park were out there, hungry and could smell my fear.

Of all the things, I didn't ever assume an animal would lunge through the wooden gate, sending splinters of wood scattering through the air. It charged directly into the side of my car and slam its giant body into the driver's door. A blood-curdling scream escaped my mouth as my car flipped sideways, flying from a strong force that it spun like a ballet dancer. It landed on the ground with a hard thump.

My head hit against the steering wheel as my body stiffened up. Bad move.

I knew once I stiffened, my neck would probably snap.

Luckily, it didn't.

My eyes were groggy as I opened them, blood was trickling down my forehead from my scalp. I had broken some bones and, I was crushed inside my car.

Trying hard to stay awake and conscious, I focused on the large black animal that had sent my car hurling through the midnight sky. It darted off, and I realised I was going to die out here alone.

I tried to move. I tried to get out and damn well run, but I couldn't. My belt was crushing against my chest. My leg was stuck under the dash. Shards of glass were covering me. I felt blood oozing from different parts of my body. My head felt like a sledge hammer went through it, causing my mind to go blank. For the last time my eyes stayed open, all I could see was another animal in front of my smashed window.

Its eyes looked furious, glowing with anger as it glared at me. I should have been petrified and screaming, but I wasn't. A sense of relief filled me as I stared at what looked like a giant wolf. It was a beautiful big black wolf that soon let out an excruciatingly loud howl.

The wolf was angry, and then slowly, everything went black.

If you enjoyed this sample, look for
Wolf in the Night
on Amazon.

DELICIOUS ROSE

AMBER MERRY

PROLOGUE

My brain is foggy and my head is throbbing slightly as I walk through the car park. The rain is pouring heavily as we reach Darcy's Red Citroen. She wraps her arms around my shoulders and kisses my cheek quickly, before getting in the car. I step back, watching her.

"I'll see you in a bit," I tell her, trying to persuade my brain that going to the gym is a good thing.

"I'll pick you up in thirty minutes. Be ready!" Darcy calls out before slamming the door shut.

Rolling my eyes, I wave dramatically as I reach my car and hop in. My wet clothes are sticking to every inch of my skin, and my blonde hair is knotted and flat. I reach for my dashboard to turn the heating on, hoping to feel my hands. Wiggling my numb fingers against the warm air, I reach into my bag for my phone and found no messages from Theo. I haven't heard from him all day and he even goes to work before I wake up.

Ever since he landed that job a couple of months ago, he hasn't been around. He always works late or starts too early. I connect my phone to my radio, opening Spotify and chucking my phone back into my bag. Humming to "Hurts's Somebody To Die For" as I start my car and pull out of the parking lot.

After singing along to the music while stuck in traffic for a long time, I arrive at the flat and park in the underground car park to avoid the rain. Making sure I have everything, I step out of my car. The cold breeze hit me hard, as I rush through the quiet car park and into the damp basement towards the lifts. Stepping into the silver box, I press my floor number. I need to grab my gym bag, spare clothes, and shower bag. I'm thankful that Theo isn't home to distract me, but I hate that I don't see him anymore.

Arriving on the fifth floor, I watch the door slide open and step into the brightly lit corridor. Hoping I haven't wasted too much time before Darcy comes to get me, I speed towards my room's front door. Blindly reaching into my bag to find my keys, I grab onto the cold steel after hearing it jingle. Finding the right key, I press it into the lock and twist it. I can smell home as I open the door slowly—our home.

I notice that the lights are turned on. Is Theo back for his lunch hour? I doubt it. I scoff to myself as I walk into the kitchen. Theo has definitely been here. I never turn the lights on until I get home in the evenings.

Rolling my eyes, I walk to the kitchen counter and place my handbag down. Grabbing my empty water bottle, I turn on the taps and let the water turn cold. My phone pings with a text message, and I reach into my bag, hoping it's Theo.

Text Message [From Darcy]: Be in five minutes, I'm coming up I need to piss, leave the front door unlocked XOX

Why hasn't he texted me back? I know he's busy at work, but how about on his lunch? I just want him to check on me like he used to. Replying to Darcy's text, I put my phone back into my bag, placing my bottle underneath the tap and filling it up. I notice a royal blue handbag on the dining room table. Is that mine?

I turn my head to look at our bedroom door. After shutting the tap off, I slowly make my way out of the kitchen and towards my bedroom. The thick carpet silences my footsteps. I stop and reach for the silver handle. My knees wobble and my heart stops beating when I hear music playing and a girl's moan getting louder and louder. I take a large step backwards, but the sound of pleasure follows me, and I can feel my trust in him slowly dying. Maybe he's just watching porn as a stress reliever, but that wouldn't make sense; he should be at work and it's only two-thirty.

My brain is coming up with different scenarios; he wouldn't do this to me. It's just the TV. I squeeze my eyes shut as I take a step forward and reaching the handle. I push the door wide open.

The sight I come to see shatters me completely. Lauren, my best friend who I have trusted and loved my whole life, is completely naked straddling my fiancé.

"What the fuck?!" I scream out with my body shaking as I take in the view.

Their heads snap towards me as I collapse to the floor, holding my chest. I lift my head slightly, watching them as they take in my reaction. I fear I might pass out, but they haven't even attempted to get off each other.

"Rose, just let me explain!" Theo's eyes widen, but his body stays underneath my best friend.

The pain doesn't subside as I stand up with my blood boiling with rage. Reaching for the TV remote, I mute the music.

"What explaination would you give me? That both of you betrayed me? Don't you fucking dare try and make up an excuse!" My hands are shaking as I yell at the love of my life.

I move my eyes from Theo to my best friend, Lauren. Her big brown eyes are full of fear and her naked body wraps around Theo in my fucking bed. Her long brown hair is a tangled mess and their skin are glossy with sweat. I think I'm going to throw up.

"How long has this been going on?" I take a step closer, trying to keep my calm for as long as possible.

"About six months," she whispers.

My eyes twitch as I clench my fist and bite my tongue. I can't take my eyes off them. How could they do this to me?

"So, for six months you've been lying and cheating and making a complete fool out of me? For six fucking months?!" I lean against the cold wall facing them. The only sound I can hear is my own breathing; loud and uncontrollable. Pushing myself away from the wall, I walk towards my bedroom. My heart is breaking with every glance I take at them.

"You need to calm down Rose. I'm not going to deny or hide it anymore. I love her. I'm in love with her," Theo growls at me.

I stop walking, and I look up at him in horror as my tears begin to fall down my face. *I love her. I'm in love with her.* I process the words before running towards them and launching myself at Lauren as a red mist takes over. Getting a tight hold on her hair, I tug her off Theo's body. Lauren screams as I pin her to the floor and smash my fist into her gorgeous face over and over again.

"You've ruined everything!" My voice is unrecognizable.

Raising my fist once again, I look down at her bloody nose and lip. But my body is suddenly pulled off her. I swing my elbow round in pure anger, catching Theo's nose. My body's thrown across the bedroom at full force. I slam into the wall, hitting my head hard. Curling myself into a ball, I cradle my pounding head.My eyes sting as I watch him pick her up off the floor and gently place her on the bed—our bed. His fingers run softly as he checks on her bloody nose and busted lip. It kills me. It kills me to see so much love and adoration as he caresses her. What the fuck is happening?

"You need help, Rose. You're psychotic! I think you've broken her nose!" He blows up. His jaw tenses as he stares at me, while wiping away Lauren's tears and holding her against his bare chest.

My heart breaks even more. He cannot make me the bad guy! I will never allow that!

"I need help? I have done nothing but love you unconditionally, Theo, and this is what you do to repay me? Slag it up with my best mate!" I yell back at him and cover my face with my hands as I sob.

I can't do this anymore; my heart is broken.

"I love her, Rose. I'm sorry but it's over."

His harsh words are crushing me. Will I ever get over this? Theo's been my rock through so much shit, but now he's telling me he has no love for me?

"So, this whole time was a lie, wasn't it?" I struggle to speak as I look at my engagement ring. I take it off my finger and place it in my palm. I remember he surprised me seven months ago with a holiday to Santorini with its beautiful view looking over the topaz water. That day, he told me everything, everything I've ever wanted to hear—to spend the rest of my life with him. The most incredible memory that even to this day I could never forget. But somehow, he manages to fuck with my stupid best friend and destroy me forever.

"It just happened, Rose. We were drunk," Lauren speaks up with a shaky voice.

I take my eyes off the ring and glare at her. "Being drunk is not an excuse, Lauren! When did it happen?" I ask both of them. Though I do not want to know the truth, I know it would drive me crazy if I didn't find out.

"Darcy's birthday party," she answers me.

I take a deep breath to control myself. I can no longer take watching them hold each other naked as he touches her bloody face in a soothing way; the pain in my heart just becomes more and more unbearable. From this day on, I will never allow myself to fall in love again. With that firm resolve, I stand up and walk over to the bedroom window and open it wide.

"You both won. I'm done. You got what you both wished for, but I do hope he would break your heart, Lauren. I really hope he would fucking hurt you," I growl at her. I open my palm, and the intricate diamond ring shimmers as the sun peeks from behind the clouds. Taking a deep breath, I throw the ring out of the window and into the flowing river below.

"Rose, what the fuck?! That cost me a bloody fortune!" Theo throws himself at the window.

The look of panic in his face actually makes me laugh. "Never promise a girl you're in love with the absolute world if you're going to shag her best friend," I hiss at him.

"You're f-fucking crazy!" he stammers, looking at the water below.

"I never knew living by the riverside would be so helpful. Good luck finding that." I smirk, trying to control the heartache as I walk through the bedroom. I stop at the door and turn to face them one last time. Their eyes are wide. Maybe it has hit them how evil they've been, or that they can finally be together. She can have the world I was promised. I hate them both with every fibre of my being.

"What the fuck is going on?!" Darcy treads into the bedroom. Her mouth opens in horror as she looks at both of their naked bodies, her eyes never leaving the sight in front of us. My eyes are still glued to the truth that my relationship with Theo is done. Six years of my life being madly in love with him has been wasted, and I am not going to marry him. He isn't my forever.

CHAPTER 1

ROSE

Six months later

I let my tears fall down my cheeks as I watch the film in complete silence. Apart from the sobbing and occasional sniffing, I know I'm wallowing in my own self-pity. I need to remind myself that life is beautiful, and I have everything I need. The love of my life didn't freeze to death in the middle of the North Atlantic Ocean, but he might as well have. There is nothing worse than catching your best friend in bed with your man.

My bedroom door swings open and slams against the wall with a loud thud, but I keep my eyes glued to the screen. I can feel her watching me. Darcy's blue eyes are studying me carefully from the doorway. "Rose, you should be getting ready." Her comment is short, and I know she's trying not to laugh at my pathetic state.

I turn my head from the TV to meet her stare. Her lips are twitching as she struggles to keep her smile hidden. I roll my eyes at her before bringing my attention back to the film.

"I'm just watching a film. Calm yourself." I scoff.

"No, you need to shower and get ready." Darcy enters the room and stands in front of the Leonardo DiCaprio movie with her eyebrows raised. She knows either way she will win this battle, and even though there is no battle to be won, I'm going out and I look forward to it. I lean my body slightly, trying to get around her slim figure to catch the film playing behind her.

"Why can't I have Jack? Why am I not that Rose?" I point at the beautiful Kate Winslet being kissed by Jack in a state of panic on the sinking ship. I really am a stupid girl; it's almost impossible not to laugh at my own stupidity.

I'm losing my mind.

"Count yourself lucky, you're not that Rose," Chloe says, announcing her presence.

I take my eyes off the TV once again as I watch her approach Darcy. Chloe is wrapped in a towel with her dark brown hair dripping wet. I cross my arms over my chest in annoyance. I just want to be left alone to watch the rest of the film in peace.

"We are going out doll. Now go shower." Darcy marches over to me, grips my ankles and tugs me off the bed, holding onto the duvet to keep myself from falling but it doesn't help. I fall on the floor in seconds with Darcy towering over me, laughing.

"Rose, you don't need to have sex tonight, just come out." Chloe's face is full of amusement; she doesn't believe it though. Ever since I caught Theo and Lauren, I've fallen down a twisted spiral of alcohol and sex with random lads, and I can't get back up.

"I don't want to be this girl anymore. Theo was the only guy I had ever slept with, well, besides Wayne, but that doesn't count. Now I'm a whore with double digits." I pull a disgusted face at the thought of the guys I've had sex with in the last six months.

"Hey, that's also an insult to me!" Darcy bends down and slaps my arm.

I sit up on my elbows, ignoring her.

"Okay, so you're both sluts! Now Rose, please come." Chloe sits on the edge of my bed.

I stand up and walk over to the mirror. Looking at my reflection seems to get harder as the days go by. I look horrendous. My blonde hair is greasy and shoved up into a messy bun. My eyes are bloodshot with heavy bags, making me look like I've been punched in the face. My black strap top is creased and my baggy tracksuit bottoms need some washing.

"We are going to Lust. I told you about it last Sunday," Darcy says as she takes hold of my shoulders and shakes me aggressively.

I push her away with a pretty weak scowl. I know getting ready will make me look and feel better, but looking like a wreck on the weekends is normal.

"Okay, let me get ready," I mumble to myself, avoiding their eyes.

"Good. Now, take a shower. You look homeless." Chloe shoves me towards the bathroom and slams the door shut behind me.

I know I'm acting stubborn. I enjoy my nights out, but I also know I need to stop what I'm doing. It's not helping me get over him. Turning the shower on, I strip my clothes off as I wait for the water to heat up.

After trying on multiple outfits, I take a look in the mirror as I slip on my final choice. The black material clinging to my figure is sitting above the knee with a low neckline. Smiling to myself, I play with the three-quarter length sleeves before pulling the low neckline down a bit. I can't deny the fact that my chest is impressive, and *that* part of my body draws attention on a night out. If I have it, I've got to flaunt it, right?

"Yes, I totally love that dress. Your tits look fucking amazing!" Darcy looks gorgeous in her pixie bleach blonde hair styled to the side, dark eye makeup, and bright red Rosy lips. She is wearing high-waisted black leather trousers and a matching black leather bandeau with silver stiletto heels.

"Are you girls ready? I need to start drinking." Chloe marches in, looking like a model as always in her thick black heels. Her dark eye makeup makes her blue eyes stand out with her straight chocolate hair. She shows off her black oversized blazer dress, flashing her amazing cleavage.

"Look at you two," I compliment them both, amused as I watch them strut and pose in my doorway. Wearing my tight dress and burgundy heels, my hair loosely curled, my makeup actually flawless for once covering all obvious signs of crying and sleepless nights. I don't look too bad.

"Rose, you look beautiful. Why the hell am I the only one with small tits? Unlike both of you." Darcy grabs both of our chests aggressively before slapping her cute B cups.

"You have boobs!" Chloe pushes her way past Darcy and out of the room, as we follow her quickly.

"Every girl has boobs, but you two are ridiculously lucky." Darcy sulks next to me as we walk down the hallway.

Rolling my eyes as we enter the kitchen, I plant my bum on a kitchen stool.

"Now, let's do some shots please?" I watch Darcy open the cupboard, picking out three shot glasses and a huge bottle of Sambuca.

I'm baffled she's hidden that from me. I could've drowned my sorrows. "Where the hell have you been hiding that?" I ask.

She gives me a grin before twisting the lid off. "You would be amazed what I've hidden in this place," Darcy answers and pouts at me.

Rolling my eyes, I look at Chloe and see her opening a bottle of champagne.

What the hell? I look at her closely as she twists the bottle whilst her other hand covers the cork with a tea towel. She manages to pop the cork and pour the sparkly liquid into a glass each without spilling it. It's official. I'm getting pissed tonight, no question. But the real question is, will I be able to go a whole night without bringing somebody home? I need to stop being so easy.

After a couple of shots, I start to feel the warm sensation in my tummy. Opening my clutch bag, I grab my cigarettes and pink lighter. Slightly raising my hand, I shake the packet and call the girls, "Fag?"

Darcy stands up and walks over to me and grabs the packet from my hand. Chloe swiftly takes a packet from her bag, too. Darcy opens the balcony doors as we step out into the chill air. Leaning against the railing, we look over at the city as it burst with light and people.

"So tonight, Rose stays a Virgin Mary. I'm on the hunt, and Chloe, you need to get laid. When was the last time?" Darcy moves closer towards Chloe, bumping her shoulder against hers.

Looking down, I watch a group of girls laugh and stumble with bottles of wine in their hands, ready for their night out.

"About five months ago," Chloe answers and I roll my eyes.

Sometimes Darcy can be so shockingly outspoken; she'd probably ask my mum the same question if she wanted to. I have so much respect for Chloe. She's beyond gorgeous and guys throw themselves at her, but she won't do it unless she feels a connection, and I used to be like that.

"Holy shit! Yeah, let's get you a hunk, then." Darcy wraps her arm around Chloe's shoulder and blows smoke out of her rouge lips.

Just before I finish my cigarette, my usual nerves kick in. What if Theo or Lauren is out tonight? I haven't seen them for five months since the last incident in the flat.

"What's going on in that head of yours, Rose? Talk to us." Chloe and Darcy look at me.

I inhale the nicotine and wait a couple of seconds before blowing it out into the starry sky. They know what's coming, but they're still the best for asking me every time. Not only did Lauren ruin my friendship with her, but Chloe and Darcy are livid. We had all been such a tight group for years. It sucks so bad but they have not left my side.

"What happens if they're out tonight? It's been months, and I know it's going to happen at some point." I look them. They are honestly spunky and will not take crap from anyone, apart from my mum. Nobody messes with her. I don't doubt for a second, they would let anything happen to me.

"You need to go for a nervous poo. That's what I do before a night out." Darcy's face turns serious, but I ignore her comment whilst trying to keep a straight face.

"We kick him in the balls, claw her eyes out. Simple. My answer to that question will never change," Darcy speaks up again, saving herself from her previous comment.

I watch her press her cigarette into the ash tray whilst Chloe leans up against me.

"I agree. Hurt the fuckers; they both betrayed you beyond repair." Chloe squeezes my arm with her fierce eyes looking at me.

I know they're not lying either, and I've seen these girls go crazy when they need to be.

"Okay, at least I don't need to worry; I have my own personal security." I finish off my cigarette before putting it out and leaning against the balcony, looking down the city lighting up from below and all around. It's breath-taking at night.

"That's right baby. Now let's go have some fucking fun!" Darcy wraps her arm round my shoulder and squeezes me tight, pulling me back inside the living room.

"You've got this girl," Chloe whispers appearing to my left. She wraps her arms around me and hugs me gently. I give her a warm smile, holding my tears that are desperate to ruin my makeup. I really don't think I could manage myself without these two beautiful, yet crazy girls.

Stepping out of the cab, we make our way over to the new club named *Lust* which has apparently been opened last weekend. It's *"fucking amazing"* as Darcy had told me and Chloe last Sunday with her head stuck in the toilet bowl. The queue outside isn't trailing around the street—*thank God*—but from what I can hear, it sounds packed inside. We only have to stand outside for ten minutes before the bouncers let us in.

Lights are flashing a range of different colours as we pay our entry and step onto the dance floor. The club is huge with a large dance floor in the centre of the room. A bar is taking up the entire wall to the right of me, a variety of booths, and deep purple leather sofas scattered around. I've never seen a club so busy.

"Fuck, this is huge!" Chloe yells into my ear.

Darcy heads in front, manoeuvring herself through the crowd, and leaves me and Chloe leaning against the bar waiting to be spotted and served.

"What do you girls want? First rounds on me." Darcy gives me a wink and I laugh nervously. "Rose, I want you drunk okay?" She really is bold.

"Tequila!" Chloe yells over to Darcy who nods just as the barman leans across the bar to talk to her.

I turn my head to study the busy floor. An old classic R&B song echoes through the room, and I cannot help but smile at my excitement. Skimming through the crowd and hoping not to see my dreaded ex, my eyes instantly stop on a muscular arm completely covered in intricate tattoos wrapping his large bicep up to his throat.

I can see the sharpness of his jaw in this dark room flashing under the captivating bright blue light. My eyes are locked on him as he grinds with a girl twenty feet away from me.

This man is hot and utterly gorgeous, but he knows it. I keep my vision on him as he grips into the girl's waist, tugging her closer towards his front. Biting my bottom lip, I try to ignore the warmth in my belly. I make my way back to his face, trying to ignore the desire of his hands to wrap around me like that. His astonishing eyes catches me, and my body suddenly freezes. His hands are not leaving the girl who is swaying her arse against his groin, but his eyes shifts to look into mine for what seem like a lifetime. His lips curl up into a smile. *Oh lord.*

"Rose, shot!"

I spin around quickly, trying to ignore the fact that I have just possibly seen the most attractive male in the entire world. Darcy raises a shot glass which I take gently. I feel flustered beyond belief as I hold the glass to my lips, tilting my head as I beat the strong spirit rushing down my throat. *God, I hate tequila.*

"Shit!" Chloe hisses, holding onto her chest as she lets the drink run through her body.

Darcy slams the glass onto the counter with a straight face before reaching out and grabbing Chloe's hands and mine, leading us to the dance floor. She finds a spot right in the centre of the packed crowd. I let the music take over me as Calvin Harris's "How Deep Is Your Love" starts to play, swaying my hips and running my fingers through my hair.

After a few songs, I start to feel the alcohol taking full swing on my body as I grind to the music. I can see that Darcy has found her "boy for the night". He is tall with shoulder-length brown hair, and he is watching her in fascination with his large hands all over her waist. I can tell he's ready to take her home, but she won't budge just yet. She doesn't cease to amaze me, and I've never met someone with such confidence and a sex drive like hers. Everyone who thinks I'm bad hasn't heard one of Darcy's stories.

Chloe is slowly holding my hand, slut dropping, and grinding on me. Her moves are floppy and stupid, but I can't help but laugh and praise her for it. She doesn't care about anything, and I know many guys are still checking her out even if she is a hot mess. I stop quickly and take a deep breath. It's so hot in here. Chloe's face lights up as her eyes fall on something behind me. Intrigued to find her source of happiness, I turn around to look through the clump of sweating bodies and saw someone familiar—my big brother, Daniel. I give him a smile as he walks over to me, lifts me up in his big arms and spins me around.

After saying hello to Chloe, he holds his hand out for me to take. "Let's get some fresh air!" he yells.

I reach out for Chloe to take my hand as he drags me away from the dance floor. I signal to Darcy that we are going outside, and she nods her head in understanding before giving her full attention to her night fling.

Stepping outside into the smoking area, I reach for my cigarettes quickly to light one, dying for some calming chemicals to kick in.

"How have the girls managed this?" He looks at me with a puzzled look.

"What the hell is that supposed to mean, dick?" I slap his arm and take in another load of smoke.

He shrugs the pain away and looks at Chloe, whose bright eyes are taking in every inch of my brother. She is so in love with him.

"The power of persuasion." Chloe leans on me and winks at Daniel.

It annoys me thinking they aren't going out on a date. I can see how he looks at her too.

"Clever. My sister is lucky to have you both. Are you doing okay?" He directs his eyes back to me and I nod at him.

When I told him about Theo, he was incredible to stay by my side from what I heard. He bumped into Theo and gave him a couple of bruises.

"It's good to see you happy, Rose. It's been so long," he says sadly.

I scrunch my face in confusion. He meets up with me every now and then after work, and I never look like shit. I think his heart would break if he sees me crying. It's an ordinary weekend for me before I glam up and come out to play at night.

"It's only been six months Dan." I scoff, inhaling the nicotine and looking around the smoking area, trying to avoid my brother's eyes. I know it's more than Theo; he's talking about Wayne and our dad. I really don't want this conversation tonight, and I don't even think about it. *That's a lie.*

"No, it hasn't. I know you hold in more than you'll let on, but I'm here. We all are." He looks deeply into my eyes.

I can't be angry with him. He's been so strong for me; someone had to be. Mum certainly wasn't okay.

"I know, Dan. Thank you." I squeeze his shoulder. I really don't want tonight to be a sob fest. My emotions are high and with the mix of alcohol, I will be a blubbering mess if this carries on.

"Danny!"

My brother's eyes divert from mine to look past a smiling Chloe. Seconds later, the familiar face of my brother's best friend Lee, pops up out of nowhere. His eyes are slightly bloodshot as he staggers over to my brother. He's at least four inches shorter than him with fluffy blonde hair and a very innocent baby face.

"Looking gorgeous as ever, ladies. Where's the slag?"

I roll my eyes at his attempt to insult Darcy. He may look sweet as hell but he is crude and unnecessary, but I love him like a brother anyway. It's what I'm used to.

"You wouldn't have the balls to say that to her face," Chloe replies, folding her arms over her chest with confidence radiating.

She's right. Darcy would eat him alive; she has done so many times in the past. But he can't seem to stop teasing her.

"Obviously not, she's scary as hell."

My brother is chuckling beside me with his voice slightly higher than normal. My friends are his friends and his are mine. We've been a tight group for years, and I couldn't imagine that changing. Even with Lauren's betrayal, I needed these guys more than ever and they had me from the moment my life cracked.

"Luca, over here mate!" My brother's attention moves past us as he yells over the dimly lit smoking area.

"Who's Luca? New friend?" I question him, feeling intrigued.

"I've known him for a few months and he's a good laugh. He actually moved in with me and Lee about a month ago," he answers with his eyes now back on me and a small smile tugging on his lips.

Obviously, my face gave away my thoughts. How did I not know about a new flatmate? I turn my gaze away from Daniel as a tall man walks over to our group. His tight black jeans are showing off his muscular legs and his fists are clenched and covered in tattoos. The ink linked onto his forearms and working up both arms and under his t-shirt and onto his throat. Realisation hits my body hard when I trace over his defined jaw and striking blue eyes. He reaches our group, towering over all of us. He's got to be at least six foot four, maybe even taller and his light brown hair is a styled mess. I can feel my heart slamming into my chest.

The same smile on his plump lips from earlier in the club, but the beautiful woman is nowhere in sight. I didn't even know it was possible for someone to actually look this mindblowing in real life. *He's a fucking god.*

"Luca this is my sister, Rose. Rose, this is Luca." My brother looks at his new friend, then to me.

I keep my head down, I don't even know if I can speak. I think I might collapse if he looks at me again. I watch as his tattooed hand appears. I'm hesitant to take it, but I know I can't be rude. His warm hand wraps around mine completely. I feel heat wash over me and my legs trembling slightly. My eyes make their way up to his face, taking him in once again. Topaz orbs shimmering in the dark lighting, he's staring right at me with that fucking smile stuck on his face. *Yes, I'm going to die.*

"Pleasure." The word rolls off his tongue like a work of art, making my knees buckle and my core aches.

His perfectly proportioned face has my heart going nuts I can hardly breathe; his jawline could slice anything in his way and those blue eyes could break the heart of any girl.

"Nice to meet you, Luca." My voice cracks as his hand still holds on tight to mine.

He looks confident as I smile at him. He knows exactly what he's doing to me. I pull my hand away from his, hiding it behind my back for him to take it and end my life. His lips curl into a grin as he ruffles his hair. His eyes are peering into mine as he reaches into his front pocket and pull out a packet of fags. I watch in awe as he lights a cigarette and places it between his gorgeous full lips. I am in serious trouble.

If you enjoyed this sample, look for
Delicious Rose
on Amazon.

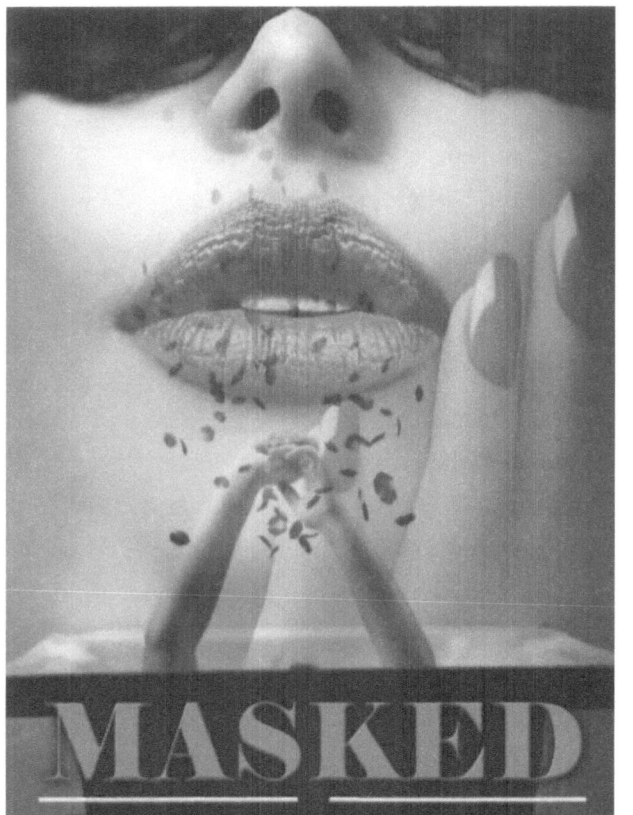

MASKED
FEELINGS

Lechna Baram

Chapter 1

The Mysterious Vixen

Sweet Delice Club

I stared at the club's sign and rolled my eyes. I still can't believe that I work here. I held my sports bag closer to me and sighed. I hated my job but I had no choice. I was helpless. Extremely helpless. I needed money right now. And with this job, I make a lot of money in one night.

Yes. I am a stripper.

I walked in the club and saw a lot of men. A lot would be an understatement. This club was really classy and posh. Yes, I know you're probably asking yourself how a strip club could be classy and posh. This one is. Not everyone could gain entry to the Sweet Delice Club. Only men with money could enter, and this job really got me a lot of money.

I snuck in the backstage, trying to avoid people since I didn't have my mask on. Normally, the girls were not supposed to dance with masks but I begged the boss to let me wear a mask as I didn't want anyone to recognize me. He conceded without any fuss because I was a pretty good addition to the club.

"Athena Amington!" Rose scolded as I walked in the dressing room to see her dressed in her skirt and bra. I gave her a sheepish smile and shrugged.

"I know! I know! I'm late!" I put my hands up in surrender, causing her to huff. I put my sports bag on the table and took a deep breath.

"Come on, get ready," she said as she opened my bag and took out my shorts and a black bra. "You're lucky you don't have to show your boobs or your ass," she grumbled.

"Yeah, but I have to dance on horny men and trust me with these shorts, I can feel each and every boner those men get." I shivered in disgust. All the other strippers were supposed to dance on stage and obviously, they end up taking their clothes off. However, the boss told me to put on those really small shorts and a bra. I was supposed to dance on the stage as well but during my show, I was supposed to go to men and give them lap dances. I think that's why he told me to keep my clothes on. I shuddered when I thought of those hands on me. I always wanted to puke but again, there were securities all around. Men didn't have the right to touch us, and I was glad it was this way.

"I hate this job," Rose mumbled.

"Same," I whispered as I started getting out of my clothes and put on my shorts which showed half of my ass. Then I put on my silvery bra. I stared at myself in the mirror and sighed. I let my long black hair hang in loose waves.

"Here," Rose said as she pushed my makeup kit and mask in front of me. I did smoky eyes, making my green eyes pop. I then stared at my mask. It was silvery and had some black designs on it. Yeah, it matched my 'clothes.' I put it on and tied it securely so it wouldn't fall. I put on my sexy black stilettos. I looked like a slut. A sexy slut. But I'm a stripper, right? It's part of my job.

"I don't wanna go out there," I told Rose as she applied her red blood lipstick before handing it to me. I turned to face the mirror and put on lipstick before returning it to her.

"Think of the money you'll get." She tried to encourage. I took a deep breath and closed my eyes.

Think positive.

"I'll rock tonight." I tried to squeal positively but they could see my fake smile a mile away. Rose laughed at my horrible effort to cheer up.

"You look sexy. Goddamn sexy." I heard a voice say from behind. I turned to see Jerry, our boss; he's pretty cool. His eyes raked my long tan legs before settling on my face. I grinned at him, earning a response.

"Thank you," Rose and I said at the same time as he approached with a tube of oil in his hand. He handed it to Rose and winked at her.

"This is for you. Make your body all shiny, honey," he said and Rose rolled her eyes. The other strippers had to put oil on their bodies to make them look more attractive and sexy. I didn't have to, because I danced on clients and we didn't want to ruin their clothes. Rose waved at me and walked out of the room to apply oil on her body without Jerry ogling her.

"You're ready?" Jerry asked, turning his attention to me. I shrugged and ruffled my hair to make it look messier.

"I feel cheap when I do that," I told him truthfully. Jerry pretty amazing; he knew how to boost up your confidence in a matter of seconds. He gave me a reassuring smile and patted my head like a dog, getting a glare from me. I hate when he did that.

"You shouldn't," he said as he jumped on the counter and stared at me. "You don't look vulgar." He pointed to my clothes. I scoffed and motioned to my ass, at which he rolled his eyes. "People wear less at the beach," he said with confidence.

"We're not at the beach,"

"Listen, you wear a mask," Jerry said as he stared at me. "No one knows who you are. You're popular because of that. I'm pretty sure nearly all the men there are here because they want to know who The Mysterious Vixen is," he said, pointing to my mask. "I don't see why you feel cheap when you see all the other girls naked while you are not." He ended with raised eyebrows.

"You're right." I concluded as I pulled him in for a hug. He wrapped his arms around me and gave me a smile.

"I'm always right, sweetheart," he said with a smirk.

"You wish."

I have always considered Jerry family. He always gave me good advice, and he said my place wasn't in this club and that I should be studying in college because I was smart. Yeah. In fact, I am studying psychology in college. Hearing that brought a smile to his face. Jerry was in his late thirties while I was just a nineteen-year-old girl who badly needed a job. He gave me the job because he knew I needed it.

"I'm done," Rose said, fixing her bra as she walked into the room. Jerry was definitely checking her out. A smile crept on my face when I saw Rose blushing when she noticed how he was staring at her.

"Ready?" Jerry asked as he jumped off the counter. Rose nodded and sat on a chair.

"Shouldn't Athena go first?" she asked and Jerry nodded.

"Rose, don't use my real name. It's Vixen," I mumbled looking around. Only Jerry and Rose knew my real name. The others only knew me by the name 'Vixen.'

"Sorry!" She quickly apologized. I gave her a smile while fixing my shorts. It was so tight that I could feel my blood having problems circulating. Now, just imagine the torture I have to go through dancing in these.

"Rose, it will be you just after Athena," Jerry told her. I smacked his arm and glared at him.

"Stop. Using. My. Name." I emphasized each word. He rolled his eyes and nodded.

"There's no one around."

"Not willing to take the risk."

"Let's go."

"Good luck," Rose called out.

"I'll really need it," I shouted back as I followed Jerry out of the room. A few strippers walked past me and gave me a nod. They never saw my face, just my mask. They didn't seem to want to know me either. As we walked to the stage, I noticed one of the girls giving me a death glare. That was Stacy. Let's just say that she is not a big fan of Vixen. Apparently, I was stealing some of her clients.

"It will be your turn in a minute or two," Jerry said as he peeked on the stage to see whether the girl before me was nearly over. I took a deep breath, trying to calm my nerves. I had to work here three times a week and let me tell you that after three months of working here, I'm still not used to this atmosphere. I was pretty sure I was going to see the same faces in there. They always come on the day I was going to perform.

"You should be happy you're not completely naked," I muttered to myself, trying to calm my nerves. Jerry stared at me in amusement. He loved to watch me fidget like this.

"Calm down," Jerry said as he shook his head in disbelief. "You've done this a lot of times and you're always nervous before stepping in front of these people." "It's quite normal to be nervous of being naked in front of horny men," I remarked, glaring at my stilettos. *Why was I doing this again?*

Oh yeah, money.

"It's your turn, honey," Jerry told me. "There's a lot of new faces," he said as he stopped looking at the people.

"Way to make me more nervous, asshole," I snapped, making him chuckle.

"You're always nervous and you'll still rock your performance as always. So just calm down and go shake your ass over there and bring me cash," he said motioning to the stage.

"You're really an asshole," I told him before taking my place on the first step of the stairs which led to the stage.

"Good luck," Jerry whispered as my song started playing. I chose "The Hills" by The Weekend as I felt really comfortable with it. I knew how to move my body to its beat.

"Next, we have The Mysterious Vixen!" I heard Jerry announce with pride. I put on a smirk on my face and stepped on stage with my head down and my hair covering my face a bit.

Time to unleash Vixen.

Following the beat of the song, I stepped towards the pole at the center of the stage. I couldn't show that I was nervous right now. I kept my sexy smirk plastered and as soon as The Weekend's song went on, I raised my head and made eye contact with some of the men present. I have to admit that some of them were a really fine sight to behold. Those lustful stares I was getting were slightly pushing me to do my job better. Once the music actually started, I wrapped one leg around the pole and twirled around it, slowing down my moves, making it sensual. Sexual.

"Damn." I heard someone sigh just in front of me. I pulled away from the pole and got on all fours. I crept my way to the man sitting in the front row. I gave him a little grin when I saw his gaze raking over my legs to my ass. He had baby blue eyes and blond hair. He seemed to be Barbie's Ken. Well, sorry Barbie, I'm about to give your man a lap dance. I slowly got off stage and made my way to him. I smirked when I saw him gulp.

"Hello," I whispered seductively as I started moving my body to the song again. I dropped down and opened his legs. Standing up, I took my place between his legs, giving him a show he was never going to forget. As I sat on his lap, I could feel his dick growing from under me. I tried not to shudder in disgust. Soon, fortunately, my song ended and I leaned to whisper a lie in the man's ear. "I hope to see you again." That's shit that all strippers had to tell the men they were giving lap dances to so they would come around again.

All lights turned off and I made my way back backstage amidst the applause. Two security guys accompanied me to the dressing room to protect me from creeps who would sometimes follow us backstage. Yeah. There were real weirdos and creepers out there.

"That was perfect!" Jerry shouted in excitement. I smiled and nodded. "Let's get to your dressing room, then we'll talk," he said, looking at the two guys behind me. He motioned for them to go as we made our way to the dressing room. I saw Rose get up from her chair and give me a big smile.

"I got a boner just by watching you," she said, wrapping her arms around me.

"If you have a dick, you're fired," Jerry joked while I rolled my eyes. Yes, that was something I tended to do a lot. "Now go. It's your turn," he said, pushing Rose out of the room. Rose glared at him but still left for her performance.

"I'm tired," I said as I leaned my head against the wall.

"Then go home," Jerry said as he handed me some cash, $500. Now you understand why I work here.

"I'll wait for Rose, so we can leave together," I told him. He nodded and clapped his hands in one firm way before wiggling his eyebrows.

"I'm going to watch Rose perform," he told me with a grin.

"Ask her out already." I teased. He gave me a smirk and wink.

"Maybe I will," he said as I sat down and turned my attention to the television in front of me. The television showed the stage. This way we could see the performance of the other strippers. I could hear Rose's song and soon, she stepped on stage playing with her hair. She definitely knew what she was doing. Every time she'd perform, I'd watch her in awe.

After a few minutes, Rose ended her performance and walked back into the dressing room with Jerry following behind her. *Didn't Jerry have other strippers to take care of?* "I need your help," Jerry said. I didn't pay attention, thinking that he was probably talking to Rose but then, when I realized that Rose didn't answer, I turned to see both of them staring at me.

"What's wrong?" I asked when I saw Rose staring at me with a wide smile while Jerry rushed and dropped down on his knees in front of me. "What the hell?" I asked as I backed away.

"You won't believe what just happened!" Rose exclaimed as she walked to us and pulled Jerry up by his ears. They'd look cute together.

"What happened?" I asked, curiosity getting the best of me. I crossed my arms over my chest, looking at Jerry.

"I just got an offer," he said, rubbing his ears.

"And?" asked

"A private lap dance," he said with a sheepish smile.

"No," I replied instantly. I've never done private lap dances before, and I'm not planning on doing it either. Rose huffed and stared at me with wide eyes.

"The man is giving $50,000!" she exclaimed, making my eyes go wide as I tried not to choke on my saliva. *What on earth?*

"Why?!" I asked in disbelief.

"I don't know! But that's a lot of money," Rose said. "He said that he wanted Vixen! Otherwise, I'd definitely dance for that man," she said as she sat down. "Accept, Athena." That was a lot of money. It was just a dance after all.

It was definitely a tempting offer.

"What if he's a creep?" I asked, playing with my fingers. I always do that whenever I'm nervous. Jerry gave me a smile and walked to the door. He motioned someone to come in. My eyes widened as I saw the blond guy who I had given a lap dance walk into the room. My hands flew to my face to make sure that I still had my mask. I mean, it was so light that I didn't feel it.

"Hello," he greeted and gave me a slight smile when he realized how surprised I was.

"Why would you pay such a huge amount of money when I just gave you a lap dance out there?" I asked directly, not wanting to fool around.

"Straightforward," he mumbled to himself. Jerry and Rose nodded at his statement. I rolled my eyes but kept quiet.

"I'll need you to do something," he said as he scratched the back of his head. He looked a little bit nervous. I knew this was bad. Really bad.

"That does not sound good...at all," I said as I sat down on my chair, waiting for him to explain.

"It's not that bad," he tried to reassure. *But again, am I supposed to trust this stranger?*

"Talk." I demanded, making him grin a little bit.

"Well you'll have to do what you do the best," he said, still wearing the grin.

"Eat?" I asked, tilting my head to the left. He stared at me in confusion.

"Dance." He sighed and sat in front of me.

"I already danced for you."

"This time, it won't be for me," he said and I bit down on my lips, waiting for him to elaborate. "My brother just went through a breakup." He clarified, making me scoff.

"And he's all depressed and shit, and I'm supposed to cheer him up?" I guessed and surprisingly, he shook his head.

"In fact, no. He's being a cold, arrogant asshole," he said, mostly talking to himself. "I need you to get an emotion out of him," he explained. "Any type of emotion...anger doesn't count," he mumbled. I could see that this situation with his brother was really bothering him.

"Why me?"

"You've got something special," he said, making me smile. "I've seen it," he added with a smirk. "I don't think any other stripper here will be able to get a reaction out of him."

"By reaction, you mean a boner, right?"

"You're really blunt," he stated and I nodded. *Why should I disagree with that fact?*

"So, I'm supposed to dance for your cold, arrogant asshole brother?" I asked and he nodded. "Is he here?" asked. He nodded again.

"Will you please do it?" he asked, or practically begged. I sighed and nodded.

"Fine, I'll do it" I exhaled. "But you must be pretty stupid to spend a lot of money on something that you're not even sure that's going to work" I mumbled.

"No, I'm not. I'm just damn rich," he said arrogantly. "And I'm sure that it will be worth it," he added as he stood up. I did the same and turned to stare at myself in the mirror. I fixed my mask and my hair before giving them my attention again.

"Where is he?" I asked.

"In the private room," Jerry told me as we all walked out of the room.

"If he's so angry and all shit, then why did he agree to come here with you?" I asked the blond dude while following him.

"I kinda blackmailed him," he said. *Blackmail? What are you? Ten?* I kept my question to myself but nevertheless, I rolled my eyes.

"How?" I asked just to make conversation by the time Jerry guided us to the room.

"I told him I'd tell my mom," he said. I stared at him for a few seconds, waiting for him to tell me that it was a joke. He just gave me a grin. *Yes. He was definitely ten.*

"What's your name?" I asked, as I turned to see Rose behind me.

"Dean," he answered. "Yours?"

"Vixen," I said, not willing to tell him my real name.

"I already know your stage name," he muttered as we reached the private sector of the club.

"That's the only name you'll know," I replied with a grin while turning to Jerry. "I want the cameras in the room turned off." "What about your security?" he asked. I knew that inside the room, there will be cameras. They were there to ensure that strippers were not in danger while giving a private performance.

"You can turn them off. My brother is not going to touch her," Dean said as his eyes trailed on Jerry's features. He seemed to be judging him. Jerry nodded and walked away.

"I'll wait for you in the dressing room," Rose said as she ran to keep up with Jerry.

"Wish me good luck," I whispered to Dean as I faced the door. I hated to perform. Now imagine how nervous I was to perform again. Twice in a night.

"Good luck," Dean said. "I'm gonna get out of here now." He laughed at how nervous I was. "There's no monster in there. Calm down." With that he walked away with his hands in his pocket. I stared at the door, fixing my shorts and bra and put my hand on the door knob.

Let's get this done.

If you enjoyed this sample, look for
Masked Feelings
on Amazon.

ABOUT THE AUTHOR

I'm wife to a FIFO miner. Mother of three. Passionate foodie, and a vivid dreamer. Living in a small beach town in the lovely Tasmania. I spend my time between home and down at the beach… making memories and capturing the moments.

When I'm not glued to my laptop, I'm either in the kitchen creating recipes, cooking, or having a Netflix binge session. Often, I find myself drifting off into the world of make believe, getting lost inside the stories I write. I write because it's my passion. I want to create a world for my readers to get lost in . . . For them to swoon and fall in love the way I do with each character made. Oh, and I love starbursts!

Sweetly, Melissa xx